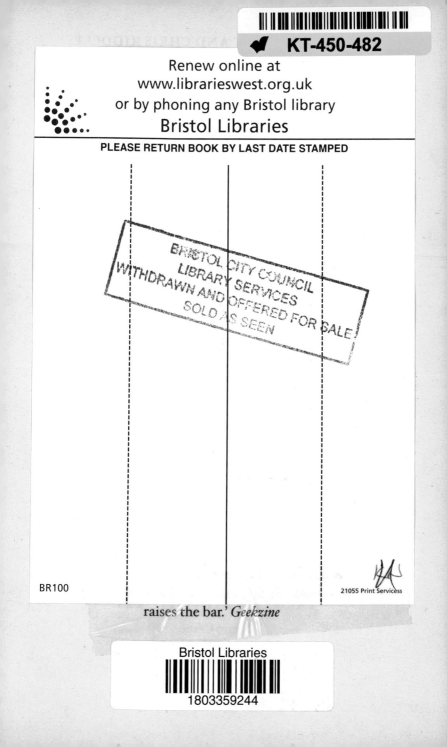

raises the bar.' *Geekzine*

BY PAUL STEWART AND CHRIS RIDDELL:

WYRMEWEALD:

Returner's Wealth
Bloodhoney
The Bone Trail

THE EDGE CHRONICLES:

The Quint trilogy
The Curse of the Gloamglozer
The Winter Knights
Clash of the Sky Galleons

The Twig trilogy
Beyond the Deepwoods
Stormchaser
Midnight Over Sanctaphrax

The Rook trilogy
The Last of the Sky Pirates
Vox
Freeglader

The Immortals

The Lost Barkscrolls
The Edge Chronicles Maps

BARNABY GRIMES:

Curse of the Night Wolf
Return of the Emerald Skull
Legion of the Dead
Phantom of Blood Alley

For Younger Readers:
FAR-FLUNG ADVENTURES

Fergus Crane
Corby Flood
Hugo Pepper

www.stewartandriddell.co.uk

WYRMEWEALD

BLOODHONEY

PAUL STEWART AND CHRIS RIDDELL

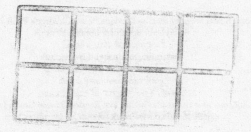

CORGI BOOKS

P.S. – For Nicky and Richard
C.R. – For Jo

WYRMEWEALD: BLOODHONEY
A CORGI BOOK 978 0 552 56089 4

First published in Great Britain by Doubleday,
an imprint of Random House Children's Publishers UK
A Random House Group Company

Doubleday edition published 2012
Corgi edition published 2013

1 3 5 7 9 10 8 6 4 2

The Random House Group Limited supports the Forest Stewardship Council (FSC®),
the leading international forest certification organization. Our books carrying the FSC
label are printed on FSC®-certified paper. FSC is the only forest certification scheme
endorsed by the leading environmental organizations, including Greenpeace. Our paper
procurement policy can be found at www.randomhouse.co.uk/environment.

MIX
Paper from
responsible sources
FSC® C016897

Set in Hoefler Text

Corgi Books are published by Random House Children's Publishers UK,
61–63 Uxbridge Road, London W5 5SA

www.randomhousechildrens.co.uk
www.totallyrandombooks.co.uk
www.randomhouse.co.uk

Addresses for companies within The Random House Group Limited
can be found at: www.randomhouse.co.uk/offices.htm

THE RANDOM HOUSE GROUP Limited Reg. No. 954009

A CIP catalogue record for this book is available from the British Library.

Printed and bound in Great Britain by CPI Group (UK), Croydon, CR0 4YY

Kith – those who hunt and trap wyrmes

Kin – those who bond with wyrmes

Keld – those who dwell underground

ONE

The *thud thud* of heavy footfalls came drumbeat steady from the far side of the ridge. A pair of foraging skitter-wyrmes paused. The footfalls crunched and squeaked in the freshfall snow. They did not falter.

They were getting nearer . . .

The skitterwyrmes stood up on their hindlegs and peered around jerkily through the driving snow, heads cocked and fluted crests fluttering. Beneath their feet, the ground trembled. They eyed one another for an instant, then with short barked shrieks darted for a crevice in the snowcrusted rocks close by and disappeared.

The thudding grew louder, anchoring the freeform wail of the wind with its relentless rhythm . . .

The hissing of the falling snow softened abruptly as the wind dropped. Above, yellow-grey clouds curdled and thinned, and a pale sun broke through. It set the dwindling display of snowflakes to sparkling and sent long shadows off across the snowdrifts. Yet there was no warmth to it.

A cowled head rose up from behind a snowcapped

ridge, the face lost in shadow beneath a heavy hood; then broad shoulders, with an immense backpack strapped to them. A white lakewyrmeskin cape creaked as it flapped to reveal legs like tree trunks, and heavy boots that were toecapped and laced ladderwise to the shins.

The winter caller paused at the top of the ridge and surveyed the rocky snowscene ahead. A gloved hand emerged from the folds of the cape. It reached up and pushed the hood back, and the cold sun fell upon a bone mask that covered the face. It gleamed on the yellowed cheekbones and eyesockets and glinted in the darting black eyes beneath.

With a gruff snort, the hulking figure pulled a piece of rag from a back pocket and, with unlikely delicacy, cupped it to the mask and breathed deeply, eyes closed.

It was fainter now, the smell. But it was still there. A telltale mix of wyrmeoil and pitchsmoke, and sweat soured by fear and disgust. It was a unique smell, unmistakable, and leading him inexorably on to his quarry.

Find them. Dig them out. Dispatch them . . . slowly.

The words of the keld mistress echoed inside his head. Ever since he had left the underground cavern he had heard them, urging him on through the weald of fullwinter in pursuit of the murderers.

The winter caller lowered the cloth and sniffed at the

air, then snorted again. Twists of mist coiled out of the bone nostrils.

He rummaged in another pocket and drew out a handful of dried meat, which he shoved through the mouth hole in the bone mask. He chewed mechanically, turning the meat to pulp – till his molars clamped down on something that jarred his jaws. He probed around his mouth with his tongue, seeking and finding a small hard object, then spat it out.

It was a milk tooth. It lay on the surface of the snow for a moment, pearly and unblemished, before fresh snowflakes hid it from view.

He pulled the hood back over his masked face and lurched forward. The thudding drumbeat resumed.

It was as he crested the next ridge that he saw them. He did not stop, nor break his stride. There were two of them, one taller than the other, the pair of them brown against the white, standing beside a tattered awning and broken staves. Then they saw him.

The shorter one waved.

It wasn't his quarry, he knew that much. They both smelled of damp buckhide and something metallic. And, as the waving grew more agitated, he noticed that the shorter one's odour was laced with buttermilk. Kithtang.

A man and a girl . . .

They started towards him. The girl was up front, wading thighdeep through the drifts of snow as fast as she could manage, her walking staff raised above her head. The man hurried after her, shouting out for her to watch her step, to probe for hidden cracks and crevasses that might swallow her up, but ignoring his own advice. They were grinning, the both of them, their gaunt faces flushed.

The twitter and chirp of their eager voices grew shrill as the gap between him and them closed up. And as they approached, the man extended a hand in greeting.

'How do, stranger,' he said. 'I am truly pleased to make your acquaintance.'

The winter caller stared down at the man from the shadows of the hood. He noted the raggedy beard, the sunken sparkle to his eyes, the broken crossbow at his shoulder. He said nothing, nor made a move to shake the proffered hand.

The man pulled back awkwardly and brushed snowflakes from his beard. 'Like I say, I . . . I can't tell you what a relief it is for us that our paths have crossed,' he told him, though his voice lacked conviction.

'We got separated from the convoy,' the girl chipped in. 'Daddy and me. On account of the bellyache I got from that bad meat . . .'

'Then the snow set in,' the man added. He shook his head. 'And a mountain still to climb before we make our winter lay-up. The winds destroyed the makeshift,' he said, nodding back at the flapping wyrmeskin canopy and splintered wood. 'And . . . and our provisions are woeful low.' He eyed the bulging backpack at the stranger's shoulders. 'If you maybe had something to barter, friend. Something to share with me and my little girl here . . . ?'

The figure grunted, seemingly in response, then swept back his gleaming grey cloak. He reached out with his huge gloved hands and clamped them gently to the sides of the man's head. The man looked up at him, smiling warily, trying not to react badly to this hulking stranger's unusual greeting. Beside him, his daughter stepped back uneasily.

'Daddy?' she said.

'It's all right, angel,' the man told her. 'He don't mean no harm, do you, stranger?'

The winter caller said nothing, but steadily increased the pressure on the man's head as if he were testing a fruit for ripeness.

'You let go of him!' the girl shrieked, fear gripping her as she saw her daddy's eyes bulge and turn bloodshot. 'Let him *go*!'

The winter caller knocked her aside with a casual

shrug that sent her sprawling to the snow-covered ground, and his hood fell back. The girl looked up and gasped at the sight of the bone mask.

'Daddy! *Daddy* . . .'

There was a splintering sound. Blood started to ooze between the fingers of the wyrmeskin gloves. It spattered down onto the snow, red on white, turning pink, like cherry blossom. The lifeless body slumped down upon it with a dull thump.

The hooded figure turned to the girl, and she shook uncontrollably beneath the emotionless gaze of the glittering black eyes behind the bone mask. Stirring herself, the girl scrambled backwards, struggling to climb to her feet, the worn soles of her boots slipping on the snow.

She began pleading, begging the stranger to spare her life. Her anguished voice rose and fell, words spilling from spitfleck lips.

Twitter twitter. Chirp chirp chirp.

The winter caller remained motionless.

The keld mistress and her colleagues would certainly appreciate the girl, he knew that. She was small, but looked strong, and Cutter Daniel had a thing for plaited braids. She would make a good slave. Then again, he had other business to attend to, didn't he? The little matter of his quarry. She'd only get in his way, and if he tied her up and left her till he was done, she would be dead and useless by the time he returned.

He reached down and grabbed a hold of her. He lifted her off the ground and the twittering and chirping grew louder and uglier and higher in pitch, till it was screeching inside his head.

Twitter twitter. Chirp chirp chirp.

He started to shake the girl, his gloved hands gripping her bony shoulders, shaking and shaking and shaking until she fell limp. And silent. Her head lolled back on her broken neck.

The winter caller released his grip on the body and it crumpled in a heap at his feet. He stepped over it and continued up the mountainside.

The words of the keld mistress returned.

Find them. Dig them out. Dispatch them . . . slowly.

Behind him, the two skitterwyrmes appeared from the crack in the rock, and were joined by half a dozen more. They scurried over the snow, which was already crusting up with the intense cold. They lapped at the blood. They probed the bodies with greedy curiosity, then sank their fangs into the still warm flesh. If they were to benefit from this unexpected feast before the carrionwyrmes arrived, they would have to be quick.

Two

'Make a wish, Thrace?' said Micah. He wiped the grease from his lips on the back of his hand and held up the wishbone.

Eli Halfwinter was over on the far side of the chamber, clattering pots and pans as he scoured them with sand and sluiced them clean in the water pail. The cragclimber didn't hold with foolish superstitions and Micah hoped he wasn't listening – though not enough to stop him from asking.

'Thrace?' he persisted. 'A wish?'

The kingirl made no move. She was staring down at the wooden bowl in her lap. Micah watched her glumly.

The winter den that Eli had brought them to was far larger than Micah had first thought. As well as the low-ceilinged store chamber he'd seen first, with its boxes and sacks and barrels and sides of salted meat hanging from hooks, there were three other chambers besides, connected one to the other.

The first of them was large and airy, and with a ceiling high enough that even Eli did not have to stoop. The floor was scattered with dozens of nubbed wyrmepelts that warmed and softened the cold, hard stone floor, apart from a large indentation at the centre of the chamber which contained the fire upon which they cooked. Eli had rigged up a kind of flue above it. Beaten from rustfleck metal, the broad funnel tapered to a long pipe that led to the chimney hole in the cave ceiling high above, and carried the smoke away. The second chamber was long and narrow, with grooves in the floor where they slept, each one lined with rag and straw bedding. There was a wedge-shaped hole in the end wall, which offered a natural vent for air. The last chamber was much smaller, and there was a pit in the corner, a heap of sandsalt beside it, where the three of them went to relieve themselves.

Back on the plains, Micah had grown up in a cramped shack with five others. Compared to that, the winter den was spacious, and despite the ebb and flow of the howling wind outside, it felt cosy. Leastways, that was what Micah thought.

Thrace did not agree. Could not agree. To her, the place was a prison and, like a wyrme in a cage, she paced about listlessly, aware of her confines, unable to escape, unable to fly . . .

'Thrace?' he whispered gently.

This time, the kingirl looked up. She was beautiful;

snatch your breath away beautiful, with her ashgold hair and dark grey eyes. But even in the dim lampglow of the chamber Micah could see that Thrace had lost weight. Too much weight. Her face was a shadow and gleam of hollowed cheeks and jutting cheekbones, while the suit of soulskin, that once had hugged her body, hung loose like a hand-me-down from some bigger sister.

'A wish, Thrace,' Micah repeated. He held up the wishbone.

Thrace looked at it blankly.

Trouble was, thought Micah, Thrace wasn't eating enough. According to the sand that had trickled through the hourglass, Eli and he had spent nigh on three hours chopping dried roots and pickled vegetables, slicing and dicing the smoked squabwyrme and boiling it up into a thick stew which, if it didn't sound too boastful, had tasted pretty damn fine. Thrace, though, had barely touched it.

'Hunger, I have,' she'd said when he urged her to eat. 'Yet no appetite for food.' She'd pushed the bowl away.

Micah stared into her eyes. Once, they had glittered slatedark and pooldeep. But now? It was like the life in them had been drained away, leaving behind two dull grey stones . . .

With a start, Micah realized that Thrace's gaze had

shifted from the wishbone, and that she was staring directly into his own eyes. He swallowed, then smiled at her.

'Pull the wishbone with me, Thrace,' he encouraged her. 'Maybe it'll come true.'

'My wish?' Thrace said wearily. She shrugged. 'Maybe you would be happier if it did not.'

A cold shiver pinched the nape of Micah's neck and tingled at his scalp. He swallowed again, and hoped once more that the cragclimber wasn't listening. 'That's foolish talk, Thrace, and you know it,' he told her. 'Whatsoever you might wish for yourself, I would wish it too.' He smiled again, leaned forward and took her by the wrist. 'There is nothing I want more in this world than for you to be happy.'

Micah raised her hand, brought it to his lips and was about to kiss it, but Thrace pulled away. Micah feared he'd angered her – he hated angering her – but when she looked away, it was not anger he saw in those empty grey eyes, but an unhappiness that was desolate and intense. And that grieved him.

'Thrace . . .' he began.

But the kingirl had climbed to her feet, the bowl of uneaten stew clasped to her chest, and was heading for the adjacent sleeping chamber.

'I could heat it up for you,' Micah offered, jumping up from the floor.

'That won't be necessary,' said Thrace, and was gone.

Micah slumped back down with a sigh. He'd hoped so much that, holed up together in the underground den for the long months of fullwinter, they might find contentment in each other's company. But that was not the way it had turned out. Despite their physical close-ness, Thrace seemed further away from him than ever.

Oh, she loved him, in her own way, and as best she could, Micah knew that. But as for being content . . . It was like she just wouldn't allow herself to be. Worse than that, it seemed there was nothing that he could do to make it otherwise.

Micah stared down at the wishbone. He'd saved it specially from the smoked carcass of the squabwyrme. It was broad and graceful, and maybe three times the size of a large turkey's.

'Eli,' he said, looking up. 'Would *you* care to pull the wishbone with me. I have a wish for Thrace that I would surely like to come true.'

'Can't make a wish on someone else's behalf,' came the cragclimber's gruff response. 'Besides,' he added, 'wyrmebone's too tough to snap by mere pulling.'

Eli did not look round. He didn't need to. Micah

knew from his words that he'd overheard him and Thrace talking after all, and he blushed at that.

'Bring me over them dirty things when you're done,' Eli told him.

Micah observed Eli's back tense and flex as he scrubbed away at a stubborn patch of burnt grease on the roasting pan. Time in the winter den was measured out with minor chores – potwalloping, knifegrinding and suchlike – and Eli filled his days with them. When he wasn't cleaning or repairing kit, like as not he'd be planning and preparing their meals, meticulously eking out the provisions in the store chamber, where he seemed to be most often.

With a small sigh, Micah gathered up his and Eli's wooden bowls, mugs and spoons, the liquor jug, and the large dish that had contained honey-sweetened barley mash, but now was empty. He piled everything into a stack, lay the wishbone across the top bowl and carried the whole lot over to Eli.

'Set it down there, lad,' said Eli, nodding towards a flat block of stone. His gaze fell upon the wishbone. 'Wishes,' he said, and snorted. 'You're too old for such nonsense, Micah,' he observed, then added, 'Besides, that fine wishbone could be turned to something useful.'

Micah frowned. He picked up the bone and turned it over in his hands. 'It could?'

'Look at it close,' said Eli, wiping his wet hands on the back of his breeches and turning to Micah. 'Does its shape not bring something to mind?'

Micah shrugged. Eli took the wishbone from him and, holding it in one hand, stroked the pitted surface with the other.

'See, Micah,' he said, 'unlike you or me or any other human being that ever lived, wyrmes have fused collarbones. Like birds.' He traced a finger lightly down each of the curved lengths of bone, pausing at the ridged nub where they joined. 'It strengthens it. Makes the creatures capable of flight.'

Eli gripped the wishbone by the thick shaft, and turned it over so that the two curved lengths were uppermost. He looked at Micah, his mouth twisted into a half smile and his pale blue eyes questioning.

'Remind you of anything now?'

Micah frowned. 'The letter Y?' he suggested.

Eli switched the wishbone to his left hand and mimed a pulling-back motion behind it with his right.

'A catapult!' Micah exclaimed.

'Maker be praised,' Eli chuckled, 'there's something going on inside that head of yours after all. I swear I was beginning to doubt it.' He nodded earnestly. 'But you got there in the end, lad. A catapult.'

He held up the wishbone and Micah appraised it afresh through eager eyes.

'You got the basic body here,' Eli was saying. 'All you need now is some stout leather, some thick twine and a couple of strips of tensible wyrmeskin, and you've got yourself a catapult that could down a man at a hundred paces.' He smiled. 'Should that need ever arise . . .'

He handed the wishbone to Micah, who raised it before him, closed one eye and, with clawed fingers and thumb, drew back the imaginary drawstring slowly, then released it.

'*Boof*,' he muttered, and looked at Eli. 'Think it'll work?'

'First things first, Micah, lad,' Eli told him. 'You still got to make the thing.' He turned and nodded towards the store chamber. 'You'll find everything you need in that old chest in the corner. When you've selected likely materials, you bring them to show me and I'll get you started.' He smiled. 'Bit of luck, it should occupy you for a couple of days at least.'

Micah laughed. Making a catapult sounded a sight more interesting than chores.

He headed for the store chamber, passing through

the sleeping chamber and ducking down to avoid grazing his head on the low ceiling. He paused. Thrace was sitting on the edge of her sackmattress, feeding scraps of stewed meat to the manderwyrme that was perched upon her shoulder. A wooden cage hung from a jutting spur of rock above her head, its barred door open.

Eli had explained to both of them how important the manderwyrme was. If the rock vent or the cooking chimney got blocked up and the atmosphere in the den grew toxic, then long before the three of them had even noticed, the sensitive creature would die – allowing them time to make good the situation before they too succumbed. Micah sighed wearily. They couldn't afford to lose the wyrme, yet it wasn't the first time that Thrace had removed it from its cage.

The kingirl missed her whitewyrme Aseel, missed him grievously, and it pained Micah to see it. But the whitewyrme had abandoned Thrace when she and Micah had lain together on the lakeshore in those last days of halfwinter. Now, holed up in this den for fullwinter, sheltering from the biting cold and deadly blizzards, this little caged creature was all she had. He knew that.

'How's it liking its supper?' he asked gently.

Thrace peeled off another piece of stringy meat and

held it up. The manderwyrme snatched it from her fingers and swallowed it whole.

'Seems to like it well enough,' he said, answering his own question. He paused. 'Which is good . . .' He paused again, looking at the uncaged manderwyrme and wondering how to phrase the words of admonishment he knew he should express.

But Thrace guessed anyhow. She spun round and glared at him. 'I know, I know,' she said, her eyes dull and sullen. 'But it's cruel to keep it caged every minute of the day and night.'

She raised a hand and tickled the manderwyrme beneath its chin. She shook her head slowly, and when she spoke again, her voice was soft and soothing, and little more than a whisper.

'Nothing should have to put up with that,' she told the little wyrme. 'Nothing, and no one . . .'

THREE

Micah's eyes snapped open. Something had wakened him . . .

He looked around the sleeping chamber, though he knew it was useless to do so. The lamps in the winter den were out and the blackness was absolute. Tiny white specks, like glittering motes of dust, danced in the air as Micah's eyes struggled, and failed, to get used to the lack of light.

He listened to the wind. It scoured the mountaintops and cliff-faces outside, wild and unrelenting, and got trapped in the cracks and crevices of the encasing rock, where it howled and yammered like some demented creature. But Micah had grown accustomed to the noise, and it was not what had roused him.

He pulled up his covers, relaxed back on his sack-mattress and laced his fingers behind his head. He stared at the void above where the low ceiling ought to be and wondered whether it was snowing up top. He wondered whether the moon was up, whether it was crescent-shaped or full, or hidden behind banks of clouds – or whether it was even night at all. The lack of light in the winter den made it nighttime for him, Thrace and Eli right now, but what if the sun was shining outside?

Down in the den, the cragclimber imposed the hours of light and dark upon them all with a fastidious rigidity, and the lamps were either lit or snuffed out at his word. It was he who turned the hourglass each time the sand emptied from the top glass to the bottom, and he who kept a tally of the days drifting into weeks, striking marks upon the wall with a stubby piece of charcoal set aside for that purpose.

Like the Maker Himself, Eli gave them night and day, Micah mused – as well as the powerful liquor that blurred the time and made their underground den as tolerable as it could be.

He had to hand it to him, Micah thought; the seasoned cragclimber seemed to have thought of everything. The winter den was well hid from prying eyes, and stocked with provisions to last them through the winter. A trickle of running water emerged from a mossy crack and dribbled into a small rockbowl in an alcove at one end of the main chamber and, thanks to some deep thermal or other, it would never freeze up, no matter how far the temperature dipped outside. They had the means of making fire, and the zigzag arrangement of fissures through the rock not only took the smoke away, but brought it out near a smoking vent a safe distance away up the mountainside, ensuring that no one – neither friend nor foe – might link the two.

Micah closed his eyes. He was feeling drowsy again.

Just then, from somewhere in the darkness of the chamber, there came a sound. Micah froze, instantly wide awake once more.

It was a whispering voice – soft yet insistent, sonorous as far-off thunder, gentle as pattering rain and keening like the wind outside.

'Thrace?' he said gently. He reached out to the sack-mattress next to his and found it empty. 'Thrace?'

The kingirl did not reply, yet in seeming response the rainpatter, windsigh whispers grew louder.

Micah propped himself up on his elbows. He cocked his head to one side, trying to determine where the sounds were coming from. One moment they seemed to be coming from his left, the next it seemed like they were right above his head, and as the air fluttered in his face, he raised his hands protectively.

The whispering grew louder, imitating the whoosh and pitterpatter of wind and rain rising up like a gathering storm. Then all at once, out of the darkness, there came a long crooning cry that started like a rumbling growl somewhere deep down at the back of the throat and grew to a hissing sigh.

'Aah . . . zheeeell . . .'

Micah sat up straight, his stomach churning. The kingirl was talking in her sleep. Though not talking so that he could understand, but instead in that curious language the whitewyrmes used, and which Aseel had taught her.

'Aah . . . zheeeell. Aah . . . zheeeell.'

The longing in her voice was unmistakable as she called his name. It sounded closer to him now, and Micah plunged his hands into the darkness, trying to find where Thrace was standing.

'Aah . . . zh—'

The kingirl's call abruptly cut short. The sound of wind and rain ceased. Micah strained to hear where she was, but all he could hear was the faint yet stealthy sound of someone moving, trying not to make a noise. The next moment, he felt a sharp stabbing pain in his chest.

'Aaaii!' he yelped, and fell back.

He felt the presence of someone standing above him, and legs straddled his body as he lay trembling, supine. The pain stabbed at his chest again, and he felt something sharp just above his quickly beating heart. With shaking hands, he reached up and grasped the stout pole that was pressing against his chest and tried to pull it away, but the pressure being exerted down upon it was powerful and unyielding.

'Thrace . . . Eli. Eli! *Eli!*' he called out to the cragclimber who, to give Micah and Thrace their privacy, had taken to sleeping in the main chamber.

The air abruptly filled with honeycolour light and Micah turned his head to see Eli standing silhouetted at the entrance to the sleeping chamber, a lamp raised in his hand.

'Don't wake her,' he hissed. 'Whatever you do, Micah, do not wake her up . . .'

Micah looked up at the kingirl standing over him, her arms braced as she gripped the end of the broomhandle and continued to push down hard. She looked awake already, her top teeth pressed into her lower lip and eyes narrowed with cold calculation.

Eli was beside her in a moment. He placed the lamp on the floor and took her by the shoulder, whispering reassuring words as he did so.

Thrace flinched for a moment, and Micah had to stifle his cries as the end of the broomhandle scraped against his ribs. But then, as Eli slowly and surely eased the broom from her grip, the pain subsided and was suddenly gone.

'That's it . . . that's the way . . .' Eli soothed as he steered the kingirl away from Micah's sackmattress and over to her own. 'This way, Thrace . . .'

Micah sat up again and looked across at them, watching their every move as Eli, one hand gripping her arm and the other supporting her back, laid Thrace gently down. Her head rolled to one side and, for a moment, her gaze met Micah's: fierce, beautiful, but bewildered, and lacking any recognition.

'She's still asleep,' Eli whispered.

Micah nodded uncertainly. He swallowed. Then, as he continued to watch, Thrace's eyelids seemed to grow heavy and the stern expression melted away. She closed her eyes. Micah swallowed again. He looked up at Eli.

'Does she really hate me that much?' he whispered.

Eli stooped down to gather up the makeshift lance and the lamp. 'She don't hate you, lad,' he said.

Micah shrugged. 'You sure about that?' he said, looking down at the growing bruise on his chest.

Eli crouched down next to him. He glanced at Thrace, whose breathing was now deep and even, then back at Micah.

'You gotta understand, lad, that it ain't easy for Thrace. Deep down inside she's more troubled than she could ever admit to either you or me – or even herself.'

He shook his head. 'When she's asleep, she's back with him, heeding his words, doing his bidding. Like I told you before, Micah, lad, the ties of kinship cannot be undone . . .'

'But . . . but Aseel's gone,' said Micah. 'He left her. He abandoned her . . .'

'And maybe they'll never see one another again,' said Eli, nodding. 'But I tell you this,' he added, resting a hand on Micah's, 'and it's something you'd do well to remember; Aseel will live on inside that kingirl till the day she takes her last breath, and there ain't nothing you nor I nor no one else can do about it. It's something you must simply accept.' He patted Micah's arm, then climbed to his feet. 'You sleep on now till m—' He paused, and his stubbled features creased into a grin. 'Till I say it's morning.'

Micah watched Eli as he climbed to his feet, shifted the lamp from his left hand to his right, and disappeared into the adjacent chamber. He turned his head and looked at Thrace. She was still asleep, her soft lips parted and dark eyelids unmoving. He heard a soft clatter from the main chamber, a breath of air, and Eli's light was extinguished.

Micah sighed and laid himself back down. He reached up and touched his chest, his fingertips gingerly seeking out the bruise. It was tender, but no real harm had been done. The stabbing pain in his heart was different, though. Micah feared it would never stop hurting.

Four

The winter caller was stooped forward, the white lakewyrmeskin cloak flapping. His breath was rasping and phlegm-clogged and billowed out in plumes of grey mist as he trudged on through the snow. Now and again, a gust of icy wind plucked at the cowled hood to reveal the bone mask beneath, which was frosted white, icicles of frozen drool glinting like stubby tusks around the leering mouth hole.

He crested a ridge and took temporary shelter in the windlee of a hollow. The sky was lightening. He glanced round. Behind him, the deep footprints he had made were already filling with snow and closing up, leaving no trace of his presence.

He reached inside his cloak and pulled out a long flask fashioned from a length of hollowed femur. He drew the cork and, raising the flask, put it to his lips.

He gulped at the sweet rustcolour liquid. It burned like fire and coursed through the winter caller's body, numbing his senses to pain and banishing weariness, and all emotions. Fear, doubt. Pity. Only the voice of the keld mistress remained in his drugged brain –

that, and an acute sensitivity to smell and sound.

She had trained him well, her favoured slave. Purchased young and innocent for a handful of gems, even back then he'd shown signs of determined spirit and prodigious strength, characteristics that careful beatings and doses of bloodhoney tamed as the keld mistress had bent him to her implacable will.

The winter caller recorked the flask and tucked it away in an inside pocket beneath the folds of the white cloak. He set off again. As the sky continued to brighten overhead, the blizzard eased some, and far in front of him the winter caller caught sight of a smoking mountain peak. He grunted, pleased that he was still on course.

The short day was already coming to an end by the time the winter caller reached the high pinnacles. The smoke emerged, not from one opening but from a whole series of crusted fumaroles that studded the summit, and rose like yellowstain sheets. Here, where heat from the molten rock beneath melted the snow before it could settle, the mountaintop was bare wet rock and strewn with gravel that crunched underfoot.

A family of jackwyrmes, crouched together for warmth in their rock nest, eyed the trespasser's approach warily.

The hulking figure paused again, shook the snow

from the hood and shoulders of his cloak and scanned the horizon. Then he drew the rag from his pocket and sniffed it deeply, then at the air, then the rag again . . .

Near. His quarry was near, he was sure it was.

He turned and wandered about the rock, seemingly aimlessly, head bowed and eyes darting. He kicked at loose stones, sending them tumbling down the narrow openings, listening to their clattered descent and sniffing at the smoke that twisted up out of the heatshimmer.

The jackwyrmes jabbered and squealed at the intrusion. There were eight of them in all. Two were fully grown, the size of turkeycocks, their garish markings stark against the dark rock, while their half dozen flightless young, though almost as large, had not yet sloughed their juvenile grey skin. The adults puffed out yellow chests and flapped red and blue wings, shrieking menacingly, crests raised, neckruffs quivering and fringed tails switching from side to side. Their drab young opened wide their jaws and hissed their displeasure.

The winter caller seemed not to notice them, or if he did, he paid them no mind as he continued to trudge to and fro, plunging his head into the wreaths of gaseous smoke and breathing deep.

The smoke was pungent. It reeked of sulphur. Rotten eggs and hot metal. All apart from one . . .

Sagebrush, he identified as he sniffed at the grey smoke. Longpine. Spit-hickory. It was, the winter caller knew, the kindling and wood favoured by kith for their fires, and he salivated with anticipation. He breathed in again, his tongue smacking against the back of his teeth, and detected wyrmeoil and pitchsmoke . . .

Unable to tolerate the stranger in their midst an instant longer the adult jackwyrmes took to the air with furious screeching and a flash of primary colours. Jaws agape and fangs bared, they swooped down at the wyrme-clad individual that threatened their young.

Heeding their clamour, the winter caller looked up. He braced himself, reached out and slapped the closer of the two jackwyrmes so hard he knocked it out of the sky and down to the ground, then crushed its head with a heavy boot. Its mate screeched and veered off, but not fast enough. With a throaty grunt, and surprising agility, the winter caller thrust out a hand and grabbed the creature by one red and blue wing. He swung it around his head, once, twice, then dashed it against the rock.

The juveniles' hissing rose to a loud screech. They shuffled about, flapping their wings frantically, uselessly, and spilled out from the rocks that ringed their nest. They clustered together, like some ungainly six-headed mutation, their long jaws snapping and cracking as a dark shadow fell across them.

Eyes narrowing behind the bone mask as strident wyrmescreech filled his head, the winter caller seized one of the young jackwyrmes and, like wringing out a dish-cloth, wrung its neck. There was a cracking of vertebrae, the wyrme went limp and was tossed aside, and he reached out for a second creature, then a third, until all of the jackwyrmes had been dispatched and lay at his feet.

He knelt down next to the hole with the sagebrush and spit-hickory smoke and thrust a gloved hand inside. It was like a chimney. The rocksides were smooth and crevice-free, and became narrower the deeper down he reached. He felt how the chimney-like opening bent off to one side, and made a mental note of the angle and direction it took. Then, pulling himself up, he reached for the carcass of the male jackwyrme and thrust it into the hole till it wedged tight. He jammed the female in on top of its mate.

He sat back on his haunches and observed his handiwork. The hole had all but disappeared, but smoke was still dribbling out from the gaps between the dead wyrmes' leathery bodies.

Hands on hips, the winter caller looked around him.

His gaze fell upon the pile of dead wyrmelings. He grabbed first one, then another, and another, and used the warm pliant corpses to plug up the gaps till the sweet smell of burning wood was extinguished and the smoke ceased.

He climbed to his feet.

Where there was a chimney, there had to be a hearth, safe and hidden and warming the unsuspecting winter sleepers huddled around it. Judging by the angle of the chimney, the den lay somewhere on the other side of the mountain.

Somewhere close.

FIVE

At the sound of rock grinding on rock, Micah looked up. Frozen air lapped at his face and turned his bare forearms to gooseflesh. He gulped at the crisp clean air, aware suddenly of how fetid and stale the atmosphere in the den was by comparison.

He was sitting on his sackmattress, his legs folded up beneath him, surrounded by woodworking tools, scraps of leather, spools of twine and gut-thread. He had his hackdagger in one hand, which he was using to cut two small holes in the square of lakewyrmeskin leather he held in the other. The catapult he was working on lay in his lap.

The grinding noise repeated. Micah leaned to one side and peered through the low opening that led from the sleeping chamber to the store, to see Eli pushing the rockslab that sealed the entrance to the winter den back into place.

Micah set the catapult aside, climbed to his feet and ducked through the narrow gap to the adjacent chamber. 'How was it, Eli?' he asked.

'Cold,' said Eli, brushing dry snow from his shoulders

32

and lowering his hood. Droplets of water glistened at the ends of his hair, his eyebrows, the tip of his nose. He hugged his arms vigorously to himself a couple times, then pulled off his gloves, his jacket, his scarf and hat, and hung them up beside the entrance. 'Coldest it's been. And blowing a blizzard.'

Micah nodded. If it had not been cold and blowing a blizzard, Eli would never have ventured outside in the first place, for it was only in such adverse conditions that he dared leave the safety of the den. The thick snow falling reduced the risk of his being seen and ensured that any tracks he made would vanish without trace.

'Can't have footprints leading up to the entrance if we want to say hid,' Eli had explained when Micah had enquired the first time he'd left the den. 'Might as well leave a welcome mat outside.'

Of course, best would have been if they could remain holed up without ever having to set foot outside. But if the winter den was not to end up a midden or cesspool, that was not possible. It took two weeks – three, if they were sparing with the sandsalt – for the shallow pit in the corner of the small chamber to fill. After that, it began to stink. Every four weeks or so, when it could not be put off any longer, and when the windhowl and winterchill indicated that the weather was at its meanest, Eli and

Micah would shovel the contents of the pit into the waste buckets, and Eli would carry them outside and empty them into the deep snow, well away from the den's entrance.

'Did you see . . . anything?' Thrace asked.

She stood by the entrance, just as she always did when Eli went outside. Every time the rockslab slid open, she would be there, poking her head tentatively outside and scanning the sky eagerly, until Eli pushed the slab shut behind him. Then, she'd wait by the entrance for his return, her arms wrapped round her slender body, teeth chattering and eyes downcast.

Sometimes Micah thought that, despite the repeated disappointments, Thrace lived for these moments, hoping against hope that each time might prove different. Once again, as the rockslab slid open, she had failed to see what she was looking for, though her hope persisted that Eli might have.

But he had not.

'Nothing and no one,' he told her, shaking his head. 'And it's unlikely we shall for a while to come. Fullwinter's truly upon us now. The wind's changed direction and the snow's already started to drift. Keeps up like this, we're going to be buried deep this time tomorrow.'

The kingirl turned away.

Eli's face registered his concern for her. 'A mug of yarrow tea would not come amiss, Thrace,' he said.

But Thrace did not appear to hear him.

'I'll get some,' Micah offered.

Eli shrugged. 'I was simply trying to occupy her some,' he told Micah quietly. 'Happen I can make a mug of yarrow tea myself. You want one, lad?'

Micah nodded. 'Surely.'

Eli poured water into the boiling pot and set it over the fire, which he poked at until flames were lapping at the base of blackened copper. He looked round.

'How's that catapult of yours coming along?'

'Slowly,' said Micah. 'I'm taking my time over it, Eli. Just as you advised.'

'It's good to have something to distract your thoughts,' Eli observed, glancing at the entrance to the narrow sleeping chamber into which Thrace had retreated. 'Specially now, with the den sealed up till the thaw.'

Making the catapult had proven to be every bit as time-consuming as Eli had planned it would, and Micah certainly appreciated having something to take his mind off the cramped and repetitive nature of life in the winter den.

On the first day of his endeavour, Micah had sanded

the wishbone, smoothing away its rough ridges and imperfections. The second day he spent carving a grip into the handle with his hackdagger, and two notches, one at the top of each of the twin prongs of the Y-shaped wishbone. Then on the third day, while the bone was hardening off in the hot ashes of the fire, he had made ready the other materials. He'd tested the elasticity of the various pelts that Eli had stored, before deciding a mistwyrme pelt would best suit his purpose. He'd cut two long strips from the soft tensible leather. Then he'd cut out a square of stout lakewyrme skin which, attached to the drawstring of the catapult, would form the pouch from which pebbles and shards might be fired.

Slowly and carefully, sleeves rolled up to his elbows and the tip of his tongue protruding from the corner of his mouth, Micah stitched, knotted and fixed everything in place. He held the catapult up.

It sure did look the part, and Micah could barely resist trying it out there and then. But there was still one last thing to do. He reached for the wooden spool of gut-thread which lay beside him on the sackmattress.

Micah remembered Eli trading for it at the scrimshaw den. How long ago that now seemed, he mused as he measured out four pieces of equal length and cut them off.

It had been the rain season back then, not fullwinter, and he and Eli had been little more than strangers. At first, the cragclimber had seemed closed off and distant, and there had been times when Micah had feared Eli was about to strike out on his own and leave him to fend for himself in the high country.

But he had not, and Micah was grateful to him for that. He knew he could never have survived on his own, for the wyrmeweald was a harsh and unforgiving wilderness, so different from the plains he'd left behind. It was a place where adventurers came – some to hunt and trap, others to thieve and swindle; all to exploit the land that had once belonged only to wyrmekind. Three seasons earlier, Micah had made the arduous journey to the high country, his head filled with fanciful notions of making his fortune, and he would have died in the attempt had Eli Halfwinter not taken him under his wing. And as they'd shared the trail, Micah had begun to get to know the cragclimber better. He'd learned when to speak and when to allow the silence between them to go undisturbed; to watch and learn, and to respect the ways of the harsh weald. Just like Eli did.

Micah pushed his thick hair away from his eyes, then bound each of the knots tightly with the thread, fixing them permanently into place.

'Looks just about ready to me,' came Eli's voice, and Micah looked up to see the cragclimber standing over him.

Micah grinned. 'Looks that way to me too.'

Eli hunkered down next to Micah and took the catapult out of his hands. He inspected it closely, but gave nothing away. Then, leaning back, he reached into a pocket and pulled out a handful of pebbles that were white and spherical.

'You mind if I try it out?' he asked.

'Go ahead,' said Micah.

Eli loaded one of the pebbles into the leather pouch and raised the catapult to his eye. Slowly, he pulled back on the drawstring.

Micah watched, his eyes wide and heart quickening at his chest. Was the bone hardened enough? Would the bands hold?

'See that mark there,' said Eli.

Micah looked at the black star-shaped mark high up on the wall opposite, and nodded.

Eli opened his fingers. The bands snapped back and the pebble whistled across the underground chamber. With a sharp crack, it struck the centre of the star, denting the sandstone before thudding down onto the floor of the cave.

Eli nodded slowly, sagely. He handed the catapult back to Micah, who held his breath.

'That is one excellent piece of workmanship,' he told him.

'You think I did a good job?' said Micah, scarcely daring to take in Eli's praise.

'I could not have done it better myself,' Eli confessed. He got to his feet. 'Gather up them stones and come with me.'

'You left, right or either-handed?' Eli asked.

'Right-handed,' said Micah.

''S what I thought,' said Eli frowning. 'Then you'd do better to hold it in your left hand and pull back the drawstring with your right. You'll get more power that way. And, any luck,' he added, 'a jot more accuracy.'

They were standing close to the back wall of the main chamber. An oily smell of frying lingered in the air from their supper, though the fire had since burned down to shimmering embers. Thrace sat folded up on a wyrmepelt by a side wall, the hood of her soulskin pulled up over her head and her arms wrapped around her raised legs. Opposite them was the rockslab at the entrance to the den, upon which Eli had drawn a charcoal target; three concentric rings, with a blacked-in circle at their centre.

Micah swapped the catapult from one hand to the other and pulled the pouch back till the drawstring bands went taut. Eli was right, he realized.

The cragclimber observed him critically. 'Keep your grip loose,' he told him.

Micah relaxed his hold a fraction. The pouch slipped quickly forward between his knuckles, taking with it the pebble, which shot off through the air, across the chamber and thudded against the slab of rock. Thrace looked up. Micah ran over to inspect his shot.

'I hit the target!' he exclaimed, fingering the small indentation between the first and second rings.

'Pretty good for a first attempt,' said Eli, nodding.

'Beginner's luck, I reckon,' said Micah modestly, though inside he was glowing with triumph.

'Natural talent, I'd say,' said Eli. 'Now, all you got to do is hone it.'

'Which means practice,' said Micah.

'Which means practice,' Eli repeated.

Micah returned to the opposite wall. He shot pebble after pebble at the target, then gathered them all up and started again.

Eli sat behind him on one of the wyrmeskin pelts, his back against the wall. He'd collected together all the knives they possessed: cooking and hunting knives, straight-edged and serrated – even Micah's hackdagger – and they lay before him in a line. One by one, he was sharpening the blades. The soft hiss of metal sliding over the block of whetstone accompanied the hollow thud of the pebbles as they struck the rock.

Every so often, Eli would look up and make some comment or other. 'Keep your elbow in.' Or, 'Keep your head still after you've fired.' And every once in a while, 'Excellent shot, lad.'

Micah would blush each time the cragclimber complimented him, but even he recognized he was improving. With each freshly collected bunch of pebbles, the average number of bull's-eyes was going up. More than that, as he kept on practising, something began to change. Something inside of him. With his stance and movement coming automatic, he could concentrate on the flight of the pebble itself, till each time he let one fly, it was like he was willing it to the target.

The charcoal circle Eli had drawn got pitted and flaked away as, time and again, he struck the very centre. And each time it happened, instead of being surprised, Micah was overwhelmed with a growing understanding that he was in control.

He glanced over his shoulder, and saw that Thrace was looking at him intently, her grey eyes glittering from the shadow beneath her hood. She climbed to her feet in one graceful movement, crossed the floor of the cave and plucked the catapult from his grasp. Then, with a single swift movement, she turned, pulling the drawstring back as she did so, and sent a pebble thudding into the very centre of the target. Turning back to Micah, she let the catapult clatter to the floor, and returned to the wyrme-pelt. Micah felt his face burning.

'Time to hunker down, I reckon,' said Eli soothingly, and Micah heard the sound of a cork being pulled from a liquor bottle.

Three small pewter beakers stood in a line, each one filled to the brim with green liquor. Eli picked one of them up and took it across to Thrace. Micah heard the two of them exchange soft words and saw Thrace shake her head, but Eli bent forward and set the beaker down next to her anyway. Then he returned and gave Micah his, and the two of them clinked metal on metal, and Micah downed the liquor in one. He wiped his lips on the back of his hand.

'It's a good batch,' Eli commented, having downed his own beaker. 'Triple distilled.' He smacked his lips. 'Fiery, yet smooth.'

Micah nodded. 'Like burning velvet,' he said, and added bashfully, 'if that don't sound too fanciful.'

Eli smiled. 'It's as good a description as I've heard. And wintersleep would be a deal harder without it.'

Micah held out his beaker for a refill, but the cragclimber shook his head.

'Moderation, lad,' he said, his pale blue eyes twinkling. 'It should soothe the senses, not destroy them.'

Micah smiled ruefully as he felt the fire fade to a warm glow in his belly. He'd helped Eli in the making of the liquor, with the cragclimber talking him through the process. It was he who'd mixed up a mash of barleygrain, water and yeast, who'd skimmed it off as it was fermenting, then poured it into the still.

Eli was proud of his still. He had made it himself. The stillpot was like an onion in appearance, and had been welded together from beaten panels of copper. At the top of the pot, there jutted an elbow-shaped pipe that tapered towards its end, and to which twenty foot of copper piping – that Eli called 'the serpent' – was attached. With the still on the blazing fire and the copper pipe immersed in a barrel of ice-cold water beside it, it didn't take long before a thin colourless liquid began to drip from the end of the pipe, and was collected in a flagon.

Micah had kept the woodfire stoked beneath the still

and used bellows to make it blaze. Inside the pot, the wash bubbled and alcohol vapours rose, then condensed into liquid as they passed down the chilled coiling belly of the serpent. Micah recalled the warm, almost medicinal smells that had filled the air, so strong it felt like drawing breath might prove intoxicating. A whole day it had taken for the still to boil empty and the flagon to fill, and another two for it to be distilled twice more.

'You want I should give you a hand finishing them knives off?' Micah asked.

Eli went to reply, then glanced across at the hourglass. The sand had all but trickled through. 'We'll see to them tomorrow,' he said. 'Give us something to do,' he added. 'Right now, I aim to watch the fire burn down some, then turn in.'

He settled himself down on a thick wyrmepelt next to the glowing embers. Micah sat down opposite him, and watched the blackened stubs of wood flush orange then blue, and the wisps of smoke that seemed to hover around the base of the metal chimney.

This was Micah's favourite time of day – when the hourglass had almost reached the end of its second turning, when the chores were done and they were all about to turn in. It was when Eli dimmed the lamp and handed out the beakers of liquor, and they took turns to talk as the embers glowed and the firelight gradually faded, until they were little more than disembodied voices in the darkness.

Thrace crossed the cavern and sat down beside Micah, her face pensive. 'I didn't mean to . . . to disrespect that wyrmebone you've been fashioning,' she told him.

'That's all right.' Micah sighed. 'You're a better shot than me, Thrace, that's the simple fact of it. Spite of all the practice I put in.'

'Thrace is kin, lad. Such things come natural to her.' The cragclimber shifted his position and his boot heel knocked a burned-down log. Sparks flew up, orange and darting, then disappeared. 'But I tell you this, Micah lad, that slingshot is a real fine weapon, and fashioned by your own hand. With patience. Precision. I'm proud of you.'

Micah smiled to himself. The dark silence settled back down, then fractured.

'I miss my kinlance. It made me feel safe . . .' Thrace's voice was low, reflective, but Micah could detect the tautness of loss. Of recrimination. 'I miss the air, the sky, and the high places where I felt safe. This . . . this cramped dark cave, with its stench of filth, our own filth – it's suffocating me . . .'

'Then talk about your life, Thrace. Your kin ways. Remember the clouds. The highstacks and the valley country.' The cragclimber's voice was touched with a yearning of its own. 'Travel back to them open places in your thoughts . . . Trust me, it'll help!'

The kingirl's soulskin creaked, and Micah knew she had raised her hood.

'I cannot.'

'Drink the liquor,' said Micah. 'It'll help you sleep.'

Thrace eyed the proffered beaker mistrustfully for a moment, then seized it and drank the pungent liquid down in two long gulps. She tossed the vessel aside.

Micah's body felt heavy and his head swam. He placed a hand tentatively on her arm. She did not shake it off. He reached out with the other hand and pulled her gently towards him – and she suddenly hugged him so tight he thought his heart would burst.

'I'm about to turn out the lamp,' Eli announced from the other chamber.

Micah lay down beside Thrace, pulled the covers up over them both and wrapped his arms around her slender body. Eli extinguished the lamp, and the winter den was plunged into absolute darkness.

'Thrace?' Micah whispered.

'Micah,' Thrace whispered back, and rolled over, and he could smell her warm spicy breath in his face. 'Micah.' She wriggled out of her silken suit of soulskin, then reached out and began unbuttoning Micah's shirt, and soon they were naked, skin touching skin. 'Micah. Micah . . .'

Afterwards, Micah lay back, an ache, raw and intractable, deep in his chest. He was so close to her, yet each day that passed Thrace seemed more distant from him. He placed one arm gently around her shoulders and rubbed his thumb up and down her temple, and crooked the other arm so that the flat of his hand was resting on her front and he could feel her heartbeat.

'You don't need that kinlance, Thrace. You've got me,' he said softly. 'I'll protect you.' He paused. 'Always.'

The kingirl did not reply. Her breathing was slow and even, for she was asleep, and moments later, so too was Micah.

Above their heads, in the cage by the rock vent, the little manderwyrme fluttered its wings weakly, then collapsed. A soft chirping noise rattled at the back of its throat as it gasped for good air that it could not find, and died.

Six

With a soft grunt, the winter caller swung the heavy backpack from his shoulders and set it down. It sank deep into the feathery snow. He undid the ties at the top and plunged a gloved hand inside.

He pushed aside flasks of bloodhoney, waxpaper parcels of sechemeat; knives, garrottes, lengths of rope and tools. Tongue-splitters and eye-scoops. Bone-shears. Liver-clamps . . .

His hand closed around the pair of snowshoes he was searching for. He pulled them out and they fell, *slap slap*, to the ground. A swirl of snowflakes warped and wefted his breath.

The snowshoes were broad and oval, the outer frame and cross-struts fashioned from wyrmeribs, with woven gut forming a webbing between. Heaving himself up out of the deep snow, he bent over and slipped first one heavy boot, then the other, into place in the snowshoes, which he strapped on tightly.

He took a couple of steps, experimental. The snowshoes flattened the surface of the snow but did not sink into it, and he grunted with approval. Rolling his shoulders, he hefted the heavy pack onto his back, and trudged on.

It had been snowing without remission for a long while. Three nights, certainly, plus the brief daylight hours between. The winddriven flakes had fallen and settled and built up and frozen, and more had settled and gone hard in turn, layer upon layer, getting thicker and thicker. And still it hadn't let up.

It masked the smell – with its earthy tang – that the winter caller was following, but did not obscure it completely. His nose was too good for that. It detected the odour of his quarry every step of the way, and the piece of rag kept him on track.

He was close, he knew that much. Very close. He dropped to his knees and, huge hands flat on the snow, took a deep breath.

These ones were cleverer than most. They had taken great care to disguise their chimney, and sited it as far from the den as was practical. And they dumped their waste just as carefully, to disguise their presence. But not carefully enough. The drip of the waste bucket had given them away, tiny specks beneath the crusting of snow that would have been undetectable to senses less keen than his own.

Straightening up and reaching round, the winter

caller unhitched the mattock from the side of his back-pack and gripped the carved beech handle in both hands. It was day, or what passed for it. The sky was yellow-grey and the wyrmegrease on the flat cutting edges of the pickaxe gleamed. Stooping forward, he scraped away the freshfall, then began chipping at the icesnow beneath. His breath billowed and snow began to pile up behind him as he dug deeper. Occasionally a frozen lump would run off down the hill, gathering snow as it did so, growing larger, scoring a line down the slope.

The winter caller paused. He pressed the rag to his face and breathed in. He sniffed at the hole he'd made in the snowdrift. Scat. He could smell it. The scat of his quarry.

From behind the bone mask, there came a wet snorting noise. The plumes of breath grew thicker.

The winter caller was laughing.

SEVEN

'Wake . . . up . . .'

The voice was muffled and echohollow, like it was calling from out of some deep cave, or a well. Micah listened to it rumble and recede, then the heaviness returned, pinning him down till he melted back into the rock itself, and it was dark, and everything was pulsing hard and regular.

'Wake . . . up . . .'

Micah stirred again. Dim red light penetrated his eyelids. He tried to open them, but could not, and his head throbbed at the effort.

The darkness tightened and hardened and held his body motionless. It crushed him, but it was warm and not unpleasant. And it was where he wanted to be . . .

'Wake . . . up . . . Micah . . .'

The red glow returned, and something was tugging his arm, pulling at him, shaking him.

'*Micah!*'

He opened his eyes. There was lanternlight that was yellow and bright and flickering.

'Micah, come on. Get up!'

'Eli?' Micah's mouth felt claggy, like it had been stuffed with damp feathers. The face before him was tight with concern. 'Eli, what is it?'

'Up, Micah. Come on, now.' The cragclimber turned to the kingirl lying beside Micah on the sackmattress and shook her by the shoulders. 'Thrace. You must wake up . . .'

Micah heaved himself onto his elbows. He felt sluggish. His body ached and was heavy, and his head was fuzzed up like bollcotton. He looked across at Thrace. Naked beneath the quilted blanket, she was beautiful. Slender, pale . . .

He noticed the purple-blue tinge to her lips. And to her fingertips . . .

'Eli,' Micah cried out, his own voice sounding distant and clogged. 'What's wrong?'

The lanternlight dimmed.

'The manderwyrme's dead, Micah,' said Eli, and as he spoke Micah saw Thrace's neck tremble and her eyelids flicker. 'The air's gone bad. Come on, now, Thrace.' Eli shook the kingirl again. 'You need to get up. *Now, Thrace!*'

The kingirl's eyes opened and she looked at Eli, but there was no recognition in her gaze. She sat up slowly and gathered the covers modestly about her.

'We don't have much time,' Eli said. 'Something must have blocked the chimney and the den ain't getting no ventilation. We've got to get outside and clear it.'

Micah hurriedly pulled on his breeches, shirt and wyrmeskin jerkin, then his tooled calfleather boots that he'd spent three days mending. He was panting, and the shortness of breath did not ease no matter how much he inhaled.

Looking up, Micah saw the lifeless manderwyrme in the dangling cage, its eyes dulled and tongue lolling, one wing sticking out through the bars. Thrace had seen it too, and she let out a low moan.

Eli grabbed Micah by the arm and bundled him out of the sleeping chamber and across the chamber beyond. It was like wading through black molasses. The walls of the winter den loomed close one moment, then telescoped off the next. There was a weight pressing on Micah's chest, and his head felt like it was being squeezed in a vice. His heartbeat hammered in his ears.

Pausing by the rockslab that sealed the den, the crag-climber crouched down and gripped the stone. Micah crouched down beside him.

'Two, three, heave,' Eli said.

And they heaved, grunting with the strain of it. But the slab did not move.

'Heave!'

They pulled again, their limbs trembling and sweat breaking out across their creased brows. The last dregs of their strength were ebbing away.

'Thrace, Thrace,' Eli called.

The kingirl appeared at their side, her face flickering in the lanternlight and soulskin loose at her shoulders. She placed her blue-tipped fingers against the side of the rockslab just below Micah's. He could feel her trembling body brace against his.

'*Heave!*' Eli groaned.

Micah closed his eyes and pulled as hard as he could. There was a scritching sound, and a small movement as the rock shifted. Not much. But just enough for a tiny crack to open up.

Eli straightened up. 'One, two, three. *Heave!*' he cried.

And this time the heavy rockslab succumbed, grinding and grating as it slid back to reveal a wall of snow, frozen and tightpacked, blocking the entrance.

Micah stepped forward. He touched the hard wall of frozen snow. It sparkled in the light of Eli's lamp. The cragclimber reached out and seized the waste shovel that was propped up against the wall.

'We've got to dig,' he said. 'Get some fresh air into the den.'

Micah picked up the broad-handled spade that lay next to the shovel, and Thrace grabbed two rockspikes, one in each hand. They turned back to the white wall, ready to attack it with their implements, only for the sound of scraping, methodical and rhythmic, to stop them in their tracks.

It was coming from the other side of the snowdrift, and it was getting closer.

'What do you think it is?' Micah asked, squinting up as the scraping grew louder. 'Squabwyrme? Greywyrme, maybe? I just hope it ain't no hungry redwing . . .'

'That's no redwing, Micah. It ain't no wyrme of any kind,' said Eli. There was dread in his voice. 'The digging's too steady,' he muttered darkly.

Micah turned to Eli, and in the yellow lamplight saw an expression that he recognized, but had never seen in the cragclimber's face before. It was fear.

'If it ain't a wyrme, then what *is* it?' Micah said.

Eli shook his head slowly, eyes narrowed, lips clamped thin. 'Den squatters, most likely – kith seeking to take shelter where they've no right to. If we're lucky . . .'

'And if we're not?' said Micah, and swallowed hard as he saw Eli reach for the heavy sidewinder that he kept loaded and propped up on the other side of the entrance.

'Keld,' came the reply.

EIGHT

Keld?

Micah's head swam. The keld were dark secretive cavern dwellers, like the one they'd killed deep down in her underground lair. Images of Redmyrtle's charnel-kitchen flashed through his mind. Bone-saws, flesh-hooks, severed heads on chopping blocks . . .

But keld above ground, out in the blizzards of full-winter? Was that possible?

'Micah. Look, look.' It was Thrace.

The wall of packed snow was thinning, and silhouetted against its pale opalescence was a dark shape, hunched in a blur of digging. Thrace let out a low moan as she stared down at the rockspikes in her hands.

'Kinlance,' she spat bitterly. 'It is my kinlance that I need.'

But the winter den was too cramped for the kinlance. Thrace had wrapped it in oiled wyrmeskin of Eli's providing, laid it beneath the twin rock outcrop down the mountainside, safe and hidden till the thaw, and Micah had watched her do it. He turned to her now, and their eyes met. Thrace looked away. The rockspikes would have to suffice.

Her chest tightened as she gulped at the stale air. Beside her, Micah took shallow wheezing breaths.

Thrace clamped the rockspikes between her teeth and, with a grunt of effort, scaled the wall above the entrance, then paused, limbs tensing and back arched as she found a purchase on the rock. Slowly, deliberately, she took the spikes from her mouth and gripped them, one in each hand. Below her, Eli panted softly as he knelt down on one knee, his sidewinder primed and raised, and index finger poised on the trigger.

At that moment, there came a grinding crunch and the gleaming iron blade of a pickaxe penetrated the snow wall. Chips of ice showered down onto the floor of the chamber and a blast of air that was cold and clean, and welcome for that, came rushing in.

The next moment, the blade disappeared. The scraping fell still.

'Micah, son,' Eli whispered. 'Don't just stand there. Fetch your catapult.'

Micah backed away from the entrance and into the shadows of the main chamber, his eyes still fixed on the snowdrift. Suddenly, with a heavy thud, a great brick of compacted snow burst into the den and shattered, followed by the massive boot that had dislodged it.

Micah turned and dashed back through the main chamber and into the sleeping chamber beyond. Behind him a fury of ice-cold air poured into the den.

He heard Eli's sidewinder give a rattling crack, and then the crumping thud of a bolt striking something hard. The next moment, Thrace's shrill screech, wild and piercing, filled the den. It was greeted by a wheezing grunt and the sounds of scuffling. Rockspikes clattered to the stone floor; first one, then the other. Eli's sidewinder clanked as the cragclimber struggled to reload it. There was a hard crunch and a small whimpered sigh, then a sharp crack, followed by another and another, and the heavy flump of a body hitting the stone floor.

The winter den fell silent.

Trembling with fear, Micah inched his way backwards, into the blackness. Eyes still fixed on the entrance to the sleeping chamber, he crouched down beside the sackmattress and felt about until his hand found the catapult. His fingers closed round its handle, then he scooped up a couple of pebbles. He listened intently for any sound coming from the other chambers as he crept deeper into the darkness.

All at once there was the sound of a match being struck on a flint box. Then something rattled and bounced along the floor of the main chamber like a rolling pebble. The next moment, there was a blinding flash and an earsplitting explosion.

Rocks crashed to the floor. Thick dust filled the air. Through the entrance of the sleeping chamber, Micah could see a sheet of flame engulf the main chamber in a sulphurous glare.

A moment later, the light abruptly dimmed as a massive figure filled the entrance to the sleeping chamber, its bulk silhouetted against the firelight behind. It held something up to its face in a gloved hand. It was black and ragged and homespun, a piece of a cloak worn by a ploughboy from the plains and found by the keld mistress, snagged on a hook in Redmyrtle's lair.

'They crept into her cavern, these kith. They robbed her. And then they murdered her. One of our own,' the keld mistress had told him, her voice low and honeyed. 'The keld must be avenged.' She had given him the rag. 'You have their scent.'

Find them. Dig them out. Dispatch them . . . slowly.

The figure pressed the rag to the bone mask and sniffed, then sniffed again. It stooped down and entered the sleeping chamber, its hooded head turning this way, that way.

With the cold stone wall pressed hard against his

back, Micah held his breath. He slipped a pebble into the sling of his catapult, which he raised slowly to his eye.

He would only get one shot.

Slurping and snuffling wetly, the monstrous figure was probing the darkness. The air was rank with the acrid stench of burning goosedown and wyrmeskin from the main chamber. But Micah could tell it had detected another odour. *His* odour.

He pulled back on the drawstring. His hands shook as he took aim.

Do it. Do it now, Micah urged himself, his eye, the stone and his outstretched arm aligned. *Now!*

He loosened his grip on the leather sling and the drawstring shot forward, sending the heavy round pebble hurtling through the air. An instant later there was a broken-egg crunch as it struck the figure full in the face. With a startled grunt, it staggered backwards, stumbled and fell to the floor with a muted crash. Its head slumped to one side. Blood trickled down onto the dusty stone.

Micah remained motionless for a moment, waiting for his heart to stop pounding. Then he approached the body. He looked down. The cloak was open at the front to reveal Eli's bolt embedded in the intricate patchwork armour of wyrmebone scapulas and clavicles beneath. The hood was still raised and it hung limply over the face.

The only movement was the droplets of blood that plashed into the growing puddle below.

Micah crouched over and pulled back the hood. A bone mask stared back at him, the nubbed ridge above the left eyesocket shattered where the pebble had struck. The blood was seeping out through the fractured bone. Behind him, in the main chamber, the blaze crackled and fizzed and he could feel the intense heat of the fire at his shoulders.

He was leaning back on his heels when, all at once, there was a deep grunt and a gloved hand shot up and seized Micah round the neck. He could feel the figure's warm fetid breath in his face and, from behind the bone sockets, the eyes glared back at him, one glittering like anthracite, the other stained with blood.

The grip tightened and tightened, and a wheezing sound emerged from the mouth hole.

'Redmyrtle,' it whispered.

NINE

There was something in his mouth keeping his jaws from closing. It was soft and padded, and it had the tang of dead meat about it.

Micah swallowed. Bile rose up at the back of his throat. He tried to open his eyes, but could not. It was like they'd been glued shut. Neither could he move his arms or legs. He was spreadeagled, arms outstretched above his head and legs splayed.

Arching his back, Micah fought to break free. But his grunts of effort were stifled by the leather gag between his teeth and the ropes at his wrists and ankles bit deep as he struggled. He slumped back, his strength spent. The cold burned into his skin, branding his shoulders, his buttocks, his calves; pulsing inside his head.

Was this it, then? Was this the way he was going to die, staked out and helpless, like a rockwyrme in a snare?

Micah flinched. There was warm breath on his face, putrid and pungent, blowing first on one eyelid, then on the other. Heaving and gagging, he tried to turn his head away, but a hand clamped round his jaw and held him still. The frozen tears which had sealed his eyes shut began to melt, and as the soft wheezing breath continued Micah was able to open his eyes and peer out through narrow slits.

The winter caller rocked back on his haunches and gave a slurping giggle. This was the part he always enjoyed the most. Before the splintering and the screams, before the cutting and the blood, was this.

The fear.

He reached up and removed the bone mask.

Micah shuddered and wanted to scream, but the leather gag stoppered all but a muted sob. Beneath the mask, the keld's face was quilted with tiny crisscross scars. They puckered his features, ridging the shapeless hump of the nose, pulling at the splayed nostrils and tightening the taut leer of the thin-lipped mouth. Pale blue eyes were sunk deep into bruised eyesockets and stared back at Micah, cold and emotionless. Muscles strained beneath the scar-tissued face, twitching almost imperceptibly as a moist tongue protruded from the mouth.

The winter caller was attempting to smile.

Micah stared at the colossal figure, unable to move, unable to cry out. He saw him reach behind his back and, following his intense gaze, found himself staring at a line of metal implements that had been laid out neatly in the snow. They glinted in the drab sunlight. Some had hooks, some had spikes, some had glinting blades; one of them had a length of compressed spring that separated two ridged metal blocks that appeared to be designed for clamping, or crushing. He watched a gloved hand hop along the line, before coming to rest on a dull grey implement.

As his hand closed around the eye-gouge, the wet hicking sound of the winter caller's laughter filled the air. He blew the snow from the implement, then brushed at the stubborn flakes that still clung on.

The winter caller leaned forward and lightly touched the metal tool to the youth's eyes. First one, then the other. He mimed a pressing and turning movement, and lest there should be any lingering doubt, he pointed to the youth's eyes again, which were filling with tears. He savoured his victim's terror, his moist tongue protruding from his lipless mouth as he carefully placed the eye-gouge back in the line, next to the marrow-spike and the bone-shears.

With a snort of derision, the winter caller climbed to his feet. He moved away.

Micah stifled a sob. He turned his head, to see the keld crouch down again – crouch down beside the figure lying beside him. His heart missed a beat.

It was Thrace. She was stretched out and fettered in the snow with ropes and stubby stakes that had been sharpened and hammered deep into the ice, and that he guessed mirrored his own. The right side of her body was badly bruised and grazed, and there looked to be blood at the fold of her ear. Beyond her was Eli, similarly gagged and bound, and with blood that had matted his hair and specked the snow about him. Like Micah himself, they were naked, their clothes lying in the snow just out of reach – boots, socks, breeches, undershirts; Thrace's soulskin – each item laid out with mocking care.

He could have finished them off in the den, Micah thought, this keld. He could have stoved their skulls in. Slit their throats.

Yet he had not. Instead, he had dragged them outside and stripped them and laid them out in the freezing snow, where he had bound them tightly, fastidiously, hand and foot.

The winter caller prodded the kingirl in the ribs. He would save her for last. Still squatting down, he turned to the kith beside her, moistening his lipless mouth with his tongue as he did so.

Eli glared up at the keld. His voice protested, but behind his gag the words were muffled and indistinct.

The winter caller hickered and slurfed. He reached back and selected the bone-shears. He touched the jags of the blades to Eli's fingers, thumbs, wrists, one by one, then twisted round and touched the toes. The ankles. The knees . . . There came another snuffling *hick hick*, and what passed for a smile plucked at the winter caller's scarred features.

He was playing with them, Micah realized, this keld. He was enjoying their helplessness, their fear, taunting them with these gutting tools laid out in the snow with such hideous precision.

The winter caller laid the shears aside and leaned over Thrace. He reached out a huge gloved hand and, with something approaching tenderness, pushed a lank strand of hair from the kingirl's face. Then, reaching behind him, he selected from the line of tools a heavy-looking implement with two rectangular plates, spiked, studded with perforations and attached to a threaded rod of metal.

It was a rib-spreader, for splitting open a wyrme's sternum and holding the rib cage apart to gain access to the precious internal organs within. The lungs, the flameoil sac. The heart.

The winter caller pressed the rib-spreader's spikes against the kingirl's skin, not hard enough to cut through, but with sufficient pressure to leave a dark red mark that made Micah want to cry out.

The winter caller sat back. The kingirl had neither flinched nor made a sound. He rested the tool on his legs, and used his flattened hands to demonstrate the working of the tool, mimicking the metal plates closing and thrusting down into something resistant, then widening again and locking into place.

There was still no trace of a reaction on the kingirl's face.

The winter caller paused. She was a tough one, this kingirl, and he was pleased. It would make her agony all the more satisfying. He drew back and was about to return the rib-spreader to the line of tools when a dark shadow passed over him.

He hesitated. The shadow crossed a second time, and this time he looked up. His eyes widened with surprise and the twisted grin melted away.

❧

TEN

With a screech of rage the whitewyrme swooped down out of the pale grey sky and struck. Its claws strafed the keld's shoulders, scoring jagged marks down the wyrmepelt of the hooded cloak.

The keld lashed out at the creature as, with a beat of its mighty wings, the whitewyrme soared back into the sky. It wheeled round sharply.

The keld threw down the rib-spreader and drew the broad gutting knife from his belt. He raised his arms, shielding his eyes with one hand and brandishing the knife with the other. In a wingchurn swirl of snow, the whitewyrme landed on the mountainside a little way off. Two tendrils of smoke rose from its nostrils.

High above, the sky was glowering and curdled. It was raw cold, but there was no wind.

The wyrme cocked its head and eyed the keld's victims pegged out in the snow. Two kith, one kin. *His* kin. She was alive, at least. The whitewyrme's gaze returned to the hulking figure of the keld standing over her, knife in hand. It arched its sinuous neck, the muscles beneath the white scales tensing as it prepared to engulf the keld in flame.

The winter caller dropped down onto the kingirl, clamped his legs round her body and put his face down near her face. He held the knife to her throat. Her wyrme was preventing him finishing off his task, and that irked him. Gripping the handle of the gutting knife, he looked up at the whitewyrme.

It was fully grown by the looks of it. He noted the pearlwhite scales that armoured its muscular body, the broad skintaut wings upon its back that were rigid and upright, and the barbels that twitched at the corners of its firebreath mouth. It would be tough to take down such a wyrme, and he'd need more than a gutting knife to do it. Beneath him, the winter caller felt the kingirl squirm and struggle. The wyrme wanted the girl, and would not breathe fire as long as the keld kept her close. But he needed his tools. He glanced over to the line of implements in the snow, just out of reach. The bolas, two lead weights attached by a leather rope. He'd need those. And the jaw clamp. The skull-hammer would be useful too, if he could reach it . . .

A soft rustling sound like the wind through thornscrub rose up from the wyrme's throat. The whitewyrme's neck dipped; its amber-coloured eyes were fixed on the kingirl's face.

'*Thrrrr . . . eeaaa . . . sssssssss.*'

The winter caller flung himself towards the line of tools.

The whitewyrme rose up on its hind legs and, with a rattling roar, let forth a blast of white flame. Like a blazing lance, it pierced the quavering air.

The winter caller raised an arm and shielded himself as best he could with his cloak. The air turned rank with the odour of scorched wyrmeskin. He grasped the bolas, the jaw clamp and reached for the skullhammer, bracing himself for another fiery blast – but the whitewyrme had dropped back down onto all fours and had hurried over to the kingirl, neck lowered and tail raised and the spurclaws at the backs of its heels kicking up snow.

Stooping down over the girl, it sliced through the tethers that bound her hands with its claws, then slashed the fetters at her ankles.

The kingirl sat up. She yanked the gag from her mouth.

'*Aseel,*' she cried out. She rubbed at her wrists, then stumbled to her feet, wincing as she did so as her numbed limbs came throbbing back to life. '*Aseel, you came back . . .*'

All at once, there was a whistling sound and a blur of movement, and two lead weights, one at either end of the long leather rope, came flying towards them. The bolas wrapped themselves round three of the whitewyrme's legs, then, as he struggled to free himself, round the fourth, binding them all together and pitching the creature to the ground. The winter caller lunged forward and was upon the wyrme's back in an instant.

Thrace cried out and threw herself at Aseel's assailant, but the winter caller kicked her viciously away and she tumbled back heavily to the ground.

Aseel reared upwards, wings flapping and back arched. He switched his powerful tail from side to side, then up over his back and struck a heavy blow to the keld clinging to his shoulders.

The winter caller fell to one side, but managed to cling on. The gutting knife was knocked from his grasp.

With a roar of rage, Aseel rolled onto his back. He felt something crack and heard a cry, and thought he must have broken his attacker's leg, or spine, but then the keld reappeared at his side – and there was something in his hands. Aseel arched his neck back and opened his jaws – but a stout leather noose was thrust over his snout and the keld twisted a bone rod that tightened the noose and clamped his jaws shut.

'*Aseel! Aseel!*' Thrace screamed.

Hobbled and muzzled, the whitewyrme pitched and bucked about in the snow. The keld leaped back, a heavy metal hammer glinting in his hand.

Thrace turned and sprinted down the snowy mountainside towards a twin outcrop of rock.

The winter caller jumped up onto Aseel's neck, avoiding the tail, which twisted and thrashed. Beneath him, the whitewyrme writhed wilder than ever, eyes rolling in his head. Smoke billowed from his muzzled snout. The keld swung the skullhammer, but was knocked off balance as Aseel dipped his neck and flexed his wings, and the blow fell on the trampled snow, sending shards of ice flying into the air. Aseel tossed back his head, but the winter caller clung on grimly, his legs braced round the neck. Slowly, gripping hold of the wyrme's neck crest, he started inching himself forward, intent on landing a clean blow.

Aseel writhed and wriggled, he flapped his wings and switched his tail, but there was nothing he could do to dislodge the keld, who was pulling himself inexorably closer to his head. Out of the corner of his eye he saw the keld raise the skullhammer . . .

He would crush the creature's head; he would spill its brains. The keld mistress's imperative echoed inside the winter caller's head. *Find them*. He had found them. *Dig them out*. He had dug them out. Now it remained only for him to dispatch them, slowly, and he would not be thwarted in his task.

He gripped the heavy hammer and—

Searing pain burned through the top of his leg. With an agonized scream, the winter caller fell from the whitewyrme's neck and tumbled down the mountainside in a flurry of churned snow. Coming to a halt, he climbed to his feet and looked up. The kingirl stood stockstill, looking back at him, a blackpine lance gripped in her hands.

Keeping a wary eye on the keld, Thrace reached up and removed the leather muzzle from Aseel's snout. She tossed it aside.

The winter caller started back up the mountainside, the hammer gripped in his massive hands and blood spattering the snow as he limped towards the kingirl. The whitewyrme was still hobbled. He would smash the lance from her grasp and stove in her head. He would take his time with her wyrme.

Thrace clenched her jaws and held her breath as the keld approached. Beside her, Aseel turned his head to one side and opened wide his jaws. With a roar, he aimed a dense plume of white-hot flame at the mountainside, where plump blankets of deep snow were piled up over a high sloping ridge of rock.

The drifted snow hissed and steamed, and thin strings of water trickled down over the snow below. The jet of flame kept up uninterrupted. There was a sharp cracking noise, followed by a low rumbling that grew louder and louder, and suddenly the whole lot began to shift.

The winter caller looked up and hesitated as the snow above began to tumble down the mountain towards him. He stumbled backwards, and was engulfed in the advancing avalanche. A leg thrust up out of the whiteness for a moment, then an arm – then both limbs disappeared inside the rush of snow as it hurtled on down the side of the mountain, taking the winter caller with it.

Eleven

Micah turned his head to see Thrace standing in the trampled snow. Her gaze was fixed on the lower slopes, where the avalanche had disappeared into the blue-shadowed depths of the valley below, its loud roar fading to a distant rumble.

Planting her kinlance in the snow, Thrace bent down and gathered up her soulskin. Micah watched as she stepped into the faded milkwhite suit of sloughed wyrmeskin, first one leg, then the other. She pulled it up over her body and pushed her arms through the sleeves in swift graceful movements, before turning to where Micah and Eli lay, gagged, bound and staked out in the snow. She crouched down, and undid the leather ties at Micah's wrists and ankles, then gently removed the gag from his mouth.

'Thrace,' Micah gasped. He sat up and reached towards her. 'Thrace, I . . .'

But the kingirl turned away. She stepped over the blooded snow to Eli and untied him, before gathering up the cragclimber's clothes and handing them to him. Eli took them, his eyes fixed on hers, and nodded grimly.

Micah tried to stand up, but his hands and feet were frozen numb and his legs felt like lumps of wood, and unconnected to him. He pitched forward onto his knees, shivering convulsively. Thrace picked up his long flannel undershirt and gently wrapped it round his shoulders, and Micah felt her breath, warm and sweet, beside his ear.

'Forgive me, Micah,' she whispered.

She straightened to her full height and walked over to where Aseel lay, hobbled by the keld's bolas. Her soulskin hung loosely off one shoulder, soot-grimed and blood-spattered, and baggy on the thin frame of her body. As the kingirl released the whitewyrme's legs from the tangle of leather rope, Aseel let out a long keening sigh and climbed to his feet.

Thrace threw the bolas aside and grasped her kinlance. Aseel bent his neck and brought his head down close to his kin. His nostrils flared.

She was tainted with the tang of kith, the scent of the one she'd lain with, and yet . . .

Aseel's yellow eyes stared into Thrace's face. Her lips parted and a soft noise like dry leaves in the wind rose from the back of her throat.

This kith of hers had helped her, protected her as best he could; had loved her with all his heart, and yet . . .

Aseel's jaws opened, and gentle clicks, like the snapping of twigs, emerged between wisps of smoke.

When he had discovered her by the lake, asleep in the kith's arms, he had thought she was lost to him, seduced back to the ways of the kith. He had tried to forget her, but beneath the kithtang, her scent had never left him and, despite everything, it had drawn him back to her, here on this fullwinter mountainside.

She had been lost to him, and yet . . .

The whitewyrme opened his jaws and blew, and thick clouds of white smoke billowed forth. Micah could feel its heat, smell its aromatic sweetness, and as he watched, Thrace was enveloped in the smoke that grew denser and denser until he could no longer see her. Then Aseel drew back his neck, and as the smoke thinned, Thrace reappeared.

The soulskin was white and gleaming and skintight once more. Her hair was no longer unkempt and straggly, but straight and lustrous, with an ashgold sheen. And as for her eyes . . .

Micah stared into them. The intensity that had first drawn her to him had returned, a dark-eyed ferocity that both thrilled him and made him afraid.

'Thrace?' he said, his voice uncertain. 'Thrace?'

The whitewyrme turned away and surveyed the sky

where banks of dark yellow-tinged clouds were gathering. Thrace gripped her kinlance and looked over her shoulder at Micah. Her face was so beautiful, pale yet radiant, the sunlight gleaming on her soft lips, her high cheekbones, her lustrous hair. A teardrop brimmed in a dark eye, then traced a path down the cheek of her expressionless face.

Aseel dipped his head up and down and, turning to him, Thrace gripped the side of the whitewyrme's wing and leaped up onto his shoulders. She wrapped her legs round his neck, then sat back, cradled in the niche of the wyrme's clavicle spur.

Aseel raised his magnificent wings and beat them up and down, stirring the untrampled snow as, with a soft grunt, he kicked off with his hindlegs and soared into the air. The kingirl turned and looked back at the kith in the tattered shirt kneeling forlornly in the churned-up snow. Slowly, deliberately, she reached up and pulled the hood of her soulskin over her head, enveloping her face in impenetrable shadow.

The whitewyrme's wingbeats grew faster as wyrme and rider rose steadily into the wintry sky. Then, spreading his wings wide, the wyrme caught the gathering wind and soared off over the mist-blurred mountaintops.

Before long, wyrme and kin were no more than a

smudge of white against the dark incoming clouds; a smudge that faded and shrank, and then disappeared.

Micah remained motionless, his eyes fixed upon the spot where they had melted into the greying sky.

'Best get dressed, lad.'

Micah stared up at the cragclimber blankly.

Eli was standing over him, the youth's clothes and boots clutched to his chest. He placed them down on the frozen ground, took Micah's arm and threaded it through one sleeve of the undershirt, then the other. He crouched down and began doing up the buttons, like a father dressing his infant son.

Micah stirred and looked down. 'I can do it,' he said, brushing Eli's hands away and climbing to his feet.

He buttoned the thick undershirt up to the collar, the warmth of the soft material letting him know just how cold he was. He put on his breeches, socks, the tooled boots and jerkin, and looked around for his hacketon, but the heavy leather overcoat must still be in the den, and he looked up to see Eli standing over by the entrance.

Beyond the tunnel of ice, the winter den was soot-blackened and smoke-filled. The cragclimber was shaking his head.

'Flameoil grenade,' he said. 'The keld's burned us out.

There ain't nothing down there to salvage, Micah. Clothes. Provisions. Tools. It's all gone. And the den itself, it can't offer us shelter no more . . .'

Micah nodded dumbly, the words barely sinking in, the image of Thrace in her gleaming soulskin filling his thoughts. Far above, the sun was blotted out by the yellow-grey clouds.

'What do we do now?' he asked, his voice flat and without hope.

Eli's clear blue eyes fixed themselves on Micah. 'We find ourselves a new place, son,' he said simply. 'Or we die.'

TWELVE

It was powerful, this musky odour that clung to the air. It seemed to have seeped into the soft yellow-grey stone of the fluted pillars and clawscratch walls of the deserted wyrme galleries. Rich, pungent and soursweet, it was the odour of the whitewyrmes who had once inhabited them.

It was this that had drawn them to the place.

Asa had detected it first; the scent of his own kind – faint, yet unmistakable on the biting fullwinter wind. And clinging to his back for warmth, swaddled in white soulskin, his kin, Hepzibar, had sensed his excitement. They'd circled high overhead, Asa's wings flexing against the gusting blizzard. Then, with his back arched, his neck braced and his tail ruddering his approach, he had swooped down out of the sky.

Yet when they had landed and looked about them, there had been no wyrmes to be seen.

They had stayed nonetheless, the juvenile whitewyrme with the pearlwhite fresh-sloughed skin and the eight-year-old girl he was kinned with. And they were grateful for the refuge.

Fullwinter had only just been breaking when they'd

escaped from the hideous underground kitchen of the keldhag, Redmyrtle. Hepzibar had felt so frightened and alone, tied up in that terrible place until Asa, the young wyrme, had been tethered beside her. He had coiled his white body around her and breathed softly in the darkness, and she had felt comforted. And then her father had come to rescue her, with the others. The boy and the man, and the kingirl, Thrace. They had set them free and killed Redmyrtle, though not before the hag had embedded a hatchet in her father's chest. He had died in Hepzibar's arms.

But then Thrace had taken them aside. She had explained kinship to them. And when Asa had shed his first skin, Thrace had helped Hepzibar clothe herself in it. And Asa had breathed on her, enveloping her in warm wreaths of smoke, until the wyrmeslough had tightened around her body, protecting her like a second skin.

Soulskin.

'Asa will take care of you now, in the kin way,' Thrace had said, as they stood on the snowy ledge outside Redmyrtle's lair. 'You will meet others and they will teach you, but first you must learn to look after yourselves.'

And then she had set them free, releasing them into the bewildering vastness of the wyrmeweald.

They had spent those first frostladen nights together in the lee of the crags that fringed the high lakes, Asa's body coiled round Hepzibar's, offering her warmth and protection. But when the water had frozen solid and fishing had become impossible, they had been forced to move on.

They had roosted in the highstacks close to the warmth of the smoking vents, but there had been no food to be had there, and they'd moved on again. They'd scavenged through the ruined nests of redwings on the high plains and had dug for damsel grubs in the frozen river gulleys. But as the drifts of freshfall snow grew deeper, food had become harder and harder to find, and by the time the scent of the great whitewyrmes had reached them, both wyrme and kin were bone-thin and famished.

Hepzibar looked up from the crackling fire of thornbrush. Asa was coiled round one of the pillars, his legs, tail and sinuous neck hugging the rough stone, and she noticed how perfectly his body fitted the contours of the sculpted rock. He was skritching himself up and down, the sound soft and insistent as he added his own saltmusk scent to the fluted column, just as generations of wyrmes had done before.

Where were they now, Hepzibar wondered,

the whitewyrmes that had once lived in this place?

There was firewood to be had here, for thornbrush and cragscrub flourished in the shelter of the undercliff, and there was plentiful water from melted snow. And as they had explored the labyrinth of ancient rock caverns, they had found lofty chambers with perches and dustbaths and ledges lined with nesting material. They had chosen a cavern at the centre of the wyrme gallery that was warm and still and safe. Only the eerie wailing of the wind testified to the fact that, outside, the weald was still in the throes of fullwinter.

And when they'd explored deeper, they had come to cool, low-ceilinged caves where long grooves had been scratched deep into the walls. Clusters of flame-dried leathergrubs and smoked bugspawn lined them, while brine pits dug into the cave floor held preserved damsel-fly larvae and bundles of stipplebeet. There was enough food here to feed a thousand wyrmes through the long months of ice and scarcity.

Yet they had abandoned it.

Hepzibar looked down and turned the skewered damsel grubs that were hissing and steaming in the flames and replacing the redolent wyrmemusk of the cavern chamber with their own tangy sweetness. Asa eased up in his skritching and peered across at her, his nostrils twitching. His eyes widened and his barbels trembled, and he opened his jaws to emit a lulling noise that pitter-pattered in the back of his throat and hissed over his teeth, like wind sighing through long grass.

Hepzibar nodded. She parted her lips and trilled her tongue, blowing out softly. *'Dinner's ready.'*

Asa purred appreciatively, uncoiled himself from the fluted pillar and crossed the cave to the fire, flexing his wings sleepily as he did so. Hepzibar took two of the laden skewers from the flames and held one out to Asa, who took it in his claws and began nibbling delicately, cautiously at the sizzling grubs. He sighed and husked.

'Tastes good,' he said, and a black tongue flicked from his scaly muzzle and lapped at the oily juice on his lips. He chittered, and Hepzibar saw amusement in his eyes. *'Much better than scraps from a redwing nest.'*

Hepzibar smiled and nibbled at a toasted grub. It was nutty and succulent, and still slightly salty from the brine pit.

'More?' she said, noticing that the whitewyrme had eaten every morsel from the sharpened stick.

'Yes, Zar, more,' the whitewyrme replied, his yellow eyes bright now and alert.

Hepzibar plucked a second skewer from the

flames and handed it to him. She took one for herself.

'*Asa.*' She frowned. '*We will be all right, won't we?*'

As she spoke, she saw Asa flinch, and understood that he was as uncertain as she was. Hepzibar laid the skewer aside, climbed to her feet and stepped towards him. She wrapped her arms round his neck and whispered softly in his ear.

'*I have you.*'

Asa inclined his head. '*You have me. And I have you . . .*'

'*We have each other.*'

Asa purred, and Hepzibar smiled and hugged him tighter. The simple words had worked, just like they always did when she felt uncertain or afraid – when the lakes had frozen, when the hunger at the highstacks had driven them both half mad, when the fullwinter wind had harried and pursued them across the snow-filled skies . . .

She let go of Asa and crouched down, and was about to stoke the fire with a grease-stained skewer when she heard a noise behind her.

She spun round, to see a pale red-headed youth leaning against a cavern pillar a little way off. She could tell at a glance that he was older than her, and though his bones showed through the white soulskin he wore, he looked taller and stronger than she was. He was gripping a long black lance which was pointing straight at her, and when he spoke, his voice was a guttural snarl at the back of his throat.

'*What are you doing here?*'

Thirteen

'I said, ain't that right, Micah?'

'Y . . . yes,' said Micah uncertainly. He scratched behind his ear. 'What? I . . .'

'Micah!' Eli said sharply, taking him by the shoulders and pushing his face up close. 'You gotta snap out of this.'

Micah tried to pull away, but the cragclimber held him tight. His thumbs dug into Micah's shoulders.

'You're kith, boy. Thrace is kin. Y'understand? She weren't never more than on loan to you, and now Aseel's come back to claim his own, that's it. It's over. She's back where she belongs, and if you truly have feelings for her, then you should be glad for her . . .'

'*If!* Eli, how could you doubt it?'

The cragclimber released his grip. He stared intently into Micah's eyes. 'Then let her go, Micah.' His voice was softer. 'And with good grace. Life in the winter den weren't no life for Thrace. You could see that.'

Micah bowed his head, scrutinized his boots. His face felt hot, his scalp tingly.

'Thing is,' Eli pursued, 'with her whitewyrme to protect her, Thrace is fine. We are not, Micah. Not fine

89

at all. If we're to make it through to the thaw, then you're gonna have to pull yourself out of your despond. I can't have no dead weight round my neck, not with the trail we have in front of us. Once we get started, we've got to keep moving, or we die. And I ain't fixing to die.' He paused, his pale blue eyes boring into Micah's. 'Y'understand what I'm saying to you?'

Micah nodded. Eli held his gaze for several seconds more, then jerked his head toward the winter caller's pack.

'Like I was saying,' he said, 'we may have lost our den supplies, but at least we ain't starting out with nothing.'

Micah stared down at the half-empty backpack slumped on the ground between them. Powdersnow was already gathering in the folds of wyrmeskin. He grimaced.

'Can't afford to be squeamish, boy. Besides, he don't got no more use for it himself.'

Micah crouched and watched as Eli stooped over and plunged his hand inside the winter caller's pack.

'This'll come in handy,' he said, laying out a length of rope on the ground. 'And this. And rockspikes are always useful. And . . .' He fell still.

Micah stared at the catapult gripped in the crag-climber's calloused hand – the catapult he'd spent so many long hours fashioning from the wishbone. Eli placed it down on the ground with the rest. A stoppered jar of flameoil followed. A copper pot. Eli's battered spyglass and a couple of his best knives, plus Micah's own hackdagger appeared next, and Eli chuckled.

'Looks like that winter caller did some ransacking of his own.'

The cragclimber drew a waxpaper parcel of sechemeat from the pack. Then another, and another. He placed them down on the snow, his face sombre. More keld stuff followed. A jar of bloodhoney. Snares and garrottes. The rolled-up pelt of a greywyrme . . .

'Reckon that's about the last of it,' said Eli, straightening up and upending the backpack.

With a soft jangle, something dropped out, and Micah and Eli found themselves staring at an oval medallion on a short length of silver chain that lay in the dusting of freshfall. Eli picked it up and awkwardly flicked the clasp with a thumbnail. The top of the medallion sprang open on its hinge. Inside was a coil of plaited hair, each of the three thin locks cut from a different head. One was crinkled and red, one was straight and black, and one, wispy and fair, was baby hair.

Micah stared at the delicate little plait. It was tradition with some parents back on the plains to mingle their hair with that of their child on its first birthday.

'Wonder what poor wretch he took that from,' said Eli. He closed the lid, turned the medallion over and squinted at the italics engraved into the back. 'Hiram. Anya. Darius.' He shrugged, then slipped the medallion over his head. 'Never know, might be able to trade it for something useful,' he said. 'Now, let's get this lot packed up, lad. We need to make tracks before sundown.'

Eli began selecting the equipment and provisions for their journey and returning them to the winter caller's backpack. Micah's empty stomach rumbled, and, without thinking, he picked up and unfolded one of the waxpaper parcels. He selected a slice of the brown sechemeat it contained and was about to put it in his mouth when Eli's hand shot out and slapped it from his grasp.

'Don't,' he chided. 'That's keld meat.'

He left the words hanging in the air as he returned to his task. Micah's top lip curled as he stared at the twist of dried flesh that lay beside him on the snow.

Keld meat. Which meant human meat, sliced and dried.

Micah's stomach lurched, and he couldn't stop himself wondering what part of the keld's victim it might have been cut from. A spasm racked his body, followed by another, and sour bile swirled around his tongue. He plunged his hands into the snow and rubbed them together, then wiped them across his lips and gagged again at the thought of what he had almost done . . .

'You ready?'

Eli was standing over him, the winter caller's back-pack strapped to his shoulders. He helped Micah to his feet and handed him the wyrmepelt. The cragclimber had cut a hole in the centre of the heavy skin to fashion a makeshift cape.

'It's a mite rough, but I reckon it'll keep you warm,' he said.

Micah pulled the skin over his head and strapped it at his middle with his belt, and the pair of them tramped off up the mountainside.

Despite the heavy pack at his shoulders, Eli was soon up in front, his gait easy and loping, and Micah attempted to copy it. He could have done with his walking staff, but like Eli's own staff, and so much else, it had been turned to ashes in the winter den.

As they crested the first of a series of ridges, Micah looked back. The line of gutting tools they'd left behind had all but disappeared beneath the falling snow. Beyond it were the packs of sechemeat, open now, a group of five or six small bearded rockwyrmes snouting at the meat and squabbling as they devoured it.

Micah's belly churned. He would never eat such meat. And yet, as he watched the wyrmes tucking in, his hunger tightened and he found himself – Maker forgive him – envying the small creatures that had no such qualms.

FOURTEEN

The youth regarded Hepzibar levelly. His eyes were pitchdark and glittered in the firelight. His cheeks were sunken and had a grey tinge to them that matched the dark crescents beneath his eyes. His nostrils flared as he took in the scent of the toasting grubs.

'*Get away from the fire.*'

Beside her, Hepzibar felt Asa bristle. His wings unfurled and his neck coiled back as a low growl grew steadily in his throat.

'*Why should we?*' he said.

From the shadows behind the youth stepped a great whitewyrme, a female, scalestained with age and scarred from many battles, yet powerful and braced to strike. Smoke coiled from her nostrils as her jaws parted. Her fangs flashed.

'*Move,*' she growled menacingly. Her jaws opened wider and she spat out a jet of flame, sulphurous and blisterhot.

Hepzibar stumbled back, her hands raised, shielding her eyes from the scorching heat. Asa snarled and reared up – but the adult whitewyrme reared up twice as high, slashing at the air with her hackdagger foreclaws and releasing another fierce blast of fire. Asa dipped his head. There was nothing he could do to protect his kin, and Hepzibar felt his rage and frustration as he submitted to the larger creature and withdrew meekly to her side.

The youth approached the fire and flicked the skewered grubs out from the flames with the point of his lance, before pouncing on them. He tossed two of them back to the whitewyrme.

'*Eat, Azura. Eat.*'

His words were guttural, and to Hepzibar, whose ears were accustomed to Asa's soft keening whispers, they sounded clipped and harsh. With his teeth bared and his eyes fixed on her, the youth began tearing at the toasted grubs with cracked and filthy nails, and stuffing them in his mouth. Oily juice ran down his chin. When he had finished them, he plucked the last half dozen grubs from the flames and divided them between himself and his wyrme.

Hepzibar watched as they devoured them greedily. She reached out and rested her hand on Asa's trembling neck. The youth and the whitewyrme were growling and snarling, and she was unsure whether this was some dark language between them that she could not understand – or simply raw hunger.

'*Any more?*' the youth demanded, wiping grease from his chin on the cuff of his soulskin.

Hepzibar nodded. '*Down in the store caves,*' she said, her rustling whispers halting and faint. '*Plenty.*'

The youth sat back on his haunches. He turned to the whitewyrme.

'*She said plenty, Azura.*'

'*I heard it, Kesh,*' the whitewyrme hissed.

'*We're happy to share*', Asa told them, his head inclined, but Hepzibar noted the barbels trembling at the corners of his mouth and knew he wasn't happy at all.

'*Share!?*' Kesh's voice hissed like geyser steam through a rockcleft. '*We want something, we take it. Understand?*'

Hepzibar nodded.

'*Who are you, anyway?*' The youth's words were still harsh, yet the blunting of his hunger had taken the edge off their tone.

'*I'm Hepzibar,*' she told him. '*And this is Asa.*'

The youth glared at her suspiciously. He sniffed at the air, his top lip drawn back and sharp teeth exposed. He looked suspicious, undecided about something, then he glanced round at the female whitewyrme. Her eyes narrowed and her voice rumbled like distant thunder.

'*They got the taint.*'

'*That's it,*' said Kesh, turning back to Hepzibar and Asa. '*That's what I could smell.*' He crouched down and picked up his kinlance, then stepped towards Hepzibar, sucking in the air over his teeth. '*You got the stench of kith upon you . . .*'

Hepzibar shrank back before the tall youth with the dark glinting eyes and pinched, feral-looking face. Asa coiled round her defensively, arching his back and raising his wings to shield her. Undeterred, Kesh moved slowly, deliberately towards them, sniffing at the air and scowling.

Azura skirted the fire and came round behind them, her nostrils quivering and a bloodstained glow turning her eyes from yellow to deep amber. She prodded lightly at both Hepzibar and Asa, and her snout probed with an odd delicacy, breathing in the scent as she too sniffed the air around them.

'*And not just kith . . .*' she hissed.

'*Keld,*' Kesh agreed.

He jabbed his lance at Asa, who trembled and would have backed away, but the great whitewyrme behind him gave a warning growl and he fell still.

'*You been with keld?*' Kesh said, the softness of his voice only adding to its menace. '*Answer me.*' He prodded Hepzibar with the lance.

'*No, no,*' she breathed, overwhelmed by the hatred in the youth's eyes. She husked and chittered, struggling to find the words to explain. '*We . . . were prisoners of a keld. We were sold to her. By kith.*' Her words poured out in a waterfall rush. '*The both of us, sold to a keld hag who chained us up and—*'

Before her, Kesh pressed the tip of the lance at Asa's chest. Hepzibar bit her lower lip as tears started to blur her vision.

'*And?*' Kesh demanded.

'*She wanted to kill me.*' Hepzibar's voice sounded spent, like dry grass. '*And eat me.*' She swallowed and lowered her head. '*That's why we have the stench of the keld upon us . . .*'

'*And you, wyrmeling,*' snarled Azura, her red eyes fixed on Asa. '*What have you to say?*'

Asa looked round at the whitewyrme, so much bigger and more powerful than he was, and when he spoke, his voice was soft and mild as mist.

'*Zar and me. We were in the dark,*' he said. '*Then others came, and we were free . . .*'

Asa flinched as Kesh jabbed at him with his lance once more. Hepzibar winced.

'*We were rescued,*' she blurted out.

'*Rescued?*' Kesh hissed. '*Who by?*'

'*By my papa, who died . . . And two kith. A man and a boy,*' said Hepzibar. '*And a kin . . .*'

'*Kin?*' Kesh's eyes narrowed, and from behind them, Hepzibar smelled the whitewyrme's smoke as she exhaled.

'*Yes. A kingirl without a wyrme of her own, but who understood Asa and me,*' said Hepzibar, her voice lilting yet breathy as she tried to sound braver than she felt. '*She told us that we had found kinship, just like she had once found kinship with her own wyrme. She killed the hag and helped the two of us to leave that place, and we've been together ever since . . .*'

'*What do you and your puny wyrme know of kinship?*' sneered Kesh.

Hepzibar cringed at his words and hot tears welled in her eyes. Kinship. All she knew was that she had Asa, and Asa had her, and nothing else in the weald mattered. She turned to the young whitewyrme, who inclined his neck until his head was resting on her shoulder.

Kesh eased back a ways. He looked at Asa, then back at Hepzibar. His grip on the lance relaxed.

'*I don't know what you are exactly – with your smell of keld and kith,*' he said at last. '*But I don't like it.*'

'*They're young,*' Azura observed. She dropped down

onto all fours and extended her long battlescarred neck towards Asa. '*Just how many seasons are you?*'

Asa looked at her, relieved to see that the red was fading from the great whitewyrme's eyes. '*I don't know,*' he admitted.

'*How many times have you shed your skin?*'

'*Once.*'

Hepzibar looked down and smoothed a hand over the soulskin she wore, which was white and pearly and fitted tight. She looked up at Azura, then Kesh, who was staring back at her intently.

'*Newly hatched,*' the whitewyrme observed. '*Three seasons old.*' She turned her yellow eyes on Hepzibar. '*And you? How old are you?*'

'*Nearly nine.*'

Kesh snorted dismissively. But he lowered the lance nevertheless, holding Hepzibar's gaze the while. His brow puckered. '*So, how did you find this place?*'

Hepzibar swallowed. '*Asa found it,*' she said. '*He followed the scent of the wyrmes, though*' – she looked around her – '*we found no wyrmes when we got here.*'

Kesh and Azura exchanged looks.

'*If the colony had been here when you arrived, they'd have driven you off,*' said Kesh. '*They don't believe in kinship.*'

Azura, who had circled round and now stood beside

Kesh, swayed gently back and forth, her wings flexing with the sound of dry leaves being trodden.

'*The great whitewyrmes of the colony don't understand,*' she said, shaking her great head. '*They don't understand that the only way to stop the kith from spreading into the weald is for whitewyrmes to take the young the kith abandon and to teach them our ways.*' She turned her head towards Kesh. '*To form kinship, so that we can fight the kith together.*'

Hepzibar nodded, but it was all so difficult to take in. She turned to Asa, her lip trembling.

'*The great whitewyrmes whose scent you followed, Asa; they would have driven you away. Because of me.*'

'*It doesn't matter.*'

'*Even though it means you'll never be accepted by your own kind.*'

'*It doesn't matter,*' Asa repeated, and he nuzzled up close to her. '*I have you.*'

Kesh, who had been tracing patterns in the sand on the floor of the cavern with the tip of his lance, looked up. His dark eyes were shot with anger.

'*The colony,*' he said, and it sounded like he was cussing. '*They upped and left as soon as the kith got too close.*' He glared at Hepzibar. '*As soon as they smelled the kith taint on the wind. We seen them flying overhead,*' he added, '*heading off to the west in a mighty flock, which is why we came here,*

Azura and me, to see what they had left.' He frowned darkly. *'Wyrmekin don't run away. We fight.'*

Hepzibar and Asa stole a glance at one another. The young whitewyrme looked tense and his tail swished back and forth, stirring up the dust.

'There are others?' said Hepzibar. *'Like you?'*

'Lots of others,' said Kesh, straightening up. *'The high-stacks might have been lost, and the kith are advancing into the valley country. But we aim to contain them, to defend the deeper weald and make sure they don't go no further.'* Hepzibar heard the anger creeping back into his voice. *'There's kin at the black pinnacles and the saltflats to the west. And more at the jagged ridge. And there's those of us at the yellow peaks who fight the hardest. The meanest . . .'*

Azura looked at her kin, her eyes bright and barbels twitching.

'Just before the snows hit, we spotted hunters up on the northern rises, heading west. Four of them. Four kith.' Kesh's eyes glittered and Hepzibar quavered inside as she saw him slowly lick his lips. *'They ain't heading west no more.'*

'What did you do?' she said.

'We killed them,' said Kesh coldly. *'Slowly and with great care, and we displayed them on the trail as a warning to others not to follow.'*

Hepzibar lowered her head. She could hear Asa's low and even breathing, and feel the warmth from his body, so close to hers – but she couldn't look at him. To them, their friendship was simple. She had him and he had her. They had each other.

But did their kinship mean that they had to learn how to fight? How to kill?

She turned away and crouched down and, with stiff shaking fingers, selected the stouter branches from the heap of firewood and placed them onto the fire. The dry wood caught, crackling and sparking. Kesh came and sat on the opposite side of the fire. He laid his kinlance carefully down behind him and warmed his hands in the flames. Hepzibar reached back for more branches. She began snapping them in half and adding them to the fire, one by one. The wood burst into pale green flames.

'*You seemed pretty hungry*,' Hepzibar observed, looking up shyly at the older kin. She broke another branch, tossed it onto the fire.

'*Food is scarce in fullwinter*,' said Kesh curtly. '*And fullwinter in the yellow peaks was harsher than usual this year.*'

Hepzibar nodded, and she noticed the way Kesh ran a hand thoughtfully over his jutting ribs. Azura lay down behind him, coiling around the fire in a semi-circle and folding her wings.

'*So you came here,*' said Hepzibar.

'*The colony had left. We thought the wyrme galleries would be deserted,*' said Kesh pointedly.

Azura growled, and Hepzibar felt Asa tremble.

Kesh lay himself down on his side, facing the fire, half curled up and his crooked arm beneath his head. The flames splash-patterned his soulskin.

'*The taint of kith and keld is strong,*' he noted, then looked up at Hepzibar, who was holding her raised palms up to the flickering warmth. '*It makes it hard for me and Azura to sleep.*'

'*Oh,*' said Hepzibar. '*But . . .*'

She fell still. It wasn't fair, she was well aware of that. She and Asa had found the wyrme galleries first. Why, they had been there three weeks or more – and besides, it had been Hepzibar herself who had laid the fire that late afternoon when the chill of the coming night had started to penetrate the chambers. But Kesh's tone was threatening, and Azura was staring at Asa, her ochre eyes reddening once more. Hepzibar had no option but to move.

'*That's fine,*' she said, ignoring Asa's low growls of protest. She climbed to her feet and headed for the shadowy side of the chamber, where the fire set the pillars flickering, but offered little warmth. *'We'll sleep over yonder,'* she said.

Kesh snorted. *'Do what you like,'* he said, and he closed his eyes. *'Just stay out of our way.'*

Fifteen

That first night, the sky cleared and the temperature abruptly plummeted. A spiteful wind got up, and the snow that had fallen started to drift. There was no shelter to be had, and Eli kept the two of them on the move.

'We fall asleep in this and we'll never wake up,' he said.

Micah groaned inside, but made no objections. 'Where are we headed?' he asked.

'Jura's cave,' came the reply.

'Jura's cave,' Micah repeated, and shivered at the memory of the hidden home behind the waterfall, where Eli's friend, the kinwoman, had lived, and died. He recalled the random destruction they'd stumbled upon; the eviscerated whitewyrme, and Jura herself, her throat slit and tongue hacked out at the root.

Eli eased his pace, allowing Micah to catch up. He turned to him.

'It's our best hope,' he said simply.

Micah nodded.

'Maybe our only hope,' he added, 'so I don't want to hear no nonsense 'bout ghosts and suchlike, you hear me?' He clapped a hand round Micah's shoulders. 'Jura's spirit has been set free. I saw to that.' He sighed. 'All we got to hope is that no one else has already happened upon the place . . .'

'How far off is it?'

'Three days by favourable conditions,' came the crag-climber's reply. 'Five days, the progress we're making. Longer than that if the weather turns.' He patted Micah on the back, then thrust his hands back deep in his pockets. 'Which is why we need to press on.'

The cragclimber pulled ahead again, and Micah trudged after him, the wyrmepelt wrapped tightly round his body. With each step, his boots broke through the crust of frozen snow, and it seemed to Micah like he'd been hearing that steady *crunch crunch* for ever.

The sun was setting when they'd crossed the high range behind the den, a crosswind blowing the smoke from the thermal vents into their faces. It had reeked of sulphur and hot metal, along with the pungent stench of rotting meat, and Eli had cursed under his breath when he'd discovered the decomposing jackwyrmes plugged into the crack in the warm rock. Later on, having followed a long ridge eastwards, they started descending, and by the time the moon had risen, they were trudging across a broad plateau, their shrinking shadows marching along resolutely beside them.

Now the terrain was rising again. It was a wondrous collage of silver and grey. The air was so cold that breathing in stung the fine membrane of Micah's nostrils and made his eyes water – and the tears, in turn, froze at the corners of his eyes.

Micah thought of Thrace. The warmth of her body next to his in the sleeping chamber. The softness of her skin against his skin. The sweet musk of her scent. Fresh tears welled, and he wiped them away with a clenched fist before they too froze.

Daybreak came swift and sudden. One moment, the sky was at its darkest, with the moon already gone and the stars looking higher up in the sky than ever; the next, the sky blushed pinky grey, and splinters of light broke the horizon and set the air to twinkling.

'What *is* it?' Micah breathed, clouds billowing from his mouth as he stared at the glittering air around him.

'Diamond dust, some call it,' said Eli. 'One of the wonders of fullwinter – when it gets so cold that every trace of moisture in the air gets turned to ice.' He frowned, then added, 'Though I've never witnessed it myself before.'

Eli paused, leaving the reason for that unspoken, and

Micah thought back to the winter den, which was warm and safe, but shut off from . . . from all this.

Micah stepped forward. He gripped the edges of the wyrmepelt, raised his arms and threw back his head. The particles of glittering ice flew around him like shooting stars. It felt to Micah as though he was flying, and when he breathed in he breathed in the glittering sparks of light, and they danced on his tongue and coursed through his veins and his head spun, delirious, exultant.

He thought of Thrace again, hunched up and pale, slowly fading away in the winter den, and for the first time he truly understood why.

Sixteen

Hepzibar lay down with Asa coiled around her. She rested her head on the curve of his belly. She felt his bodywarmth and, with her ear pressed against his scales, she could hear the regular beat of his heart. Slowly, the gentle purr of the whitewyrme's breathing became more rasping as Asa drifted into sleep, and Hepzibar, feeling safe and secure, soon followed him.

She dreamed of whitewyrmes. Hundreds of them.

They were bustling through the caverns, or perching on the ledges, and beyond the teeming galleries the air was full of the great creatures, looking just like Asa only bigger, circling overhead in the warm sunshine, their white wings flexed and jaws opening and closing as they called to one another.

She laughed with joy and wonder as she craned her neck to watch them, then turned round, eager to share her happiness with Asa. But he was nowhere to be seen, and when she looked back, the whitewyrmes had gone. Every last one of them. The leaden skies were empty. She walked sadly back inside the wyrme gallery, and her footsteps echoed around the deserted chambers.

A cold wind was blowing. It chilled her body, and she fought against it, but it penetrated deeper and she could not get warm . . .

Her eyes snapped open.

'*Asa?*'

Hepzibar uncurled and sat up, her cold joints protesting at the sudden movement. She looked round.

At the centre of the cave, the previous night's fire was little more than a glowing nest of embers. Kesh was still asleep before it, soaking up the fading dregs of warmth. Azura was curled round him in a broad arc, her eyes closed and soft breaths wheezing from her slightly parted jaws. Asa was standing a little way off, his back to her.

Hepzibar climbed stiffly to her feet, stretching as she did so. She crossed the floor to Asa and crouched down next to him.

'*What you got there?*' she whispered, but even as she spoke she could see what Asa was holding.

It was Kesh's kinlance.

Asa was running a sharp claw gently up and down its length. The curve of his claw exactly matched the lines carved into the blackpine.

'*A whitewyrme made this,*' he said. '*With claws like*

mine . . . and firebreath.' His voice was soft and thoughtful.

Hepzibar reached out and gripped the lance towards one end, where it was ridged and smoothed and moulded to the shape of a human hand.

Kesh's hand.

Hepzibar examined the other end of the lance. It had been filed to a point so needlepoint sharp, it pierced the skin at the ball of her thumb and drew blood. This was what Kesh fought with . . .

'*What do you think you're doing?*'

The words broke the silence of the cavern, sibilant and menacing.

Hepzibar and Asa looked up to see Kesh glaring at them, his skin livid and a vein pulsing at his temple. His eyes turned to narrow slits.

'*Put it down,*' he hissed.

Behind him, Azura stirred.

Hepzibar flinched as she realized that she was gripping the lance instinctively, and pointing it straight at Kesh's chest. She swallowed. Did she have what it took to kill? She blinked and shook herself, as if waking from a trance.

'*Here,*' she said. '*We didn't mean no harm . . .*'

Kesh snatched the kinlance from Hepzibar's fingers, gripped it at its centre and spun it round, till that needlesharp point was lowered and aiming at Hepzibar's heart.

'*Ever try that again,*' he told her, '*and I'll kill you, and your wyrme.*'

Hepzibar nodded and looked down, unable to hold Kesh's intense glare. Azura had climbed to her feet and was standing beside Kesh, ready to lash out at Asa.

'*It was me,*' Asa confessed. '*I took it!*'

Azura snorted. She surveyed the smaller white-wyrme with his gleaming white freshslough skin. The long barbels at the corners of her mouth quivered. '*I fashioned that lance,*' she said quietly. Her eyes stared off into the mid distance, and her voice grew quieter still. '*I flew high over the yellow peaks for days, until I found a branch from one of the thousand-year pines that grow only at the top of the highest crags. I hacked it down with my jaws, I shaped it with my talons, I forged it with my breath . . .*'

She opened her jaws and spat a jet of flame at Asa, who shrank back in alarm.

'*And you, little wyrmeling, dared to touch it.*'

Beside her, Kesh smiled meanly and turned away. '*Leave them, Azura,*' he said. '*They're not worth our time. Come, let's explore those store caves.*'

The pair of them left Hepzibar and Asa standing by the cold embers of the spent fire. Hepzibar looked at Asa. His crest bristled and his tail switched, and when he returned Hepzibar's gaze, she saw that his eyes seemed a darker shade than she'd seen before.

'*I shall fashion you one of those,*' he declared.

SEVENTEEN

They made good progress the second day. The clear skies that had rendered the nighttime so cold now favoured the sun, and it shone down hot and squint-dazzle bright.

They tramped across a bleak plain and up into a ridge of low crags beyond, and when darkness fell, they rested up in a narrow cutting in a sheltered cliffside, with Eli at the entrance and Micah deeper inside the rock.

They were both bellygnaw hungry, and Eli searched his pockets for something they might eat. He happened across a few pieces of dried wyrmemeat from an inside pocket, which he shared out. They chewed the meat slowly and to a pulp, putting off swallowing as long as they could. When it was finally gone, they were still ravenous.

'Can't we scavenge?' said Micah. 'Or snare us something to eat?'

The cragclimber shook his head. 'We stop to forage or trap, Micah,' he said, 'most likely we'll fall prey to something ourselves. Like I told you, lad, we got to keep moving fast as we can, or we'll die for sure.'

The third morning broke while they were sleeping, and Micah would have slept on longer still had Eli not shaken his boots and wakened him. He sat up, grazing his head painfully on the low ceiling of rock as he did so, and cursed.

Eli had poured some of the flameoil into a battered cup, then lit it and used the flickering flame to melt snow he'd gathered in the copper pot, and bring it to the boil. He and Micah sipped at the hot water one after the other, passing the pot back and forth between them. When the pot was empty, Eli packed up and got to his feet.

They left the narrow shelter behind them and set off, back into the craggy landscape. Micah's belly felt full and warm, but it would take more than hot water to sustain him.

'You got any more food stashed away in those pockets of yours?' he asked.

Eli shook his head. 'But we're making good progress, lad,' he said. 'Must be halfway there, by my reckoning. Let's just pray the weather holds.'

They fell into silence, and continued trudging through the crunching snow side by side.

There were clouds high above and a breeze had got up that chivvied them across the sky like dogworried sheep. Micah watched the cloudcast shadows skitting over the snowfields before him – then screwed his face up in surprise when some of them seemed to come to a halt.

He looked up. The clouds were still moving, and when he looked back at the plains he realized that the motionless grey shapes were not shadows at all.

'Greywyrmes,' said Eli, following Micah's gaze. 'And having a hard time by the looks of it.'

The great creatures were bone-thin, their skin hanging in folds, like canvas over tent poles. They lumbered across the snowy plain in phalanx formation, the males in a circle surrounding the females and their firstyear young. As Micah watched, the herd came to a halt again, and the adults lowered their heads and with their neck muscles bunched up like thick ropes began sweeping their heads from side to side, down through the snow.

'There's grass to be had you dig deep enough,' said Eli, 'though there's precious little nourishment to it this time of year.' He tutted softly. 'Them greys get much weaker and the redwings and ridgebacks'll start picking them off – and us with them, we stray too close.'

Micah watched the greywyrmes enviously. Nourishment or no, they were biting and chewing and swallowing and filling their bellies, and his own belly grumbled in protest. Eli strode on and Micah hurried to catch up with him, scanning the skies for signs of predators.

It was maybe an hour later when Micah spotted a wyrme hovering in the sky ahead. It was a skitterwyrme, red-ruffed and sharp-beaked, but too small to do them harm. He borrowed Eli's spyglass, put it to his eye and watched as the thin creature cocked its fluted ears, turned its head, then swooped down and dived deep into the snow. Emerging moments later, it flew back into the sky and dived again, then again. The third dive was rewarded by a small plump wyrme squirming about in the skitterwyrme's jaws, which it shook to stillness and swallowed whole.

'So, there's wyrmes hiding out under the snow beneath our feet?' said Micah.

'Scratwyrmes, mainly,' said Eli, taking back the spyglass. 'It's their strategy for making it through fullwinter. Insulated by the blanket of snow. They build tunnels down there to get about, and there are others, like that skitterwyrme there, that are grateful they do – for hunting them is their strategy.' He shrugged. 'As for us, scratwyrmes won't repay the effort expended in catching them. We must . . .'

'I know, I know,' said Micah hungrily. 'We must keep moving.'

He watched the skitterwyrme sit up on its hindlegs, then scamper away, its delicate claws skating over the surface of the snow before it took to the wing. Eli set off again, and Micah followed.

After a long slow climb, Eli and Micah finally reached the top of a steep incline and crested a sharp ridge. The land fell away before them in a broad sloping plain. Micah sighed out loud at the emptiness of it, and stopped, breathshort and lightheaded, and wondering if they were lost. Eli must have read his thoughts, for he stopped beside him and pointed to the tops of a distant cluster of tall rockstacks that were smoking like chimneys.

'Them's the highstacks,' he said. He swung his arm full about. 'And there, to the north, see that mountain that looks like a sugarloaf, that marks the start of the valley country. We're on track, lad.' He looked up ahead. 'Over them mountains up yonder, there's the high plain that you yourself have already crossed . . .'

'Twice,' said Micah with excitement. 'It's where Jura's green haven lies, ain't it?'

'That's right.'

'Yeah, I remember thinking the shape of them mountain peaks was the spit image of a bolt of lightning, laying on its side,' said Micah. 'Looks more like it than ever right now, white-tipped with snow and all.'

Eli smiled. 'You're learning, lad. You're learning.' His smile faded. 'But we best make haste and find some shelter before it gets dark – out of sight of predators and suchlike.'

The two of them strode off down the mountain slope. Their worn boots slid and skidded. Behind them, the sun sank low in the sky, and their shadows slowly lengthened before them.

Suddenly Micah saw movement out the corner of his eye, and turned his head. Four . . . five creatures with sleek silver bodies were sliding down the mountainside in the distance, seemingly swimming through the snow in fluid rippling movements, one after the other.

'Silverbacks,' said Eli. 'And off fishing most likely.'

Far below them now, Micah watched the line of wyrmes ripple across a shallow dip and over the lip at the far side, then disappear from view. Fishing. Just the word was enough to conjure up the sizzle and aroma of fish frying in a skillet, and Micah's stomach cramped up like a miser's fist at the thought of it.

As they neared the bottom of the incline, Micah heard the sound of rushing water, and the pillows of snow ahead stopped abruptly, to reveal a torrent of dark water cascading over a jumble of rocks.

'If a river's fast enough, it won't never freeze up,' Eli said.

He pointed at five bobbing heads in the river as the silverbacks battled against the current. One of the wyrmes had a large pink and brown fish clamped in its jaws, and Micah's stomach cramped up again. He looked beseechingly at Eli, who shook his head.

'We can't risk fishing. Not with fullwinter predators all round.' And he jerked a finger at the far side of the river.

There, pacing up and down on a jutting iceshelf, was a blackwing, its pointed snout twitching and yellow eyes fixed on the fish in the silverback's jaws. All at once, with a strident screech, it launched itself off the ice and made a dive for the fish. But the silverbackwyrme was too quick for it. It slipped down under the water and disappeared beneath the crust of ice that fringed the fast-flowing river. It emerged a moment later, the fish nowhere in sight.

Screeching louder, the blackwing soared into the sky, doubled over, then dived back down, not at the water, but at the icecrust itself, which shattered as the creature's sharp snout struck. It plunged into the water beneath, then rose again, water showering from its back as it flapped its wings. The pink and brown fish that the silverback had concealed beneath the ice was clamped in its own powerful jaws.

'Come on, Micah,' said Eli. 'The light's beginning to fade.'

They headed up the river a ways, till it disappeared beneath a roof of snow. Then, taking small tentative steps, they crossed it. The fragile ice cracked and groaned beneath them, but held up under their weight, and the two of them continued up the mountain on the far side. Far behind them, the sun had just set when they came to a shallow hollow in the side of a cliff.

Eli laid down the winter caller's backpack as a wind-break and curled up beside it. Micah lay down next to him, the ice-covered scree squeaking as he pulled the wyrmepelt cape up around his ears.

'We'll rest up till first light, then make for the high plain. When we get down into the green haven, we'll do all the fishing and trapping you want, Micah . . . Micah?'

But Micah didn't answer. He was already asleep.

Eighteen

A manderwyrme flitted over the snow, its outstretched wings flexing and striped tail quivering. It was sleek and bright-eyed, and seemed oblivious to the intense cold.

It came to a halt next to a pile of greywyrme dung, dark against the brilliant white of the snow. It sat back on its haunches and looked up at the cloud of plump black flies that had risen at its approach and were hovering above its head. Then it started leaping. Up and down it went, time and again, snatching the insects from the air till its belly was full. It swiped a long thin tongue around its snout, grunted contentedly, then continued on its way.

It hadn't gone more than a dozen yards, when the snow beneath it began to tremble and crack, and its sensitive ears picked up a scritching scraping noise that made it pause, and—

With a sudden explosion of snow and ice, a clenched fist drove up from below and grabbed the manderwyrme. There was a second, larger explosion, and a head appeared – a huge head, with a shapeless hump of a nose and skin quilted with crisscross scars. Pale blue eyes snapped open, and the hand pulled the struggling manderwyrme to its lipless mouth. It sank its teeth into the creature's neck, tore off its head and, holding the dead body aloft, let the blood pour down into its open mouth . . .

Micah gasped and sat up. He was sweating, despite the cold. Beside him, Eli muttered in his sleep, but did not waken.

'It was a night terror is all,' Micah murmured. 'The winter caller's dead. And the dead can't do no harm.'

NINETEEN

Hepzibar and Asa headed through the caverns and out onto the broad snowcapped ledges. A light wind was blowing. It whispered through the great shadow-filled chambers that had been excavated between the strata of rock; it sighed round the fluted columns that supported them.

A fullwinter blizzard of three days had finally passed, and already a new snowstorm was threatening from the velvet greyness of the south-west horizon. But overhead, the sky was crisp and cloudless blue, and the sun beat down, casting soft grey shadows over the rolling expanse of deep snow below.

Asa stepped to the very edge of the jutting slab of rock and flexed his wings. Hepzibar climbed up onto his back. She gripped the crested ridge that ran down the centre of his neck, one hand behind her and one in front, and looked round.

Azura and Kesh were nowhere to be seen.

'Where do you think they—?

A shadow passed over them and, looking up, Hepzibar saw the youth and the great whitewyrme swoop down and barrel over and over, before rising up once more in the clear blue sky. As she and Asa watched, Kesh and Azura looped and dived and soared and rolled, putting on a display of effortless grace and aerial mastery.

Despite their surly menacing manner that had meant Asa and Hepzibar had kept their distance for the past week, the wyrme and her rider were obviously enjoying showing off. As they passed overhead, Kesh threw back his head and gave a savage whoop of delight, while Azura sent a jet of shimmering white flame spurting out into the icy air.

Caught up in the excitement of the moment, Hepzibar urged Asa to launch himself from the ledge and take to the air. Asa leaped from the overhanging slab of rock and dropped a little in the air, then rose again, the sound of his beating wings like handclaps.

It felt so good to be out in the open air, Hepzibar thought, with the cold wind against her face and the full-winter sun glinting on Asa's scales.

Asa flapped away from the whitewyrme galleries, his shadow gliding over the snow far far below. Hepzibar turned her head and her hair swept across her face. She pushed it back – to see Azura and Kesh speeding towards them.

Kesh had his lance braced in his hand. Azura's eyes

blazed red. And as they sped closer, Hepzibar saw the kin youth raise the hood of his soulskin, masking his face in deep shadow.

She looked desperately about her. They were too far from the galleries to make it back to the cover of the pillared ledges, and there was nowhere to hide in the snowy wilderness beyond. Asa's wings beat blurfast at her sides, but Hepzibar could already feel the heat of Azura's smoky breath at the nape of her neck, and hear the hum of the kinlance as the wind whistled past its deadly tip . . .

She wrapped her arms round Asa's neck.

'*Aaaaaiiii!*'

The cry ripped through the cold air like metal through metal – cold, violent, inhuman.

Hepzibar trembled, eyes closed, waiting for the lance to pierce her soulskin, slice through her body and skewer her heart. The metallic screech sounded a second time, and Hepzibar turned, her eyes open now. Above, she saw a blur of white speeding down at Azura and Kesh as they bore down on her and Asa. The blur coalesced.

It was a second wyrme; a male. A kingirl sat astride his shoulders. Her hair streamed back as, face grim set, she gripped her kinlance. The whitewyrme tilted his wings and the kingirl leaned to one side – and they clashed with Azura and Kesh.

Kesh's kinlance was knocked from his grip and sent tumbling down to the snowy ground, turning over and over in the air as it fell. As they flew past, the white-wyrme's tail lashed round and struck Azura hard on her haunches, sending her into a spin that pitched her and Kesh spiralling down to the ground after it.

They landed awkwardly in the snowdrift that fringed the scrub-covered undercliff below the wyrme galleries. The second whitewyrme and his rider landed next to them, and the kingirl jabbed the tip of her lance at the red-haired youth. Her eyes glittered with a mixture of fury and contempt.

'*Kin don't do that to kin,*' she said, her voice ice-cold.

Kesh's top lip twitched. He glanced up at Hepzibar and Asa, who were hovering in the sky above. Asa's wings were outstretched, the air plumping up the leathery white skin stretched between the fine bones.

'*They ain't kin,*' he snarled, and the air around them fuzzed with smoke as Azura snorted her concurrence.

The whitewyrme male reared up and fired a plume of yellow-white flame. Azura stopped snorting and, as the air cleared, she stared at a dark zigzag scar that coursed down the side of the male wyrme's neck. She dipped her head in submission and fell back, cowering and trembling so hard Kesh had to hold on tight to stop himself from being shaken from her back.

Asa extended his legs beneath him and touched down lightly on the snow-covered ground. Hepzibar stared at the lean yet powerful-looking kingirl.

'*Thrace?*' she said.

TWENTY

'I don't much like the look of that sky,' said Eli.

Micah rolled over, opened his eyes.

Above them, the sky was leaden, and already small flurries of snow were being carried on the icy wind. Micah shivered and clutched at his belly. It was empty and cramped and growled at him like a neglected barn dog. He glanced at the winter caller's pack questioningly.

'Ain't there nothing in there to take the edge off this hunger?' he asked. 'What about that jar you stowed away, Eli?'

The cragclimber eyed him levelly for a moment, then climbed wearily to his feet.

'Bloodhoney,' he said, pulling the backpack onto his shoulders. 'Keld stuff. I hung onto it in case we got into a fix and there was no way of getting out of it. But if we make good time, we'll be at the haven by nightfall, and we'll not have a need of it.'

'So, you reckon we'll make it there by nightfall?' Micah said, brightening up.

'I intend we should give it a try,' said Eli. He looked

up, and his expression darkened with concern. 'But I still don't like the look of that sky.'

Micah had never experienced snow like it. It fell so heavy the entire world was whited out.

It had started as he and Eli had left the cliffside, fluttering down light at first, but soon thickening up till Micah struggled to see for more than a few footsteps in front of him. But Eli pressed on, and Micah knew that they had no option but to keep walking.

The snow grew deep. Their boots pressed and squeaked with every step, and Micah's feet became numb.

Eli paused and looked back at him.

Micah saw how the snow clung to the cragclimber's stubble and eyelashes, and the wisps of hair that stuck out from his hat. He noted the deepsunk cheeks and the raw rims to his eyes, and the eyes themselves, shiny and threaded with red. He saw how the cragclimber stooped into the wind, gnarled and bent as a blackhickory, and he knew he must look the same.

'You all right, lad?'

Micah nodded stiffly. 'I'm all right.'

But he was not all right, and as the cragclimber turned away again, and Micah followed after him, he felt his energy drain away, till his legs felt like rocks and every dragged footstep was a trial. Slowly, the air began to darken about them as the day wore on, and the snow kept falling.

Eli paused a second time, and Micah stopped beside him. He wanted to lie down, and had to lock his knees to remain standing. Without saying a word, Eli removed the rope from the backpack, tied one end round Micah's waist and the other round his own. Then he turned away and kept on, and when Micah felt the rope tugging at his middle, he stumbled forward after him.

As the light faded, they left the mountains behind them and set off across an undulating plain that was flatter, but no easier to navigate. Cracks and crevices in the surface of the rock had to be skirted, and the tips of snowcovered boulders formed obstacles that should not have troubled them, but did.

Micah pulled the wyrmepelt tight around him, but the wind and the snow penetrated anyway, soaking into his breeches and jerkin, chilling him to his core. If they were travelling in the right direction, surely by now they should have come to the gash in the rock that marked the entrance to the green haven. Surely . . . But they had not, and Micah was plagued by the thought that they had wandered off course, or were heading round in circles, and when he tripped and fell, he could not stir himself.

'Get up,' said Eli.

'I . . . I just need to rest up a moment,' said Micah, his voice rasping and fragile.

'Get up!' Eli reached forward and dragged Micah to his feet. 'We must keep moving.'

They kept on and, with every step he took, Micah heard the cragclimber's words repeating inside his head. *Keep moving. Keep moving.*

Micah's stomach tightened and grumbled.

If only he had something to eat. If only it would stop snowing. If only he could rest up . . .

Keep moving.

Micah trudged on, the rope between him and Eli – first tightening, then going slack – letting him know when he was falling back, and when he was keeping up. He was bent forward, his head down. Every time he looked up, the speckled void was the same, until he became aware that the darkness was fading once more.

Another night had passed. The greyness was shot with white. Another day had begun.

Keep moving. Must keep moving . . .

And then, with an abruptness that caught them both by surprise, the wind dropped and the snow stopped falling. Micah rubbed his eyes. It made no sense. The blizzard was over, but he still could not see anything, and he was suddenly hot with fear that the whiteout had robbed him of his sight.

'Eli, Eli,' he called out.

The cragclimber appeared before him, ghostly and pale, the outline to his body fuzzed.

'It's fog,' he said simply. 'Freezing fog. Keep moving, Micah.'

The freezing fog seemed to suck the moisture from Micah's skin till his face felt like ancient parchment, and it froze the sweat-drenched clothes to his back. His body was chilled, but his head burned feverhot. He shook violently, and every step was an effort of will.

Keep moving. Must keep moving, he told himself, and was saying it over and over when he fell to his knees and sprawled forward, face down in the snow . . .

'Drink it.'

Micah struggled to open his eyes.

'Drink it.'

He was lying on his back now, and Eli was knelt down next to him, an arm wrapped round his shoulder, supporting him. There was something pressing at his lower lip.

'Drink it, Micah.'

He opened his lips a little, and liquid filled his mouth. It was viscous and sweet, and tasted faintly metallic. He swallowed, then swallowed again, and as the liquid hit his stomach, his hunger left him. He gulped down more of the liquid, greedily now, and when the jar was removed from his mouth, he looked up expectantly, eager for more.

Eli sat back on his haunches and raised the jar to his own lips. He drained what was left in the jar, then passed the back of his hand across his mouth, wiping away the residue, that Micah noticed was a deep sumptuous red, like blood.

'Is that . . . ?' he murmured.

'Bloodhoney,' said Eli, climbing to his feet and heaving the backpack onto his shoulders.

Micah stood up. His limbs pulsed with vigour and his stomach felt full. The fever had cooled, but his whole body was suffused in a warmth that seemed to be glowing deep inside him. He no longer felt tired, and his senses were taut and jangling. He was acutely aware of the soft squeaking crunch of Eli's footfalls in the snow as the cragclimber turned away and resumed their journey, and the stale tang of his own wyrmepelt cape filling his nostrils as he followed him.

TWENTY-ONE

Thrace sat crosslegged on the floor, her kinlance lying across her folded legs. She was oiling the blackpine, working claggy damsel-grub grease into the smooth dark wood with her fingertips. On either side of her, coiled round the fluted columns and dozing fitfully, were Asa and Aseel. The older wyrme dwarfed the younger one, his neck, body and tail winding round the right-hand column from ceiling to clawscratch floor.

One day, thought Hepzibar, stopping by the left-hand column, her arms full of firewood, Asa would be as big and powerful as Thrace's wyrme.

In the shadows behind Thrace, Hepzibar was aware of movement and, narrowing her eyes, she made out the indistinct shapes of Kesh and Azura. Since Thrace and Aseel had saved her from them, the kin youth and his wyrme had kept their distance. Neither of them wanted to risk angering Thrace further.

Kesh caught Hepzibar's eye and sneered, and Hepzibar blushed and turned away again. She busied herself with making a fire, constructing a lattice pyramid of sagebrush on the bed of silver ash at the centre of the cavern. When she was done, she nodded to Asa, who uncoiled himself from the column and approached the wood. He opened his jaws and sent a jet of flame into the centre of the pyramid. The sagebrush sparked and gave off twists of sweet aromatic smoke.

Hepzibar raised her chilled hands to the flames. Then she looked up, to see Thrace staring back at her, and she was struck, not for the first time, by the intensity of the older kingirl's gaze.

'*Sit, little one,*' said Thrace softly.

Hepzibar settled herself next to the fire and Asa coiled himself around her in a circle. She smiled and stroked him, her fingertips playing with the fold of skin beneath the young wyrme's chin.

'*Your kinship is growing strong,*' Thrace observed.

Hepzibar nodded, and Asa turned his head towards her. His warm breath enfolded her.

Thrace sat back, her hands flat on the ground behind her.

'*It is good to see,*' she said, '*but if it is to grow further, you have much you need to learn . . .*'

There was a derisive snort from the shadows behind her. Thrace ignored it. Her dark eyes were fixed on Hepzibar's upturned face.

'*And I shall teach you.*'

'*You will?*' said Hepzibar, feeling her chest tighten and a lump come to her throat.

Hepzibar nodded. '*Yes, little one. Just as soon as the snows of fullwinter have thawed.*'

She fell still for a moment, and when she spoke again her voice was hushed and intense, like something gnawing at dried grain.

'*Aseel was full grown when he found me. And he taught me the ways of kinship – though it cost him dear . . .*'

Aseel, who had unwound himself from the column and come to share in the warmth of the fire, raised his head. He stared at Thrace evenly from beneath heavy-lidded eyes. Hepzibar noticed the way the end of his tail twitched from side to side, and she found herself watching the twin coils of smoke that rose up from his flared nostrils.

'*But Asa is new hatched,*' Thrace went on, '*and you are young. You will both need the guidance that we can give you.*'

She carefully laid her kinlance to one side, then unfolded her legs and hugged them to her chest. She looked at Hepzibar and Asa.

'*We are in the midst of a great struggle,*' she said quietly. '*A struggle being fought here in the valley country between kin and kith.*'

Hepzibar swallowed uneasily and glanced at Asa, who

was staring into the flames. She could not tell what he was thinking. Aseel had closed his eyes.

'When the thaw comes, the kith will be on the move again, so you must both learn fast.'

From the shadows came Kesh's voice, low, guttural and full of hatred. *'The kith need to be taught a lesson,'* he growled. *'A lesson they'll never forget.'* He paused. *'Like the one Azura and I taught them in the yellow peaks.'*

The four at the fire – Thrace and Aseel, Asa and Hepzibar – all turned and looked at him, and Hepzibar wondered if she was the only one who noticed the look of distant pain in Azura's eyes, or the way her barbels twisted and coiled. Thrace turned back to Hepzibar, and she nodded.

'There has been great cruelty, it is true,' Thrace told her, *'and there will be more. But kith understand no other way – at least,'* she added softly, *'most kith . . .'*

She fell still, and Hepzibar saw her eyes moisten. Aseel raised his great head and blew a cloud of warm smoke at Thrace that enveloped her, warmed and comforted her. She turned and smiled at him, but Hepzibar saw how sad that smile was, how full of longing. Then Thrace's face hardened.

'After all,' she said, *'it was kith who took you and sold you to Redmyrtle. Both of you.'*

Hepzibar nodded and Asa growled menacingly.

Neither of them would ever allow themselves to be captured and imprisoned again. They would fight, whatever the cost.

Thrace looked at her whitewyrme, who was still lying with his eyes closed, listening. Her fingertips traced the length of the gleaming kinlance.

'*The first thing is for Asa to find a lance for you. We will help. He will fashion it and you will use it to defend yourself, so you will never be vulnerable to attack again.*'

From the shadows there came only silence now. And when Hepzibar looked round again, she saw Azura staring intently at her kin, while Kesh, for his part, was biting into his lower lip and staring at the ground, his eyes ablaze.

'*The whitewyrmes may have departed,*' said Thrace, '*but the galleries they've left behind shall afford us food and shelter this fullwinter.*'

Aseel sighed, and when he spoke, there was a sadness in his windbreath voice. '*I was once of this colony and the wyrme galleries were my home. My wyrmemate, Aylsa, still flies with the flock . . .*'

The great whitewyrme shifted forwards on his haunches and turned his neck. The firelight flickered in his eyes.

Paul Stewart and Chris Riddell

'*They have ventured into the lands beyond the mountains, to strange lands. Wild lands . . .*' His eyes glowed a deep shade of red. '*Lands where the* others *are said to dwell.*'

TWENTY-TWO

It was light, the air an impenetrable matt grey, when they came to a cleft in the snowplain that cut down deep into the rock. Micah stopped and peered over the edge of the rock. The thick fog swirled below him, growing thicker, then thinner again, revealing trees and bushes cobbled with snow that plunged down the valleysides and into the depths.

'The green haven?' he said, turning to the cragclimber.

Eli did not reply, and when Micah turned, he could see disappointment in his face. 'It's a ravine, right enough, and possibly deep enough for a haven,' he said at last. 'But it ain't Jura's green haven.'

Micah frowned. They had walked over the snowclad high plain for most of the day and on through the night, the bloodhoney coursing through their veins and quelling all feelings of fatigue. But now, in the early light of dawn, the effects had begun to wear off and Micah felt increasingly giddy and unsteady on his feet.

'Maybe there's somewhere to shelter anyhow,' he suggested. He knew he couldn't go much further.

'Maybe,' said Eli. 'And maybe there's some who've already made their winter den down there.'

'We could take a look,' said Micah. 'Couldn't we?' he added uncertainly when Eli remained silent.

The cragclimber shrugged. 'Most kith don't take kindly to den squatters invading their winter hold-ups. Freeloaders seeking shelter they've not earned don't usually get a good reception.'

Micah swallowed uneasily. 'We can't turn back,' he said quietly.

'No,' said Eli gruffly. 'We can't.'

Still tethered to one another, the pair of them started down into the precipitous crevasse. Clambering over boulders and scree, they found themselves in a frozen gorge that was frosted white with snow and wreathed in fog. Further down, blackpine and spruce grew out of cracks in the valley walls, and as they passed by, pillows of snow slipped from overladen branches and flopped to the frozen ground below.

Beneath their boots, the snow squinked and squeeched.

They went deeper. The freezing fog persisted stubborn, and Micah took care where he placed his boots as the ravine steepened. The air fell absolutely still and was silent. Micah's ears popped when he swallowed.

Around him, the snowclad trees stood tall, leaning together conspiratorially like marble giants.

Micah began to worry at how long it would take to retrace their footsteps should the steep descent prove to be in vain. Ahead of him, Eli's pace slowed, and Micah wondered whether the cragclimber was having the same reservations.

The fog thinned momentarily. Micah looked down into the depths. He heard the unmistakable sound of boots tramping and, peering into the white gloom, saw a figure climbing up towards them.

Micah was pricked by the sudden recollection of his nightmare of the winter caller bursting out from the snow. Next to him, he saw Eli crouch low and stiffen. There were rockspikes in his hand. Micah reached for his belt and drew out his catapult. With his other hand he fumbled in the snow at his feet and unearthed a few jagged shards of flint.

Whoever was approaching was just below them now. Dressed in a heavy cloak and a broadbrim hat, and clutching a wyrmehorn in one hand, the figure stopped and looked up.

Micah raised his catapult, then hesitated as he found himself looking into a face that was fresh and open-featured, eyes the colour of shards of turquoise looking back at him. Freckles crossed the bridge of an upturned nose, and there was a slight cleft to the full pale lips, which parted as the girl smiled.

'Welcome,' she said. 'You'll not need those weapons here.'

TWENTY-THREE

Far from their abandoned galleries, the wyrmehost flew across the mottled sky in skein formation, the gleaming white of their scales shimmering in the sunlight that broke through the high clouds. It was bitter cold, and the crisp, ordered lines of the mighty flock were blurred by the tumbling white clouds of breath that billowed from the mouths of a thousand wyrmes.

They were flagging, particularly the very old and the very young, and those females who were heavy with wyve. Up front, at the apex of the skein, was their leader, Alsasse, scar-scaled and grey-tainted with age but, with his high crest and powerful wingbeats, commanding. Just behind him flew the second of the host, Alucius. He was younger than Alsasse, gleaming-scaled and alert, his clear yellow eyes scanning the desolate landscape below.

Behind them, in a line, came three more wyrmes, and after them, five more. Then nine. Then thirteen . . . And so it continued, line upon line, each one longer than the one before, and forming a vast triangle of creatures that moved through the air like a gathering storm.

The mothers and their young flew at the centre of

the formation, along with the oldest of the wyrmes. The males flew mostly at the fringes of the skein, maintaining its shape and ensuring no one strayed. Some of the older, more experienced males, however, flew in and out of the formation, keeping a watchful eye on the yearlings, who were struggling on this, the longest and most challenging flight of their young lives.

Occasionally, if one of the young wyrmes showed signs of exhaustion – wingbeats slowing, neck drooping, tail losing its sinuous ruddering shape – a powerful male would glide beneath it and support the yearling's weight until it had recovered sufficiently to continue. But even with this watchful care, the young and the old among the host had suffered cruelly in this fullwinter exodus.

'*Storm ahead!*'

Alsasse's words rippled back through the formation, and were confirmed a moment later when the entire host plunged into the darkness and bitterchill of a swirling bank of snowdense cloud. They kept wingtip to wingtip, their eyes fixed on the swishing tails of the whitewyrme ahead. They did not waver . . .

Many weeks had passed since Alsasse had led the colony out into the brooding skies of the weald, his eyes set on the horizon to the west. They had abandoned the magnificent wyrme galleries which had been home to their kind for countless centuries, and set off into the unknown.

It was a heavy responsibility, but Alsasse had had no choice. The two-hides were already in the valley country and, judging by their taint on the wind, there were many of them. The deep weald, beyond the range of even the most adventurous of the great whitewyrmes, was the only answer. The two-hides could never follow them there, of that Alsasse was certain. And Alucius had agreed.

But it had been hard, this exodus in the teeth of full-winter. When they'd left the wyrme galleries, the first snows were falling, and it had soon got worse. Over the smoke ridges, the host had been pursued by unrelenting blizzards. They'd flown on through the ravines beyond, finding shelter of sorts, but little food. The first of the whitewyrmes had begun to die in the jagged peak country further on, with the young dropping out of the sky with exhaustion and the very old seeking out ledges and crannies in which to curl up and die of cold.

With a heavy heart, Alsasse had kept the host moving. He sent out the ablest hunters to forage as they continued, but the pickings were meagre. Several females laid wyves, but the host could not stop to prepare nests for them, and the precious eggs were lost.

Alsasse grieved, but still he drove the whitewyrmes on.

Beyond the peaks were more mountain ranges, then more, each higher and more desolate than the ones before. And still they had kept on.

Eventually, the host had got used to the terrible rigours of the exodus, accepting losses when they couldn't be avoided, but cleaving to each other in an ever-closer bond. The skein formation became tight, efficient and all but unbreakable. The forages became more skilful, even as finding food in the fullwinter snows became harder.

No one complained and the sorrow in Alsasse's heart had eased as he saw their courage.

But now they were hungry and thin, and even the strongest of the males was finding it difficult to maintain the steady wingbeat in the face of exhaustion. They had to find somewhere to rest up, and soon, Alsasse realized, or the host risked catastrophic losses.

Yet the bank of stormcloud continued. Mile after mile. Hour after torturous hour. Above them, the blurred grey sun slipped down slowly in the sky, then disappeared beneath the horizon. It seemed as though the flight through the chill opacity would never end.

But then, as abruptly as it had enveloped them, so the cloud cleared. The whitewyrmes emerged from the stormclouds and entered the dark twinkling clarity of night.

Behind Alsasse, Alucius stared down at the landscape beneath, desperately searching for a possible roosting place. They had left behind a pleated labyrinth of high valleys, jagged ridges and pointed summits, the sharp angles of the rocks softened by thick snow. Now, the land below them had changed utterly. Black basalt slabs and glass obsidian flows created a dark brooding rockscape that was cracked and haphazard, the blocks of rock glowing infernal red from the molten lava that flowed in the depths of the cracks and crevices that cut through them.

It looked, thought Alsasse, like a world only half-finished in its creation, and as they flew over it, the flock fell into fearful silence. Alsasse dipped his head and surveyed the primordial desolation, and was aware that behind him, the whitewyrmes could sense his growing unease.

Where in this terrible landscape were they to land?

To the north, Alucius's keen yellow eyes spotted the glint and gleam of water. He called ahead to Alsasse in that soft screeslide sigh of a voice of his, calm and steady and reassuring to the host and its leader.

Alsasse gave the word to descend. The mighty flock

dipped in the sky and the skein broke formation as the wyrmes came in to land. They wobbled down through the air on hot sulphurous upcurrents, their wings outstretched, then lowered their legs and touched down in this new and unfamiliar land.

Coils of souryellow smoke streamed out evenly from clefts in the expanse of black rock on which they'd landed, while all around them, from dips and basins that were filled with algae-choked pools, plumes of steam exploded intermittently into the air. Crusty lichens of orange and red, bright in the molten fireglow, clung to the rocks at the fringes of the pools. Long diaphanous filaments of cottonweed swayed in the swirling water like sheets in the wind. Skimming the bubbling surface were saltbugs and sulphur flies and plump lacewing damsel flies – and there were small unfamiliar wyrmes of bright blue and gold feeding on them.

Alsasse raised his long neck and looked around. He noted the warmth which seeped up from the rock. He noted the water, the vegetation and the insects. He breathed in the air, long and slow, sifting through the patchwork of odours. Brimstone. Charwater. Hot rock. Ferrous, sour, brackish . . .

It was the smell of a landscape newly formed – and free of the taint of the two-hides.

He turned to Alucius, his eyes shining brighter than they had in a very long while. '*I believe we have travelled far enough.*'

But Alucius made no reply. Instead, his gaze was focused on the lip of the nearest glowing crevice – a great crack in the black rock that seemed to descend into the fiery centre of the earth.

Alsasse twisted his sinuous neck and followed the second of the host's intense gaze. Around him, the rest of the flock did the same.

A massive taloned hand gripped the lip of the crevice. It was blueblack and gleamed like burnished pewter.

As the whitewyrmes watched, the razor-sharp talons dug into the rock for purchase and powerful muscles flexed at the wrist and knuckles. Another hand appeared, and then a crested head, a massive body and broad dark wings.

Slowly, deliberately, an enormous male blueblack-wyrme pulled himself from the crevice and stepped out onto the sleek rock. He was broad-chested, thick-necked and blunt-snouted, and he looked to be twice as big as the largest of the whitewyrmes. His dark scales shimmered in the orange fireglow of the crevice; his sapphire-bright eyes, small and glinting in his brutal face, regarded the host narrowly.

He opened his jaws and the sound the blueblack-wyrme released was grinding and heavy and bubbled like the molten lava flow in the crevice depths. It sounded dark. Unfamiliar. But it was recognizable. Just. And when it was repeated, the words were unmistakable.

'*You are not welcome here.*'

Twenty-Four

The girl raised the horn to her mouth and blew. A deep mournful sound boomed and throbbed, then faded away. The girl lowered the horn.

'Follow me,' she said, turning away. 'If you have need of shelter.'

Micah turned to Eli. The cragclimber had made no move, but remained where he was on the snowcapped outcrop, the rockspikes clenched in his fists. His eyes were dull and sunken, his stubbled cheeks hollowed out, and as Micah watched, he saw him begin to sway slightly on his feet.

The cragclimber was every bit as exhausted as Micah himself.

'What shall we do?' Micah whispered.

'Don't seem like there's a whole load of options open to us,' Eli muttered gruffly, his eyes fixed on the back of the girl in the long grey cloak and wide-brimmed hat as she made her way down the side of the valley.

She was agile and sure-footed, Micah observed, stepping lightly from rockslab to boulder, neither slipping nor hesitating.

'This haven's occupied, that much is clear,' Eli was saying. 'But if we retreat back up there . . .' He glanced back the way they'd come, and shook his head. 'We do that, we'll freeze to death for sure. Reckon we're gonna have to follow her, Micah,' he concluded. 'But I ain't fixing to surrender my weapons.'

Micah nodded, and followed the cragclimber as he lurched forward and stumbled down after the girl. Dislodged rocks skittered before them, and their halting breath fletched the cold air.

The sides of the ravine became steeper the further down they went, and began to close up. The freezing fog thinned and lifted. It hung in the air above them, creamy and opaque, and with the weak sun shining through, looked like folds of muslin.

They trudged down into a narrow defile that steepened further, the cliffs almost vertical on either side of them, stumbling, steadying themselves with their hands against the rock. The pinched trail turned sharply, and Micah looked up to see that the way ahead was barred by a wooden stockade that spanned the tight gap between the rockfaces. Stout pinelogs, stripped of their bark, had been carpentered and set in line, then braced and latticed with crossbars that were riveted into place.

The girl came to a halt in front of the wall of

wood. She looked up, cupped her hands to her mouth.

'It's Cara. Midwatch sentinel,' she called. 'Did you not hear the horn? I bring strangers to Deephome.'

As if in reply, a rope ladder sailed over the sharpened jags that fringed the top of the stockade, and tumbled down till it dangled in front of the girl. She reached out and seized it, and climbed up the wooden rungs with swift efficient movements. Below her, Micah and Eli exchanged exhausted looks.

'I'll go first,' said the cragclimber. 'You watch my back.'

Micah nodded.

Eli pocketed the rockspikes and began pulling himself up the rope ladder. When he'd reached the top and clambered awkwardly over the stockade, Micah followed. He had his catapult gripped between his clenched teeth, and two sharp flints were wedged up his shirt sleeve. His arms and legs ached and, with the air in the ravine growing warmer, feeling was returning to his fingers and toes, setting them to a painful and fiery throbbing.

Micah grasped the top of the stockade and braced himself for a moment, his face bathed in a film of clammy sweat. His stomach grumbled and nagged.

Almost there, he told himself.

With his jaws clamped, he hauled himself over the sharp spikes. His body was shaking and his head swam, and when the wyrmepelt cape snagged and he slipped and almost fell, Micah knew that he had expended the last of his strength.

Two hands reached out and grabbed him by the arms. The girl was on one side of him, Eli on the other, and Micah found himself tripping and stumbling as they supported him down a wooden staircase that was lit up by lanterns fixed to the inside of the stockade wall. At the bottom, on a broad apron of rock that had been swept clear of snow, there stood a tall figure, dressed in a grey cloak that matched the girl's and a broadbrim hat of woven straw, lacquered with a varnish of deep red.

Micah tried to focus on the figure's face, but all he could see was the deep red swimming before his eyes in the flickering lanternlight. He reached up and took the catapult from his mouth with fingers that throbbed and cramped and were all but useless. Beside him, Eli swayed on his feet, his jaw jutting out defiantly and his hands reaching into his pockets for the rockspikes.

'Return to your watch, daughter,' said the figure in the grey cloak and red hat.

Behind him, in some kind of vast vaulted space, Micah was dimly aware of other grey shapes moving about, smudges of red and flashes of white shimmering in the background.

'I am Kilian, prophet of Deephome.'

Deephome. The word repeated inside Micah's head. Deep home.

He forced his eyes to focus. The voice that had spoken was kind and lulling, and belonged to a tall firm-jawed man who stared at him from dark deepset eyes that were shadowed beneath tufted eyebrows, and which rose sympathetically as he spoke.

'It is the heart of fullwinter, a hazardous time to be wandering the weald . . .'

'We ain't no den squatters,' Eli said gruffly, 'and our business is our own. We were making for a refuge when a snowstorm drove us off course.'

'No one is turned away from Deephome,' said the prophet, extending a smooth hand, uncalloused by rough labour, from the folds of his grey cloak. 'You are welcome to shelter among us.'

Micah was waiting for Eli's reply when he felt his legs begin to buckle. The red hat swayed and shimmered before his eyes, and the last thing he remembered was the catapult slipping from his burning fingers and clattering to the ground.

TWENTY-FIVE

There were people down at the bottom of this great gash in the rock. Lots of people. Grey-cloaked figures in red straw hats and starched white bonnets, going about their business in the vast vaulted chamber. And as he watched them, Micah realized with a jolt just how cut off he, Eli and Thrace had been in the winter den – and how unused to the company of others he had become.

Three men were sitting with wyrmebone quills and pots of sootblacking, labelling large jars of salted and pickled produce; a fourth was climbing up and down a ladder set against a vast stack of open shelves, fetching and replacing the jars as required. A little way off, two women were beating thick plaid rugs that hung from a long line slung between more shelfstacks, while another two were shuffling awkwardly across the floor of the cavern, a large liquor barrel swaying between them.

And in among them all, playing some kind of game of tag – and using the silently labouring adults as cover – were half a dozen children, all dressed in miniature versions of the grey cloaks, red hats and white bonnets of their elders. One of them noticed Kilian standing over by the strangers, who were seated at the foot of the stockade stairs.

'Brother Kilian!' she exclaimed, and the others interrupted their game and joined in.

'Brother Kilian! Brother Kilian!'

The adults paused and looked up, then returned to their tasks as the children clustered around him, jumping up and tugging at the folds of his cloak. Kilian beamed down at them benevolently.

'Who are they? Who are they?' the children clamoured, pointing at Eli and Micah.

'This is Eli Halfwinter,' Kilian told them, refilling the cragclimber's beaker with honey-coloured liquor. 'And this,' he said, turning, 'is Micah.'

Micah smiled and took another gulp from his beaker. He still felt shaky after his fainting spell, but his head was beginning to clear, and the liquor glowed in the pit of his stomach, warm and soothing.

Kilian looked around at the excited faces of the children, his unblinking gaze resting on each of them for a moment, then raised his hands for quiet. 'The two of them have travelled a long way and are sore in need of food and rest. So stop pushing, stop shoving – Mattie, that means you too – and accord them the respect that we always accord our guests. That clear?'

A harsh edge had crept into Kilian's voice. The children fell back and lowered their heads.

'Yes, brother Kilian,' they muttered. 'Sorry, brother Kilian.'

Kilian nodded, but his mind had already moved on to other matters, and he turned to Eli and Micah.

'If you'll both excuse me,' he said, 'I have business I must attend to. Cara will be back shortly. Since you arrived during her watch, she'll be the one to look after you.' With that, he turned and strode off into the cavern, disappearing through an entrance in the far wall.

Micah shook his head. 'This cave's got to be twenty times the size of our den,' he marvelled, gazing up at the vaulted ceiling. 'And with a hundred times the stores . . .'

Beside him, Eli shifted on his haunches as he eyed the foodstuff and liquor shelves lining the vast chamber. 'I ain't never seen nothing like it,' he admitted. 'Such abundance gathered together in one place.' He frowned and rubbed a hand over his grizzled jaw. 'Though don't it strike you a might odd?'

'Odd?' said Micah, turning to look directly at Eli.

The cragclimber put down his beaker on the stone floor. 'Odd that, with riches such as these to defend, they ain't more wary of strangers.'

Micah looked at the contented faces of the

grey-cloaked people around them, calmly going about their tasks, and at the happy smiling children playing at their feet. Just then there came the sound of footsteps on the stairs behind them, and looking round, Micah saw that the girl, Cara, had returned.

'Perhaps,' he conceded. 'Though I sure am grateful for their hospitality.'

As he watched, the girl descended the stairs and handed the horn she was carrying to a tall youth in a grey cloak and red hat, nodding to him as she did so. Then, as he set off up the staircase for latewatch, she turned away, undid the clasp at the neck of her cloak and slipped it off, before hanging it on a hook beneath the stairs, next to a row of others.

Without the shapeless outdoor garb, Cara looked slimmer, almost slight. She wore a skirt of heavy home-spun that stopped just below the knee, long thick stockings and moccasins. Her blouse was blue and long-sleeved and buttoned high at the neck. And when she removed the heavy broadbrim hat, which she hung up on top of the cloak, Micah saw the skulltight bonnet she wore beneath – a starched folded piece of headgear that held, but did not entirely conceal, a mass of auburn curls.

Unaware of Micah's gaze upon her, Cara smoothed down her skirt and, with movements that were graceful and lithe, reached for a dry cloak and put it on. When she turned back, Micah found himself staring into her clear blue-green eyes.

He held her gaze for a moment, and was pleased to see her face colour blush-red beneath the freckles. Lowering her eyes shyly, she approached the spot where Micah and Eli were sitting.

'You are my guests,' she began, and Micah noted how she looked at Eli, but not at him. 'I shall show you to your sleeping place, and serve you at table, but first . . .' She caught Micah's eye and the blush deepened. 'First, I shall show you where you can bathe, and I shall bring you dry clothes . . .'

'Bathe?' said Eli, and whistled through his teeth. 'That's a rare luxury in fullwinter for kith such as us, eh, Micah, lad?'

'And welcome for it,' Micah observed.

The pair of them climbed to their feet and Micah was suddenly aware of how rough and rugged the two of them must look in their wyrmepelts and heavy boots beside these neat, clean, grey-cloaked folk. He felt a certain pride and swagger as he followed Cara across the cavern, past the children, who looked up at him, wide-eyed and wondering.

At the far end of the cavern, hanging from a rod, was

a pleated wyrmeskin curtain, which Cara pushed aside. As she did so, light came flooding into the dimly-lit cavern that bathed Micah and Eli in a curious rose-blue glow.

'Come with me,' she said.

TWENTY-SIX

She led them down a short tunnel and out into another cavern, even larger than the first. Beneath their feet, the floor was lightly strewn with chopped straw and barkchip that crunched beneath their feet and lent a musky fragrance to the air. Micah frowned. There was something else besides. And as he looked more closely, he made out a fine web of lucent fungus growing upon the scattered vegetation, and realized that it was these shining filaments that illuminated the cavern with the rose-blue light.

The glowing floor lit up the limestone formations. Stalagmites and stalactites blazed like torches, while the flowstone that encased the gypsum bedrock glowed like candlewax. Light was carried up towards the vaulted ceiling high above, where sparcrystals glittered.

'This is the great chamber,' Cara was saying. 'It's where we gather – specially in fullwinter.'

Micah could see men and women, little more than shadowy silhouettes against the glow, in various parts of the cavern; alone or clustered together in small groups. Some were standing, heads lifted, eyes closed and palms upraised. Some sat crosslegged in circles, their heads bowed together, almost touching. Others lay on the floor, staring unblinking at the ceiling in awestruck contemplation, while solitary figures wandered slowly about in their grey cloaks, their heads down and hands clasped behind their backs, gently murmuring, and the sound was like a hive of smoke-lulled bees.

As Eli and Micah followed Cara through the chamber, she drew their attention to the entrances of other caverns leading from it.

'Up yonder is where the elders meet,' she told them. 'Beyond that, the eating chamber. And there, and there – and there,' she said, pointing to various points at the sides of the cavernous hall, 'are the sleeping galleries, and the kitchens, and . . .'

'Welcome, strangers,' came a soft voice, and Micah turned to see a tall bearded figure stepping towards him from the shadows.

The man was smiling, his face beatific, and prominent teeth seeming to glow in the rose-blue light. His features had the weatherbeaten look of a seasoned weald traveller, and when he raised a hand in greeting, Micah saw he'd lost two of his fingers, perhaps to a gutting knife or a wyrme snare.

'Or should that not rather be, welcome, *friends?*' the

man corrected himself. 'For, as the prophet has taught us, are not all strangers simply friends we do not yet know?'

Micah nodded awkwardly and, as the figure shrank back into the shadows, turned to Eli, who looked back at him, shifted the heavy backpack about on his shoulders and shrugged. He glanced at the girl, but she avoided his gaze and instead addressed Eli when she spoke.

'Ezekiel endured many trials and tribulations before he came to us. But now he has found peace, Maker be praised.'

She turned and, indicating for them to follow her, headed off along a narrow tunnel to their right. The same unearthly glow illuminated the hewn rock. Moments later, the tunnel turned and they entered a dome-shaped cavern that echoed with the sound of water, sluicing and bubbling and splashing over rock.

Before them was a dark pool, its surface blurred with twists of steam that glowed pink and blue. The air was warm and moist and smelled faintly sulphurous.

'We cherish our hot spring here in Deephome, for its waters are both cleansing and health-giving. But be warned,' she added, her nose crinkling with concern, 'the water is hot.' She gestured toward the far end of the pool, where a trickle of water poured down into it from the lowest of a series of rocks that jutted out like supplicant hands and sent up clouds of billowing steam. 'So it's best to bathe over yonder, where cold water mixes with the hot.'

Micah nodded. 'I been so cold of late, there were moments I feared I might never be warm again,' he said to Eli, who had removed his hat and was flapping it in front of his face.

The hot pool looked so inviting that Micah could hardly wait to plunge into its steaming waters. He undid his belt and pulled the wyrmeskin cape over his head, and was reaching up and fumbling with the buttons of his shirt with clumsy fingers when he heard Eli clear his throat.

Micah looked up to see the girl Cara blushing furiously and averting her eyes.

'I . . . I'll go fetch clean clothes,' she told Eli and, still avoiding looking at Micah, she turned away crisply, a hand raised to her face.

Micah watched her, this shy kithgirl, as she hurried off. He saw how her long auburn hair was contained neatly within the confines of the tight bonnet; how the heavy folds of her homespun skirt flapped about her legs, concealing her figure; how she couldn't seem to risk meeting his gaze.

And he thought of Thrace.

TWENTY-SEVEN

Micah sat himself down on one of the stone benches that lined the cavern walls and, lifting his feet up, one after the other, slowly removed his boots. He wiggled his toes, which were dirty and wrinkled, and he winced at the pungent odour that rose up from them. He stood up and pulled off his jerkin, his shirt, emptied the pockets of his breeches, then folded them neatly and added them to the pile.

He was tired. Bone-tired. His body ached from the nightmare trials of the past few days.

He looked down at himself, his chin pressed against his chest. His body was pallid through lack of sun, grimy through lack of washing and thin through lack of food, and he barely recognized it as his own. There was downy hair on his chest which he had not noticed before, and dark bruises from the beating he'd taken in the winter den. He traced his fingertips lightly up and down the slatboard ribs, and grazed the circle of the old scar where the kinlance had penetrated . . .

Where was Thrace now? he wondered. Where had she and Aseel gone?

Wyrmes and their kin wintered in pinnacles and high peaks near thermal vents and hot fumaroles far from the trails of the kith. Most likely she would be up there now, distant and out of reach in the vastness of the weald. And he would never see her again.

Micah sighed.

She had shed a tear when she had departed. The sight of it had made his heartbeat quicken and, for a moment, he had dared to believe that she might stay with him. But she had not. Eli had been right. Thrace had never been more than on loan to him. Her true kinship was with Aseel. The old familiar ache in his chest returned.

'You coming in, Micah, lad?' Eli's echoing voice enquired, and was accompanied by the sound of splashing and swilling.

Dragged from his thoughts, Micah looked across at the pool. Eli was standing at the far side beside the trickling stream, neckdeep in the steaming water.

'How is it?' he called back.

'Hot water in fullwinter?' said Eli. He raised his arms above his head and sank down slowly beneath the surface, then, in a stream of bubbles, burst back up again. He wiped his face. The blood and soot fell away to reveal a heavy bruise over one eye and a scabbed cut to the jaw. 'Just about as good as it can get, I'd say,' he murmured, and he leaned back against the side of the pool.

Micah got up from the bench and crossed the cavern to the water's edge. There were steps cut into the rock, which led down into the pool. Micah descended them. The rock was warm on the soles of his feet. Halfway down, his left foot splashed into the water that lapped the step, and just for a moment, he couldn't tell if it was freezing cold or scalding hot. Then his foot started to tingle and itch, and he withdrew it smartish, and sucked in air between his teeth.

'It's boiling,' he muttered.

'You get used to it,' said Eli, dunking back under the water.

Micah placed his foot down a second time, and set his right foot next to it. He stood there, waiting for the sharp burning sensation to subside, then took another step down, and then another. As he went deeper, the water seemed to grip his legs, tightening around his ankles, his calves, his knees. He reached down and swirled the water about, mixing the hot and the cold together as he continued to the bottom of the rockcut stairs, where he bent his knees and submerged himself completely.

The water wrapped itself around him, hugging him,

cradling him; hot, but not too hot now, for he had got used to it. He sat down next to Eli on a ledge cut into the side of the pool and closed his eyes, and it was like he was a flatwyrme in fullsummer, basking on the rock, the heat gently warming him through, from outside to in, soothing his knocks and bruises.

'Here,' said Eli, 'I found this on the side,' and he handed Micah a broad flat slab of pale yellow soap.

'Thank you,' said Micah.

The soap looked pearly, smelled of coaltar and almonds, and felt gritty on his skin as he rubbed it against his neck, his armpits, up and down his legs and through his hair, before slipping down under the sudfleck surface and rinsing it off. Around him, the water smudged with milky brown as the dirt of several weeks lifted from his skin and floated to the surface.

'Feels good, don't it?' came a voice that was quavering and cracked.

Micah and Eli both turned, surprised, to see an old man emerging from the dense steam at the far end of the pool. Only his head was above the water, thinning grey hair plastered to his scalp and sunken blue eyes twinkling eagerly.

'Well, don't it?' he asked again. 'To wash away the filth of the past feels good.'

'A rare treat in fullwinter,' Eli replied, and Micah nodded his agreement at the man, who rewarded him with a beaming smile.

'Not here in Deephome, it ain't,' the old man said, and as he took a step forward the water waked at his jutting chin. 'In Deephome, you can bathe every day if you have a mind to.' He threw back his head and cackled. 'And I, brother Absolom, have a mind to! I soak my old bones most days in the hot spring – though I don't recall meeting you before.'

'My name is Micah, and this is Eli,' said Micah, smiling. 'We're new to Deephome. We're—'

'Just resting up for a night or two till the weather improves some,' Eli interrupted, with a glance at Micah that warned him not to be too forthcoming with a stranger.

'Pleased to meet you, brother Eli, brother Micah,' said Absolom, his blue eyes smiling. 'Though take the advice of an old scrimshaw carver who's seen more seasons in the high country than most,' he continued, fixing Eli with an intense stare. 'Travelling in fullwinter is as foolish as sticking your head in a strangle-snare. Stay until the thaw and accept the hospitality offered to you by the prophet.'

'Kilian,' said Micah.

'Indeed,' Absolom said, nodding earnestly. 'Brother Kilian is a true stone prophet. He cares for and protects all in Deephome. Thanks to brother Kilian, we have all we need and nothing to fear, and he asks only obedience in return.'

'Obedience,' said Eli, turning and wading across to the far end of the pool where the water was at its hottest. 'Reckon that can be a high price to pay.'

'Not for an old weald traveller like me,' Absolom chuckled. 'I've been in more scrapes, backstabbings and trailwhacks than I care to remember, and I have the scars to prove it.' He stood up and Micah saw the nubbed lines and ridges that crisscrossed his chest. 'But ever since I happened on Deephome, the prophet has kept me safe, and for that I am happy to do his bidding . . .'

'As we all are, brother Absolom,' came a soft voice, and Micah looked round to see Cara standing at the cavern entrance.

She had clean clothes in her arms, which she placed on the stone bench beside Eli and Micah's soiled ones, before withdrawing.

Micah stepped out of the water, his body glowing with warmth, and shook the water from his limbs. Crossing the chamber to the bench, he picked up a linen towel and dried himself off with it. Then he slipped a crisp undershirt over his head. The material was soft and smelled fresh, like new mown hay, like rainfall. Micah hadn't had anything so clean next to his skin for longer than he could remember and he thrilled at the sensation.

Beside him, Eli grabbed a towel of his own, dried his body, then put the linen aside.

Micah grabbed the neatly folded homespun breeches and stepped into them, pulled them up. He slipped the fustian waistcoat on. He did up the buttons, enjoying the soft snugness of the material, and was just reaching for his boots when he caught sight of Eli and stopped.

The cragclimber had ignored the clean folded clothes and instead was pulling on his old gear; the scuffed breeches, the wyrmeskin jerkin and heavy jacket. When he saw Micah watching him, he paused.

'Not quite ready to look like one of brother Kilian's faithful,' he said, 'however sweet they might smell.'

Micah blushed and, picking up his boots, sat down on the stone bench. In his crisp fresh-laundered clothes, he had to admit he did look like everyone else in Deephome. Yet he could not bring himself to put on the soiled musty-smelling gear he'd arrived in. He pulled on his boots. They, at least, were old and battered and bore testament to the hard trail he and Eli had walked together.

Eli put on his own boots, then gathered up Micah's old stuff and stored it away in his backpack.

'I'll hang onto these for you, lad,' he said. 'But humour me by hanging onto these yourself and keeping them close.' He handed Micah his catapult and hackdagger, which Micah put in the waistband of his breeches.

'I will, Eli,' he assured him, though, with the hospitality Deephome had already afforded them, Micah found it hard to believe he'd ever have need of them here.

As if in answer to his thought, Cara's voice sounded from the cavern entrance. 'Old Absolom's a gentle soul,' she said sweetly, as she peered into the chamber to check that they were dressed, 'and one of our best loved elders.'

Micah pushed his tangled wet hair out of his face and looked up.

'You could use a haircut,' Cara said, blushing.

She entered the cavern, rummaging in the pockets of her skirts as she approached. She produced a bone comb and a small pair of shears, then wrapped the damp linen towel about Micah's shoulders.

'Sit still,' she told him.

Micah closed his eyes, and took pleasure in the soft scratch of the wyrmebone on his scalp and the touch of Cara's hands as she combed through his hair, working at the tangles, knot by troublesome knot.

'You have nice hair,' she observed shyly. 'Thick and curly.'

It was Micah's turn to blush as Cara set to work, lifting his hair with the comb and shearing it off, section by section, making it short and even all over, while Eli watched from the stone bench opposite. As the hair fell, Micah remembered the last time it had been cut.

He'd done it himself that time. He had just arrived in the weald from the low plains. It had been fullsummer and, sweathot beneath his tousled mop, he'd knelt down next to a stream, dipped his head in the cold water, then cropped his hair with his hackdagger. He'd watched the cut hair float off on the surface of the turbulent water, and it had been like shutting a door on his past.

'Glad the clothes fit,' Cara observed, breaking into his recollections. 'They suit you, brother Micah.'

Micah tried not to look at Eli, but he could feel the cragclimber's blue eyes on him.

'Thank you,' he said. 'But I'll only have need of them till I get a chance to launder my own undershirt and breeches.'

Eli cleared his throat.

'As you wish,' said Cara sweetly. She stood back and admired her handiwork, snipped at some stray strands, then pronounced him done.

Micah climbed to his feet and as he did so, his stomach gurgled and rasped.

Cara smiled. 'Is that your belly I hear calling for sustenance?' she enquired.

Micah nodded. 'Happen it is.'

'Then we must satisfy its needs,' she said earnestly. She turned. 'Eli, are you also hungry?'

'A mite ravenous,' Eli replied, getting up from the bench.

Micah picked up the grey cloak lying folded beside him, swung it round his shoulders and toggled it at the neck, but he left the deep red straw hat that was next to it.

'Follow me,' said Cara.

Micah and Eli fell into step behind the girl. Micah felt refreshed, clean and sweet-smelling thanks to Cara. As he walked beside Eli, Micah's nose twitched. The musky odour of sweat and woodsmoke and wyrmeoil that arose from the cragclimber's clothes was reminding him of the winter den and the world outside.

Thrace came into his mind again, but Micah pushed the thought aside.

❖❖❖

TWENTY-EIGHT

Micah and Eli followed Cara down a short tunnel and back into the great chamber, with its high-vaulted ceiling and astonishing carpet of glowing fungus. Checking over her shoulder that they were following, she led the two of them toward an arched entranceway set into the back wall.

Halfway across the glowing floor, Micah's attention was grabbed by the sight of a dozen Deephomers – five men and seven women – moving in unison at the centre of the cavern. They were engaged in a sequence of slow movements that were graceful and languid, and demanded balance and coordination. Micah was transfixed by their strange weightless dance.

As he watched, they stepped forward as one, the motion arched and exaggerated. They remained poised on one leg for a moment, before twisting to their right and, arms outstretched at their sides, thrusting the other leg forward in a measured unfurling kick. Then they gathered themselves, leaned forward and, palm flat against the air, pushed one arm out in front of them while the other arm drew back, elbow crooked and fingers splayed.

'Keep up, Micah, lad.'

Looking round, Micah realized that Cara and the cragclimber were over by the arched entrance. He hurried across to them.

'Fullwinter is long and hard, even here in Deephome,' Cara told him as he caught up. 'The dance occupies the mind and calms the spirit.'

Micah nodded. Deephomers certainly looked absorbed and serene as they turned and repeated the slow sequence of movements once more.

'Doesn't do to let down your guard,' said Eli darkly. 'Even in fullwinter, there's always those ready to exploit the unwary.'

Cara looked at him, her blue-green eyes gleaming. 'The prophet protects us,' she said simply, and turned away.

On the far side of the arched tunnel, they stepped into a cave that was smaller but no less grand than the cavern they had just left. It was circular and dome-ceilinged. The walls were rippled curtains of creamy limestone that gleamed in the bright rose-pink light emanating from the mattress of straw on the floor. Six sturdy straightback chairs with ball feet and padded seats stood in a circle around the walls and, glancing up, Micah saw that high above their heads, suspended from thick ropes beneath the dome, was a round flat slab of rock.

He shuddered. With its smooth polished surface of black stone, the slab reminded him of Redmyrtle the keld butcher's table. He looked away, but the image was harder to push from his mind.

'This is where the elders meet,' Cara said, and gave Micah a concerned look. 'But you look tired and hungry. The eating chamber is just this way.'

They entered yet another rock-cut tunnel. The air there droned with low discourse, and smelled delicious.

Micah and Eli followed the kithgirl down a set of shallow stairs and into a sunken cavern that was broad and deep and low-ceilinged. Micah paused and looked about him in surprise, for despite the hushed atmosphere of the place, the eating chamber was all but full. There must have been a hundred or more Deephomers there: men, women and children. They were seated on benches that stood on both sides of a pair of long trestle tables, the two of them set parallel to one another and taking up most of the cavern. There was straw on the floor, but the rose-blue light of its lustrous fungus was supplemented by lamps that stood in a line along the centre of both tabletops. The men and boys had removed their red straw hats, and these stood behind them, propped up against the benches where they sat.

At the right-hand end of the cavern, the ceiling dipped down and the eating chamber opened up into what looked like a second cavern beyond. Flamelight flickered on the walls, and it was from here that the mouthwatering smells were coming – as well as a stream of servers, both boys and girls. They appeared from the shadows, steaming bowls and laden platters balanced on their crooked arms, delivered them to table, then returned with stacks of empty dishes clasped to their chest.

The kitchens, Micah thought. Cara had mentioned them earlier, along with the various other caves and chambers that went to make up Deephome, this vast series of subterranean spaces interconnected by manmade tunnels. It was certainly an impressive achievement, Micah conceded, and around him, Deephomers seemed to be utterly content in this haven from the harsh weald.

'This way,' said Cara.

She made her way down the aisle between the two tables, and Eli and Micah went with her. The diners glanced up as they passed, then returned to their meals. Micah saw little curiosity in their eyes.

'May we sit, sister Abigail?' Cara asked, pausing beside the hunched figure of a diner.

A middle-aged woman looked round. Her skin was pale and waxen, and there were grey rings under her eyes. Dark smudges on her blouse and skirt suggested a chore she'd been engaged in before being called to supper. For a long moment, she looked at the three of them standing behind her, then smiled and scooted along the bench to make room. Cara gestured for Eli and Micah to sit down, before squeezing herself in between them.

A server appeared behind them at once. He set a platter, two bowls and a jug on the table before them. Micah looked round. The server was young and tall but prematurely stooped. His cheeks and chin were pockmarked. His hands were pink, and looked soft. Micah inspected his own hands – the calloused palms, the chipped and ragged nails, the scarred knuckles. He looked up and caught Cara's eye, and noted that she had also made the contrast.

'Guests, sister Cara?' the server enquired.

'Guests indeed, brother Simeon,' said Cara, and Micah heard the ease with which she spoke to this fellow Deephomer, so at odds with her hesitant shyness with him. 'This is brother Eli,' she said, and turned. 'And this is brother Micah.'

'Welcome to Deephome, brothers,' said Simeon. 'And may you enjoy our simple repast.'

Simeon moved off to serve other diners, and Micah looked at the food before him. There were racks of wyrmeribs, slices of salted haunch, blackbread and rootmash, and pickled beets of orange and purple that glistened in spiced vinegar. Micah's stomach gurgled noisily. He grasped the wooden spoon beside his plate and was about to start eating when Cara reached out and clasped his left hand with her right, and Eli's right hand with her left, and raised her eyes to the ceiling.

'For the bounty of the weald and the fellowship of Deephome, we are truly grateful to the Maker,' she intoned.

Eli bowed his head, but not before shooting Micah a quizzical look from beneath his furrowed brow, which made Micah smile. Beside him, Cara let go of their hands and they all tucked into the food in front of them.

Micah savoured every mouthful. It was a joyous relief from the leathery sechemeat and watery stew of the winter den. Even the pickled beet tasted good.

His hunger seemed to come in waves. After two mouthfuls, he felt sated, his shrunken stomach tricked into believing it was full. After four mouthfuls, his appetite returned with full vigour, and he spooned up more slices of cured wyrmemeat and rootmash. Then his hunger began to diminish as his stomach became fuller and he sat back at last and wiped his mouth on the back of his hand.

He looked round the eating chamber, and noticed a figure winding his way between the diners, crouching down next to first one Deephomer, then another . . .

It was Kilian, and Micah was impressed. Rather than sitting at the head of the table and being waited upon, the prophet was passing through the eating chamber, talking to each of the diners in turn.

Micah observed his easy smile, his understanding nods and shakes of the head, and the look of intense concern that registered on his face as he listened to some complaint or petition, only to move on with a reassuring pat on the shoulder or squeeze of a hand once his reply had been accepted. And when, having made his way slowly along the length of the table, Kilian crouched down next to sister Abigail, Micah heard the prophet's words for himself.

'You look more rested, sister,' he said gently.

'The letting has left me weakened, brother Kilian,' Abigail told him. 'Yet with this fine food and drink, my strength is returning.'

'I'm glad of that, sister Abigail,' said Kilian warmly. He straightened up and squeezed Abigail's shoulder.

'We must all contribute what we can for the good of Deephome.'

'I know it,' said Abigail, 'and I am grateful for your protection, brother Kilian.'

Kilian hesitated, then leaned forward and whispered into her ear. 'I know you are, sister, but perhaps in future you might change from your soiled clothes *before* suppertime.'

Abigail flinched, and fingered the smudged stains on her blouse. She looked mortified.

'Yes, brother Kilian,' she said. 'Of course, I'm sorry . . .'

Kilian patted her back lightly and moved on. He crouched down next to Micah, who turned to find himself looking into the prophet's smiling face.

'Sister Cara has been looking after you?' he said, his dark eyes holding Micah's gaze.

Micah nodded. 'She has,' he said. 'I have bathed. I have clean clothes.' He indicated the empty plate before him. 'And I have eaten better than in longer than I care to remember . . .'

Micah heard Eli clear his throat, and he fell still, suddenly guilty that the cragclimber might consider him ungrateful for all the meals he'd shared with him in the winter den.

'I'm pleased to hear it,' said Kilian. 'And you, daughter, you have risen to the task?'

'I hope I have, Father,' Cara replied softly.

'Yet I see brother Eli here is dressed in his old clothes,' he observed. He stood up and moved on to the cragclimber. 'I trust you were offered clean ones.'

'I was,' said Eli, turning to Cara, then Kilian. He smiled. 'But I'm more comfortable in these. Just as soon as the weather has cleared, Micah and I shall be on our way,' Eli said gruffly. 'Ain't that right, lad?'

Micah nodded, but inside his heart sank at the thought of leaving this warm safe underground haven, with its hot spring and good food and heady liquor and contented inhabitants, and returning to the unforgiving harshness of the fullwinter weald. And as he pictured the world outside, he was suddenly overwhelmed with weariness. His limbs ached, his eyelids felt heavy, and his mouth spasmed into a gaping yawn that would not be swallowed away.

Kilian smiled. 'Sleep calls,' he said, and as he continued along the table he turned and added, 'You are both welcome to stay as long as you wish.'

Micah could scarcely keep his eyes open as Cara led him and Eli back through the tunnels and caverns. He dragged his feet, he stumbled. The air sparkled and the walls blurred.

'What's down there?' he heard Eli asking, and saw that the cragclimber had stopped and was peering into a tunnel that was narrow and unlit and descended into the darkness.

'That?' Cara faltered. 'It leads to some kind of store place. For old equipment, I think,' she said. 'Nobody goes down there, except for brother Kilian once in a while . . .'

They kept on. Micah's head swam. And when Cara announced that they had arrived at the sleeping galleries, he stopped and looked ahead of him without comprehension.

They were standing at the entrance to a wedge-shaped cavern, the roof low over their heads but rising at an angle before them. The wall opposite was of banded sandstone, into which lozenge-shaped holes had been cut in rows, horizontal and vertical. The ones at the top were in deep shadow, for the glowing straw was sparse upon the floor and the cavern bathed in gloom. Ladders were propped up against the steep cave wall.

'You'll find two sleeping places at the top,' said Cara, positioning a ladder beside each of two dark openings. 'They have been prepared.'

Drawn by the promise of rest, Micah stumbled

forward. He heard Cara wish him a good night's sleep, and Eli doing the same, but was too tired to respond to either of them. He climbed one of the ladders, rung by rung, ascending into the welcome darkness, and slid into a deep niche at the top, directly beneath the cavern roof.

There was a straw-stuffed mattress inside it; thick blankets, a pillow of down. Micah pulled off his boots, slipped out of the grey cloak and lay himself down. His head sank into the softness of the pillow and he pulled the covers up to his chin.

He lay on his back in the shrouded darkness, his arms folded across his chest, and as he stared up into the velvet blackness, the faces of Deephomers in the eating chamber filled his head. Untroubled faces. Contented faces. Happy smiling faces. And one face in particular, shy and serious, blushing as her blue-green eyes gleamed.

'Sister Cara,' Micah muttered drowsily. 'Cara . . .'

His eyelids flickered and closed, and he fell into a deep dreamless sleep.

Twenty-Nine

Micah stirred and opened his eyes. It was the second time he'd woken. Voices had roused him earlier, but he'd rolled over drowsily and drifted back to sleep. Now he was wide awake, and aware that, for the first time in days, he felt fully rested.

He fingertipped the gritty sleep from the corners of his eyes and rubbed his hands over his head, puzzled for a moment at the shortness of his hair. Then he remembered its shearing, when he was seated beside the hot spring, and Cara, the kithgirl who had shorn it.

Shifting onto his front, Micah inched himself forward and peered out of the narrow sleeping niche. On either side of him, and below, were similar holes excavated from the soft sandstone of the cavern wall. He ran his hand over the gritty surface of the rock and noted the telltale chisel marks that grooved its surface. Beneath him, the floor glowed muted rose-blue. He saw no one, and when he listened, the lack of either conversation or snoring suggested the sleeping galleries around him were empty.

Where's Eli? he wondered.

He pulled himself up onto his knees and was reaching back for his boots when something caught his eye – a flash of movement, scuttling out of the shadows below and darting towards the centre of the floor.

It was a wyrme. No, two wyrmes, both of them white and tatterwinged. He had encountered their like before, rawking and screeching as they squabbled over scraps of food in Jura's cave. So long ago. He watched them, surprised to see similar wyrmes living in this series of caverns and chambers that had been taken and occupied and bent to the will of the men and women who dwelled in them. Most kith would have trapped or hunted such cavern wyrmes, and Micah was impressed that these Deephomers tolerated wyrmes amongst them. Just like kin did . . .

The wyrmes started abruptly back. Their heads shot up and they looked about them. One of them jabbered, and the pair of them turned tail and flap-ran back into the shadows. Footfalls sounded, and Micah saw wyrme-hide boots and breeches and a familiar battered jacket as Eli entered the great wedge-shaped chamber. He looked up at the sleeping niches.

'Micah? You up yet?'

'Good as,' Micah called back.

'Well, get down here, lad,' he said.

Micah pulled on his boots, the undershirt and the fustian jerkin, grabbed the grey cloak, then started down the ladder. Glancing around as he neared the bottom, he saw the cragclimber's face looking up at him. The glow from the floor uplit his face in light and shade which exaggerated the grimness of his expression. His pale eyes looked anxious, expectant.

'I've been having a scout round,' Eli said.

Micah jumped down the last few rungs and landed with a thud. He turned to Eli. 'You have?'

Eli nodded. 'That tunnel. I took a look down it.'

Micah nodded, and knew at once that Eli meant the tunnel they'd passed the previous night; the dark pitch-steep tunnel.

'What did you see?' Micah asked.

'It was dark,' Eli said, 'and I didn't go too deep. But by the looks of it, it drops down a fair ways.'

'Didn't Cara say that that there was some kind of equipment store down there?' Micah asked.

'Maybe so,' Eli said, 'but if there is, it must lie a good deal deeper than the rest of these caverns.' He paused. 'I found a bunch of kith clothes, though, piled up a little way down the tunnel, tucked away out of sight. Muddy boots. Worn, trailbattered hacketons and overmantles, the kind trappers and gutters and such favour.'

'Clothes like ours,' Micah murmured.

'Looked like it,' said Eli. 'Though these were a whole lot more scuffed and scratched than most.' He reached across and rested his hand on Micah's shoulder. 'Perhaps you might like to enquire about them, Micah, nice and gentle like.' He smiled. 'From your new friend.'

Micah cringed. 'You mean Cara?'

''Less there's some other new friend you've made I know nothing of,' said Eli. He rubbed his hand over Micah's cropped hair. 'She seems to like you.'

Micah reddened, twisted his head round and pushed Eli away.

'She does,' Eli persisted.

'Her father asked her to look after us is all,' Micah protested. 'She don't mean nothing more by it.' He turned away, angry with Eli for teasing and embarrassing him, but hoping he might be right – and turned redder still when he saw Cara come walking into the cavern.

'Sleep well?' she asked.

Micah nodded. He swallowed.

Cara frowned and looked from Micah to Eli, and back again. 'If this isn't a good time,' she began uncertainly, 'I can come back later – only breakfast is nearly over . . .'

'We thank you, Cara,' said Eli formally. 'I for one am ravenous. You hungry, lad?'

'Yes,' said Micah. 'Yes, I am.'

'Then come with me,' said Cara, turning and heading back to the entrance to the cavern.

The pair of them followed the kithgirl. Halfway across the floor there was a loud clatter. Cara spun round, and Micah looked down to see that he'd tripped over a metal tray that was lying on the straw. It had scraps of bloodied wyrmeskin and glistening fat and lengths of marrow bones upon it, and he realized that it was these the two tatterwinged wyrmes must have been bickering over – and that someone had put them there for them.

'So you feed the wyrmes?' Micah asked.

'Guests to Deephome come in all shapes and sizes,' said Cara lightly. 'And the prophet welcomes them all.'

THIRTY

'That sure was tasty,' said Micah. He patted his stomach. It was hard and round, like a small pot at the base of his ribs. 'I ain't had corncakes and syrup in a long while.'

'Barley,' Cara corrected him. 'It grows wild on the eastern slopes of the valley. We harvest it in early half-winter. And we have our own millstone for grinding it to flour.'

Micah nodded, once again impressed by the ingenuity and resourcefulness of the Deephomers.

The pair of them were seated in the eating chamber, side by side on a bench at the table farther from the entrance. The cavern had been full when they'd arrived, but it had emptied out. Eli had scarcely touched his food, and had excused himself before Micah had a chance to ask him where he was headed. Now the servers were clearing the tables and swabbing them down, while the tardier diners were scurrying off to attend to whatever chores they'd been allocated.

Micah watched a young couple over by the entrance. The man was square-jawed and so tall his grey cloak barely reached to his knees; the woman had long dark curls that coiled down from beneath her tight bonnet. They were each politely trying to usher the other one out through the entrance before laughing, holding hands and leaving together.

'That's brother Elijah and sister Ruth,' said Cara, following Micah's gaze. 'They've both been tasked with laundering the clothes.'

Micah smiled, one eyebrow raised. 'Don't look like they got too many objections to working together.'

Cara blushed. 'The dullest of tasks can be made joyful,' she said, avoiding his gaze, 'with a willing helpmate.'

Micah was tempted to smile again, at her earnestness, at her innocence. But he did not. Instead, he nodded, his expression equally serious. 'And is there a dull task that I can help *you* with, sister Cara?'

Cara's face relaxed. She climbed to her feet and stepped over the bench.

'Actually there is something,' she said.

'The trick with a blackgage,' said Cara, as she gripped the paring knife tightly, 'is to slide the blade . . . all the way round the outside of the rind without . . . without . . .' She paused, and Micah watched her graze her lower lip with her top teeth, frowning with concentration as she worried at a stubborn bit of skin – and finally broke through. 'Without cutting into the fleshy part inside.'

The fruit was one of dozens that had been laid out in a deep wooden box, with straw separating the layers. Cara had explained to Micah how they were laid down green and left to ripen, and that it was her job now to preserve them.

Perched on his low stool opposite her, Micah watched her turn the fruit over in her hand. The pair of them were sitting opposite one another in a small alcove to the right of the store chamber. A bucket of water with a rope handle stood between them; the wooden box of fruit to one side and a large earthenware pot to the other. Micah had neither heard of a blackgage, nor seen anything like it. It was purple-black and a tad larger than his clenched fist. There were ridged hoops in the rind which, when the light caught them, formed stripes down the bulbous body of the fruit, from the stalk at the top to the tassel of fibres at the bottom.

'Looks like a fine and delicate skill,' Micah observed, watching Cara's hands as she continued the incision, cutting carefully round to where she had first dug the point of the knife in.

A strand of auburn hair had fallen loose from her

white bonnet, and she paused to push it back into place with slender fingers. Then she looked up, and Micah was struck once again by the startling duck egg turquoise of her eyes.

'That should do it,' she said. She clamped both hands round the ends of the fruit, gripped tightly, then gave it a sharp twist. With a soft grating sound, the two halves of the thick outer rind turned in different directions and came loose, and Cara deftly removed the soft pale orange fruit from inside. There wasn't a scratch on it. 'Perfect,' she murmured, sitting back and smiling.

The kithgirl's skin looked so fresh and soft, Micah wanted to reach out and brush her freckled cheek with his fingertips, and he held her gaze for longer than he'd intended. It was his turn to blush.

His nose twitched at the smell the fruit gave off, which was citrus and musky. He edged his stool forward and tried to concentrate.

'Now all we do is wash it,' said Cara. She dunked the fruit into the bucket of water that stood on the floor between them. 'Bottle it.' She pushed it gently inside the pot. 'And when it's full, we'll add liquor and spices, and seal it up. Long as there's no nicks or bruises, pickled blackgage'll last for years.' She selected a second fruit from the box and handed it to Micah, together with the paring knife. 'You care to try?'

Micah took the fruit in his left hand, the knife in his right, then jabbed the point of the blade into the rind. It barely penetrated. He tried again, and with the same result, then laid the paring knife down.

'If it's all the same to you,' he said, sweeping aside the Deephome cloak he was wearing and pulling his hackdagger from his belt, 'I'll use this.'

The knife felt good in his hand. It was well balanced. The blade was thin and slightly chipped, but razor sharp, and the worn handle was moulded to his grip. He looked up at Cara, to see her staring back at him, her eyes wide.

She gestured toward the knife. 'We have no need of weapons in Deephome,' she said.

'I don't think of it as a weapon,' said Micah, flicking the knife up into the air, then catching it again. 'I think of it as a tool.' He smiled. 'Like your paring knife.'

'And that?' She pointed at the catapult tucked into Micah's belt.

'Why, that's just a wyrmebone catapult,' said Micah, looking down. 'I made it myself.' He grinned. 'I could show you how to use it. If you'd like me to.'

'A catapult,' Cara repeated. She pushed the strand of hair back off her face, her gaze fixed on the catapult.

'Made it yourself,' she said, and there was admiration in her voice. 'Well, brother Micah, whether we get the chance to try it out or not is going to depend on just how long it takes us to bottle up all these blackgages.'

'Then I guess we better get started,' said Micah.

This time, with his hackdagger in hand, he scored a line into the rind that was clean and even and deep, but not too deep. Then he gripped the fruit at both ends, just as he'd seen Cara doing, and twisted. The soft fleshy ball of fruit came away, and he rolled it round the palm of his hand.

'Beautifully done,' said Cara, looking up from her own half-finished fruit, and Micah bathed in her obvious delight.

'Beginner's luck,' he said modestly, then took another of the fruits to show that it was not. 'Sister Cara,' he said slowly, as he drew the blade through the thick rind, 'can I ask you a question?'

Cara hesitated. 'Of course, brother Micah.'

'Eli found clothes in the tunnel,' he said. 'The one you said led to an equipment store . . .'

He didn't look up, but he was aware of Cara's eyes on him. She was sitting very still.

'They were kith clothes,' he went on. 'Heavy wyrme-skin hacketons. Stout boots . . .'

'And your question?' said Cara softly.

Micah continued peeling the fruit. 'Who do the clothes belong to?'

Though his head was down, concentrating on the incision he was cutting through the rind, Micah saw that Cara kept looking up at him. Short stolen glances, time and again. He continued working at the blackgage, not looking at her, waiting for her reply.

'There *were* some kith,' she said at length.

Micah paused.

''Bout a year and a half back. Somewhere twixt half-summer and full as I recall.' She frowned. 'Seven of them. Four men. Three women . . .'

Micah picked up another of the purple-black fruits.

'We welcomed them, as we welcome all travellers to Deephome, but . . .' Cara's face clouded over. 'They . . . they did not want our hospitality, only to help themselves to our stores . . . And worse.'

'Worse?' said Micah, gripping his hackdagger tightly.

Cara was silent for a moment, head down, eyes focused on the fruit in her hand. She shuddered, then gathered herself, and when she looked up, her face was radiant, a smile on her lips. 'But my father protected us,' she said brightly. 'He told us to gather in the great chamber and he told us to sing loudly, to the glory of

Deephome and to the Maker. And that was what we did.'

She shook her head thoughtfully, the knife pincered in her fingertips. Her eyes gleamed with fervour.

'Oh, Micah, you have never heard such a wonderful sound as our voices rising up and echoing round the air. Singing together, as one. Powerful. Exultant . . .' She fell still and fixed Micah with her intense gaze. 'Then my father went out of the store chamber and told the kith to leave,' she said. 'And they did.'

Micah frowned. 'Just like that?' he said. 'Leaving their jackets and boots behind?'

Cara nodded. 'They were worn and useless,' she told him. 'My father gave them new clothes, and wished them well. As he always does.'

'You mean there have been others?' said Micah.

Cara nodded again, her eyes sparkling. 'The weald is a wild and dangerous place. You know that yourself, brother Micah,' she said solemnly. 'We welcome all to Deephome, but those who wish to harm us, my father tells to leave, and they do.'

'Always?' said Micah.

Cara smiled. 'Always,' she said.

❧✠❧

THIRTY-ONE

'Micah!'

Micah turned at the sound of his name, to see Eli striding across the store chamber towards him. The crag-climber was dressed in his heavy wyrmeskin jacket, and his battered wide-brimmed hat was pulled down low over his eyes. He wiped crumbs from around his mouth with the back of his hand.

'Where is she?' he asked.

'Cara?' said Micah, looking up from the jars of pickled blackgages he was patiently stacking on a crowded shelf. 'She's getting her cloak.' He nodded out through the store chamber towards the steps that led down from the top of the stockade.

Cara herself appeared a moment later, a heavy grey cloak toggled at her neck, and a dark red hat covering her white bonnet. She observed Eli with curiosity for a moment, then returned his smile.

'Do you mind if I join you on your watch, sister Cara?' he asked her. 'Only I've a mind to take a look outside myself. You leaving now?'

'When brother Abel gets back,' Cara nodded.

Just then, a stocky bearded figure appeared at the top of the stockade, the long curved horn slung from its strap over one shoulder. He straightened up, shook the snow from his cloak and started down the stairs. Cara went to meet him.

'Greetings, sister Cara,' he said.

'Greetings, brother Abel,' she replied. 'A quiet watch?'

'A quiet watch,' Abel confirmed. He reached up and rubbed the snow from his beard, then unshouldered the horn and handed it to Cara. 'But a cold watch,' he added. 'I swear that fullwinter wind has teeth.'

Cara nodded. 'And anything to report?'

'Yeah,' he said, then laughed. 'My prodigious hunger.'

Cara patted him amiably on the arm, then turned to the cragclimber. 'If you're still set on joining me, brother Eli, I'm about to depart,' she called from the foot of the steps.

Eli nodded grimly and marched out from the arched entrance of the store chamber and over to the stockade to join her. Micah watched him for a moment, then set the jars of blackgages aside. Pulling the heavy homespun cloak up at the back to form a makeshift hood and wrapping it tightly round him, he hurried to the foot of the stockade staircase. Eli and Cara turned and looked at him.

'Well, I ain't fixing to stop here on my own,' said Micah.

Cara smiled and Eli nodded, and the three of them climbed the wooden steps. They'd been swept of snow and salted, but freshfall was already mottling the dark boards. At the top, Cara, then Eli, climbed over the pointed stakes of the stockade wall and made their way down the rope ladder on the other side. Micah went last, and was shocked by the intense cold that snatched his breath away. The frozen rope of the ladder made his fingers throb, and his boots slipped on the icy rungs. At the bottom, he readjusted the cloak and clutched it to his chest with clenched fingers, then he trudged after Cara and Eli, who were already setting off up the steep northern side of the valley, following the trail of footprints that Abel had left in the deep snow.

A thin mist hung in the air, turning the snow-covered trees that clung to the steep sides of the chasm into eerie silhouettes. They crested the first ridge, and the swirling wind snarled and snapped. The trail steepened sharply, and soon they were above the mist. From the slategrey gash of sky above them thick snow fell as large ungainly flakes that stuck to them like wet feathers.

The incline steepened further, and their progress slowed. Vertical rock was to their left and a growing drop to their right. After five minutes of steady trudging, Cara came to a halt on a jutting snow-capped rock. Eli and Micah stopped beside her, and the three of them surveyed the valley which cut down below them, then rose up ahead, steep and snow-clogged. Micah could just make out the dim glow of the lamps at the stockade in Deephome, smudged by the mist.

Above them soared the sides of the valley, sheer and vertiginous. The daylight was already beginning to leech from the sky beyond.

'We'll stand sentinel here,' said Cara. 'Till the cold begins to bite, then move on. It isn't wise to stop still for too long in such conditions.'

The jutting rock was the first of several vantage points where Cara stopped. The next time was at the turn of a rising crag. The time after that, beside a tall pine, piebald with patches of snow, that grew at an angle from the side of the valley. And later on, as the subdued daylight grew dimmer still, on a flat slab of rock with a view down over a frozen waterfall. The snow was thin beneath their feet, and Micah guessed that Abel must have stood in that selfsame place, idly kicking the clods of snow off the rock and into the drop below.

Each time she stopped, Cara would raise her spyglass to her eye and survey the valley up ahead.

'I check for flashes of colour against the snow,' she said. 'Or movement.' Cara lowered the spyglass, her gaze still fixed on the head of the valley. 'A few weeks back, there was a woman. She had stumbled into the haven, but her strength must have failed her before she got down as far as Deephome. She was still breathing when I found her, and I got her back, but she died soon after.' Cara sighed softly, wisps of breath fluttering from her lips. 'Sometimes the Maker's will is hard to fathom.'

They tramped on up the rising valley side, and were not far short of halfway to the top of the haven when Cara turned sharp right and headed down through the trees. Micah went with her, relieved that they were climbing no further, for though it had stopped snowing, the higher they went, the stronger the wind became. It howled and whistled through the stiff branches; it cut through his clothes. He hated to think what it must be like up on the exposed plateau above.

Ahead of him, Cara ducked down beneath a prominent ledge of rock. She sat down on a bare boulder in its shade and looked up expectantly at the others. Eli and Micah exchanged glances, then, stooping low, followed her.

'This is the last sentinel point,' Cara told them. 'It was from here I spotted your approach yesterday afternoon.'

'And we're glad you did, Cara,' said Micah with feeling, pulling his cloak tightly round him and sitting down. 'Ain't we, Eli?'

The cragclimber grunted, his gaze directed at the sky, and Micah could tell he was attempting to calculate their chances if they left the shelter of the haven in weather like this. He must have concluded that they were slim, for he shook his head and turned his blue eyes on Micah.

'So where were you this morning while I was checking our kit for our onward journey?' he asked.

'I . . . I was helping Cara out,' Micah said. His face reddened, and he hoped the cragclimber would not make some wisecrack that would make it redder still.

'We pickled fruit,' said Cara. 'Blackgages.'

'Blackgages?' said Eli.

'They got thick skins,' said Micah. 'Sort of a purply-black colour on the outside, but a pale orange once you get 'em peeled.'

Eli smiled strangely, his eyes distant. 'If they're what I think they are, then Jura used to call them sweet lemons, for that was their taste.'

'That's right,' said Micah nodding, 'like lemons dipped in honey.'

'Why, Micah!' Cara said, and she placed a hand on his arm. 'I suspected the blackgages were disappearing. You were meant to be bottling them, not eating them . . .'

'Just a couple,' said Micah, smiling guiltily, enjoying the feel of her delicate fingers. 'Ones I accidentally nicked with the blade.'

'Pah,' said Cara, her eyes twinkling. 'There weren't no nicking, save for on purpose.' She turned to Eli. 'I have never seen a person more dextrous with a knife,' she said. 'And quick. Why, we completed in three hours a task that would normally have taken me all day.'

Eli pulled himself back from his thoughts. 'Good to see you're helping out, Micah, lad,' he noted. 'After all, we ain't no den squatters, expecting hospitality for no return . . .'

'I know you're not, brother Eli,' said Cara. 'For if you were, my father would have asked you to leave.'

Eli did not answer. Instead, his gaze was fixed on the base of the frozen waterfall below them. Slowly he climbed to his feet, pulling his spyglass from inside his jacket as he did so. He put it to his eye and focused on the frozen pool to which the icy stalactite of the waterfall was fused.

'Have you spotted someone?' asked Cara, training her spyglass on the same spot. 'I see no movement.'

'Not exactly,' said Eli, 'though if you follow me . . .'

The three of them scrambled awkwardly down the

valleyside. The thick mattress of snow rendered the ground featureless, and their boots stumbled over rocks they could not see, or slammed down between them. They fell back on their hands. They barked their shins.

Micah stared ahead, but the air was thick with snow once more and he could not see where Eli was leading them. He wished the howling wind would ease off for a moment, but then Cara slipped and seized hold of his cloaked arm for support, and he was glad it had not.

'There,' said Eli at last, coming to a halt on a humped boulder that glistened like a semi-precious gemstone in a setting of ice.

In front was the frozen waterfall. Micah looked up to see the mighty column of fluted ice rising and disappearing into the blur of whiteness high above him. The water had become solid in the absolute chill that had robbed it of movement, yet preserved the illusion. There were pleated folds and tallowdrip lines and blobs. Some of the ice was a pale milky green colour; most of it was clear as glass. And at the bottom, where the waterfall had landed in the pool below, the splashback of water had frozen to form something that resembled a crystal crown.

Eli was crouched down next to it, and at first Micah thought it must have been the curious twists and curves of ice that had caught his attention. Then he saw the wyrme. It was squat and round, about the size of a large turkey-cock.

Micah placed a hand on the cragclimber's shoulder, and Eli looked round at him. 'A squabwyrme,' he said, 'all fattened up for fullwinter – but killed by its thirst.'

Three of the plump wyrme's feet and one of its stubby triangular wings were encased in ice. Trapped, the creature must have fought to free itself. Frozen blood around the claws of the fourth foot bore testimony to that. In its exhaustion, it had slumped down onto its belly, where it had succumbed to the cold that stopped its heart and frosted its eyes.

'I seen it from up there on that sentinel point of yours,' Eli explained to Cara, pointing back the way they'd come.

He drew his knife from the sheath at his belt and leaned forward. Then, clasping one of the squabwyrme's back legs, he began to saw at the ankle joint with the glinting jags.

'In the name of all that's sacred,' he muttered, reaching up and wiping sweat from his brow, 'it's like cutting through rock.'

He doubled his efforts, then kicked at the incision he'd made in the bone and the leg snapped off at the knuckle. The second hindleg soon followed, then the foreleg, and when he had cut through the base of the wing, the body rolled free. It looked like a boulder. Eli wrapped his arms around it, pulled it to his chest and climbed awkwardly to his feet.

'Let's head back,' he said, 'before we end up as frozen solid as this wyrme here.'

'Squabwyrme!' Kilian clapped his hands together in delight. 'How wonderful. A welcome treat indeed.'

He raised a hand and clicked his fingers, and two Deephomers came running outside. They tipped their red hats at Kilian respectfully, then, at his command, relieved Eli of the squabwyrme and disappeared back inside.

'The cooks will honour it with their preparation – and we shall honour it in its eating.' He turned to his daughter, who had passed on the horn and hung up her cloak and was standing with Micah at the entrance to the store cavern. 'Isn't that right, daughter?'

Cara smiled and nodded. 'Brother Micah and brother Eli have honoured Deephome with their endeavours.'

'And I am most grateful to them for that,' said Kilian.

'The poor creature was caught out by the severity of the weather. I simply spotted it,' Eli said modestly. 'But

I'm glad I could contribute something to your table.' He shrugged. 'With the storm up top the way it is, looks like the lad and I are fixed for a long stay . . .'

'Stay as long as you like,' said Kilian generously. He turned to his daughter. 'If you wouldn't mind, my dear, old sister Hester has been asking for you to sit with her.'

'Of course, Father,' she said, and glancing back and giving Micah one of her quick shy smiles, went with him.

Micah watched the two of them walking through the store chamber, side by side. Kilian the prophet, protector of Deephome, and his daughter, Cara.

Cara . . .

He watched how her hips moved, setting her long skirt swaying from side to side. Thanks to the harshness of fullwinter, he and Eli would be staying in Deephome a while longer, and he was glad.

He turned to Eli.

The cragclimber's expression had turned grim. 'Micah,' he said gruffly, 'we need to talk.'

THIRTY-TWO

'Micah, I am not your father.'

'I know it, Eli . . . My father died of plains fever way back. And since you've never taken a belt to me or shown me the back of your hand, I'm guessing you're not my big brother neither . . .'

'What I'm trying to say is, we got no blood ties, you and me. So I ain't fixing to give you no fatherly advice. Here in the weald you are your own man, and as such, you should make up your own mind. But . . . there's something not right about this Deephome place.'

'But what? What? Eli, you spoke of my father. I tell you, compared with the hovel I grew up in back on the plains, Deephome is like a glimpse of the Maker's paradise. Everyone looks out for everyone else, concerned for their needs and welfare – not just looking after themselves. What's wrong with that?'

'I'm just saying something don't sit right.'

'Cara says it's simply a matter of learning their ways.'

'Well, what I seen of them, their ways trouble me, Micah. In my experience, settling in one place comes at a cost in the high country. You got to defend what you got with force, or it'll end up getting taken from you by those more powerful and ruthless. Seems to me a set-up like Deephome should be a good deal better defended than it appears to be. Hidden away down here it might be, but it's still a tempting target for marauders, and that stockade wouldn't keep hardened kith out for long.'

'It wouldn't?'

'No. That's why I prefer to keep on the move, to avoid trouble rather than waiting for it to come and find me. Yes, we have to hole up in fullwinter. It's the only way to survive. But I have always preferred to find my own den, rather than squatting in someone else's . . .'

'But trouble found us in our den, Eli. Maybe trouble just can't be avoided, and maybe it's good to have folks around you when it does find you. Besides . . . I like it here.'

'You like it here.'

'I do, Eli. I like it here a lot.'

'I went down there again, Micah.'

'Into the tunnel?'

'Into the tunnel. Only this time I went deeper than before. I took me a lamp . . .'

''Bout them clothes and all, Eli, I been meaning to tell you. Cara said that a while back, they did take in a bunch of kith. She said they were rough and violent, said how they tried to take their stores . . .'

'And?'

'And brother Kilian spoke to them. Persuaded them to leave.'

'Persuaded?'

'I know, Eli, and it sounded strange to me too. I don't know, maybe it's them eyes of his. You seen the way he looks at you, like he can read your thoughts. I reckon he sure can be persuasive when he wants to be. Cara said he gave the kith clean clothes for their old wornout gear, and that they went on their way.'

'Maybe, Micah. Maybe . . . Anyway, like I was saying, I went deeper into the tunnel than before. I came to a door . . .'

'The door to the equipment store?'

'I don't know.'

'You didn't take a look?'

'I couldn't, Micah. The door had no handle.'

'Jura charged me with your education, Micah. She was afeared that if I did not, then others would, and that they would learn you bad things. How to steal and plunder and kill . . .'

'I know it. You told me before.'

'I did. But what I did not tell you, Micah, is that I have been honoured by the task. Oh, I confess, I accepted the undertaking with reservations. Reluctance, even. Last thing I ever had in mind was to get weighted down by some greenhorn. But you was a quick learner, and willing and keen, and seldom discouraged, and I . . . I'm proud of what you have become, Micah, even if I might not always show it.'

'You do show it, Eli. In your own way. And I'm grateful.'

'There ain't no need to be grateful. It comes from you, Micah. From the inside. I take no credit for it. Whatever hardships and privations you endured as a child, something went right . . .'

'You think so?'

'I know so . . . Micah, I intend to check on the weather every day, and if it improves then I shall leave Deephome, fullwinter or no fullwinter, and should you decide to leave with me, I would be glad of your company. But should you decide not to, then I shall respect that decision . . . son.'

Thirty-Three

Every afternoon for the next two weeks, Eli dressed in his winter gear and set off outside. Every afternoon – sometimes after a few hours; more often after only a few minutes – he would return, his face sombre and thoughtful.

'Still no respite,' he would say, and the weight on Micah's chest would lift and he'd breathe easier.

Then came the day that Micah had dreaded.

'I believe it's easing off,' Eli told him. 'At last. And the skies are clearing to the west. Maker willing, we should be able to set off tomorrow morning.' He paused. 'At least, *I* shall . . .'

Micah nodded. 'I'll need to sleep on it,' he said.

Micah awoke the next morning to find a neat bundle of folded clothes at the foot of his mattress. He looked at them for a moment.

They were his clothes. His old clothes. He picked up the undershirt, which was spotless and smelled fresh. Eli must have washed it for him, he realized, and discovered that the other clothes were just as clean.

He pulled off the undershirt Cara had given him and slipped his old one on. It fitted him better, and he'd forgotten its crisp coolness. He pulled on his shirt, his breeches, and the feel of the broad leather braces at his shoulder was familiar and kind of reassuring. He picked up the heavy wyrmeskin pelt he'd worn as a cloak. Eli had been busy. The pelt had been cut and tailored into a hacketon jacket, double-stitched at the seams and lined with grey homespun.

Micah slipped it on with a mixture of elation and pride. It was a fine piece of work, and he felt honoured to wear it.

He climbed down the ladder to the foot of the sleeping gallery to find Eli waiting. The cragclimber was grim-faced, yet his blue eyes glistened as he looked at Micah.

'I reckon we could make it to Jura's cave by sundown if we set off now,' he said simply, shouldering his backpack and handing Micah a pack of his own. 'Cara packed this for you herself,' Eli said. 'Last night I went and asked for any provisions that might be spared for the journey and she insisted on it – even though I told her you'd yet to make up your mind whether you were leaving or not . . .'

'I must thank her,' said Micah. 'I . . . I need to say goodbye to her. To explain . . .'

'Of course you do,' Eli said. He patted Micah's shoulder. 'I'll meet you by the stockade steps.'

Micah found Cara in one of the alcoves at the back of the kitchen cavern. He'd known where to look. The previous afternoon, they'd been working there together on a flitch of cured wyrmemeat, removing the outer skin, scraping off the layer of stringy fat and cutting the smokestain meat below into thin slices that they placed on trays to dry. Half the wyrme had been completed, and now Cara had started work on the second half on her own.

'Brother Micah,' she said, looking up from the cutting block, a short-handled scraper in her hand. Her gaze took in the clothes he was wearing, lingering over the fine hacketon jacket of wyrmeleather. 'So, you are leaving us,' she said softly.

'Cara, I . . .' Micah saw tears welling in her blue-green eyes. 'I . . . I don't want to,' he said. 'But I just can't let Eli go alone. I'm a seasoned weald traveller, and young, and strong, and he can't manage without me . . .' He fell silent, wondering whether she knew he was lying.

Cara nodded uncertainly. Then she sniffed and turned her attention to the half-stripped wyrme carcass.

'Let me help you with that,' said Micah.

'There's no need,' said Cara, without looking up.

'I want to,' said Micah.

He sat down at the table opposite her. He pulled out his hackdagger, wiped the blade on a bunched up cloth that lay on the table, and started the painstaking work of slicing the meat she'd prepared to a fine lacy thinness. He could feel Cara's gaze on him, and when he looked up, she smiled sadly back at him.

'You look nice,' she said, and averted her gaze, and Micah recognized that her shyness had returned.

He made a show of the cutting, brandishing his knife with confidence and dexterity. He clamped his jaw in concentration. And when he took the first of the filled trays across to the drying racks, he rolled his shoulders as he walked, his head held high, pretending not to care as much as he realized he did.

And he knew that Cara had noticed.

Drawn by the sweet greasy smell of the meat, several wyrmes had turned up in the small recessed chamber. There was a stout grey buffwyrme. A handful of gaudy jackwyrmes with their elaborate neck ruffs, barbels and crests, that sniffed the air and chittered with frustration. And two tatterwings, like the ones Micah had seen on the floor of the sleeping gallery – or maybe even the same ones, for the wyrmes that lived in Deephome pretty much came and went as they pleased. They kept the place clean, scavenging any scraps they could find.

'Them jackwyrmes are always so hungry,' said Cara, laying her knife aside and tossing them a handful of scraps, and watching as they squabbled over the spoils.

Micah nodded. 'That buffwyrme seems mighty interested in their breakfast,' he said. 'Reckon I'll give him some of his own.'

'You got to be careful of buffwyrmes, Micah,' she warned. 'With them bladesharp teeth of theirs.'

Micah sliced off a piece of the fatty skin and climbed to his feet. Stooping down, hand outstretched, he approached the buffwyrme, which drew back and eyed him with suspicion. He stopped. He jiggled the skin about.

The buffwyrme took a few steps toward him, then lunged at the meat, but Micah pulled it back at the last moment. Puzzled, the wyrme cocked its head to one side. It was grey and the size of a small sheep, and when it stood still it looked more like a boulder than a living creature. Micah held out his hand again. A long black tongue flicked out from the creature's scaly muzzle. Then, with uncharacteristic delicacy, it took the proffered food in its fangs and withdrew.

Micah returned to the table. He smiled at Cara. 'It's about not showing fear,' he said, and hoped she wouldn't notice his hands were trembling. 'You learn such things out on the trail.' He paused. 'It's tough going out there in the weald, but I have learned to deal with its harshness and brutality. A single buffwyrme don't hold no fear for me.'

Cara's eyes widened with admiration. 'You got a way with them,' she said.

Micah nodded thoughtfully. He picked up his hackdagger, turned it over in his hand, pretending to find interest in the flex of the blade, the curve of the handle. He swallowed.

'I knew someone who truly did have a way with wyrmes,' he said at last. He did not look up. 'With whitewyrmes . . .'

Cara breathed in sharply. 'Whitewyrmes?' she said. 'You . . . you mean a kin?'

'Her name was Thrace,' said Micah. 'She—'

'You knew a kingirl, Micah?' Cara's voice trembled with incredulity.

'I did,' said Micah. 'I stumbled across a nest that she and her whitewyrme were protecting, and she nearly killed me . . .'

Cara nodded slowly, then tossed more scraps to the jackwyrmes and tatterwings. When she looked back, Micah was staring back down at his knife.

'I . . . I know a little bit about kin,' she offered. 'Not much . . . just how girls and boys, orphans and such, get enslaved by whitewyrmes and turn as wild and dangerous as the wyrmes they ride.'

'They ain't enslaved, Cara,' Micah broke in. He looked at his blurred reflection in the back of the blade. 'They . . . they form a union, and the bond between them can't never be broken.' He swallowed again. 'Thrace's wyrme was called Aseel . . .'

'Aseel?' Cara sounded surprised. 'They got names?'

'They got names, Cara. Just like you and me. They're intelligent, whitewyrmes – and we men and women, we threaten them. That's why they kin, so that the whitewyrmes might get a better understanding of the way humankind thinks.' He frowned. 'Aseel would do anything to protect Thrace, and she would do anything to protect him.' He looked up. 'She carried a kinlance that he fashioned for her. It was with it that she nearly killed me. I still have the scar.'

Cara stared back at him, and Micah was unsure whether she believed him or not. Then she climbed to her feet.

They held each other's gaze as Cara walked round the table. She stopped at Micah's side, and he climbed to his feet and stood before her. She reached out, unbuttoned the hacketon jacket and pulled aside the undershirt beneath, exposing the nubbed ring of scar tissue at Micah's chest. There was pity and awe and exhilaration in her eyes. She leaned forward and kissed the scar.

'I could never hurt you,' she said softly, and kissed it again. 'Not ever.'

Micah trembled as all the heartache of Thrace's leaving him came flooding back. He wrapped his arms around the girl and drew her close. He closed his eyes and pressed his lips to hers. He could feel her heartbeat fluttering against his chest. The darkness seemed to spin.

Suddenly Cara pulled away. She turned. Micah followed her gaze, and there was Eli, standing at the entrance to the small chamber, staring at the two of them, his face impassive.

'I'm guessing, Micah, that you won't be joining me after all,' he said.

Thirty-Four

'We could bid us farewell here,' said Eli. 'Ain't no reason on this earth for the two of us both to get chilled.' He shifted the winter caller's heavy backpack on his shoulders and glanced out through the arched entrance of the store chamber at the stockade steps. 'What I'm saying is, Micah, you don't have to accompany me all the way to the top sentinel point.'

'I do,' said Micah simply.

Eli turned to him and, despite the easy smile he gave, his pale blue eyes were troubled. 'I don't doubt we'll meet up again some time, lad,' he said. 'Any time you want, for I shouldn't be too difficult to locate.' His voice sounded hollow and unnaturally cheerful. 'Just stop by at any gutting post or scrimshaw den or rock hut in the valley country and ask for Eli Halfwinter, and there'll be someone able to put you on my track . . .'

He paused, as if he could no longer believe his own words and recognized that Micah did not either. The weald was large and wild and it swallowed up those who ventured into its vast wilderness. It was easy to lose yourself in the high country, and Micah knew that it was this that the cragclimber craved.

'So you come find me,' Eli said, 'if and when you leave Deephome.'

'I ain't fixing to spend the rest of my life here,' Micah told him. 'Just till fullwinter's finally done.' He stepped through the chamber entrance and looked up. He frowned. 'Mind you, that blue sky sure is looking promising . . .'

Now it was Micah's words that sounded hollow. He knew the cragclimber was taking a terrible gamble travelling in fullwinter; they both knew it.

Eli squinted up into the sun. 'It ain't too late to change your mind.'

But Micah recalled the wind and the snow and the cold that had been so biting it had nigh on chewed him to bits, and he was glad he would not be going through that again.

'Come on, then, if you're coming,' said Eli, clapping him on the back. 'But only as far as that top sentinel point, you hear?'

Micah nodded, and the pair of them headed up the wooden steps to the top of the stockade. Eli clambered onto the rope ladder and, without once looking back at the safety and comfort he was leaving behind, climbed down to the ground on the other side. Micah followed him, the wyrmeskin hacketon that Eli had so carefully fashioned for him creaking as he manoeuvred himself onto the wooden rungs of the rope ladder. The air was cold in his nostrils and plumes billowed when he breathed out, but the sun felt comforting warm upon his back, and he dared to believe that Eli might actually stand a chance on this reckless journey.

They traipsed up the steep track that scored the side of the valley in silence, passing by the various sentinel points that Cara had shown them, until they came to the flat slab of rock. The frozen waterfall was behind them. In front of them was the head of the valley, the jagged tops of the pines black against the piercing blue sky beyond.

'Guess this marks the parting of the ways,' said Eli gruffly. 'There ain't no point you going further.' He smiled. 'Wouldn't want you getting lost on your return.'

Micah smiled. He knew the cragclimber was trying to make light of the moment, to make it easy on him, yet the good-natured banter jarred inside him and he bit his lower lip, horrified at the thought that he might cry.

'I think we said all we need to say,' Eli told him. His pale blue eyes looked moist. 'You take care of yourself, you hear me?' he said, and cleared his throat.

'I shall, Eli,' said Micah.

Eli turned away and set off up the valley side on his own. Micah watched him go, and his gaze fell upon the heavy pack on his back that swayed gently from side to side as the cragclimber got into that familiar easy loping gait of his.

'You take care too, Eli,' he called after him, and Eli raised a hand in acknowledgement. He did not look back.

Micah stood staring. Despite his new hacketon, he felt chilled. The sun had slipped across the sky and was now behind the narrow cleft of the valley. The wind was getting up some. Eli shrank against the snow as he climbed higher. Micah hugged his arms around himself once, twice, to get the blood moving, then set off back down the trail of footprints.

At the first sentinel point he came to, he stopped and, with one hand on his hips and the other raised to shield his eyes, he surveyed the whiteness until he spotted movement. At the next sentinel point, by the jutting pine, he did the same; and at the sentinel point below that, by the twisted crag. And each time he spotted him, Eli looked a little smaller. By the time Micah reached the lowest sentinel point, at the snow-capped rock, he needed a spyglass, and he remembered that his had got left behind at the winter den.

He squinted into the greying shadowsnow, and

suddenly it became vital to him that he had one last sight of the cragclimber. Maybe Eli was behind some ridge or other, or maybe he had put a spurt on and had already reached the top of the valley. Whatever, Micah could not distinguish him from the rocks and shrubs, and he gave up trying and turned away, feeling distraught and empty inside.

As the stockade came into view up ahead, Micah couldn't stop himself from having one last look. He found a large boulder, brushed the snow from its top and climbed up onto it. He turned and surveyed the steep valley above, and cursed his lack of a spyglass all over again, for Eli was nowhere to be seen.

'Snowload clouds closing in from the north,' he observed, and realized he was muttering to himself the way he would have muttered to Eli had the two of them still been travelling together.

But they were not.

Tears stung Micah's eyes and he wiped them away on the sleeve of his hacketon. The leather smelled muskrich and new-oiled. He stared at the bank of clouds hunkered down at the head of the valley, crabby and glowering.

'Maker protect you,' he whispered, and swallowed. 'And bring you safely to Jura's cave.'

He climbed down from the boulder and continued

deeper into the valley. The sky above his head was a pale yellow-grey colour by the time Micah reached the stockade, and a fine sandy snow was already falling.

As Micah entered the kitchen alcove, Cara looked up and smiled. She'd plaited the sides of her long auburn hair, taming the errant curls, and in the golden lamplight glow, her skin looked like honey.

'You took your time,' she said, a teasing smile plucking at the corners of her mouth. 'I thought you must have changed your mind again.'

Micah smiled back, shook his head. 'And leave you?' he said lightly, though in truth he felt like burying his head in his hands and weeping like a whipped ploughboy.

Cara's smile grew wider and her eyes all but disappeared as the soft skin around them crinkled into lines of happiness. She picked up the cloth and wiped the wyrmegrease from her fingers, then patted the seat beside her.

'Now you set yourself down here,' she said. 'I want to hear about brother Eli's departure.'

Micah sat on the stool next to Cara, who skitched up closer next to him, till their shoulders were touching. Her closeness felt comforting, and he felt a lump in his throat. She looked up into his face.

'Well?' she said.

Micah shrugged. His jaw was set and his face expressionless. 'We went up to that sentinel point on the flat rock, and we parted. That was about the sum of it.'

Cara nodded, and her eyes were wide with concern. 'It must have been hard,' she said, 'parting and all, after the two of you had travelled together for so long.'

Micah shrugged again. He did not mention the tears he'd struggled so hard to hold back when they had finally bid each other farewell, nor the ones that had fallen freely as he stood on the boulder, staring back up the valley. Sitting there beside her in his fine new hacketon and well-worn gear, he must look to her like a seasoned weald traveller, and he was suddenly desperate not to disabuse her of the notion.

'Eli Halfwinter's been a good friend to me,' he said as casually as he could, then smiled. 'I guess we'll meet up again come the thaw, when I leave. Eli only needs to ask around to get a hold of me. Happen I'm well-enough known out there in the valley country to the east for someone to put him on my track,' he added boastfully. His chest felt constricted and his mouth dry.

'When you leave,' Cara said softly, and Micah saw hurt in her eyes.

Micah nodded. 'It was what I always intended, Cara,'

he said. 'To leave Deephome come the thaw. I only wish Eli could have seen his way to staying also.'

'You regret him leaving,' said Cara, staring deep into his eyes. 'And yet you stayed behind . . .'

'I regret him leaving,' said Micah thoughtfully, truthfully. 'But Cara, you gotta understand, Eli's mind was made up and there weren't nothing I could have done to stop him going. As for me staying here in Deephome, out of the bite of that fullwinter wind, warm and safe and with you . . .'

He leaned forward till their foreheads were touching, then he tipped his head and kissed the top of her freckled nose.

'That part, I don't regret.'

Cara blushed and gripped his shoulders and kissed him back.

'Brother Eli is not with you?' Kilian noted as his rounds of the eating chamber brought him to where Micah and Cara were sitting.

They had spent the day completing tasks in the kitchen cavern; curing meat, checking stores and filling water jars. And through it all, Cara hadn't left Micah's side for a moment, as if afraid that, if left alone, he might change his mind and follow Eli out into the gathering fullwinter storm already howling outside.

'He's gone,' Micah told the prophet. 'He set off late this morning.'

'*Late* morning?' Kilian observed, and his mouth pulled down at the corners in surprise. 'A cragclimber of Eli Halfwinter's experience, I'd have expected him to leave at sunup.'

'He was waiting for me,' Micah admitted. He looked at Cara. 'But I decided to stay here in Deephome.'

'And we are happy to have you, brother Micah. Aren't we, daughter?' said Kilian, his tufted eyebrows drawn together as he calmly observed Micah, then his daughter. 'It's blowing a gale out there according to the latewatch,' he observed. 'Maker willing, brother Eli did not leave it *too* late.'

The prophet moved on, and Micah felt Cara's hand beneath the table fumbling for, then grasping his own. She squeezed it tight.

'I'm sure Eli will be fine,' she whispered.

'Your father was right, though,' said Micah bitterly. 'To stand a fighting chance of getting to where he was going, Eli should have left at sunup.' His face grew serious. 'But Cara, he was held up.' He paused. '*I* held him up.'

Cara looked at him, and as she saw the pain and guilt

in his face, her grip on his hand tightened. 'Trust in the Maker, Micah,' she said. 'Eli is tough, resourceful. I'm sure he'll pull through.'

Micah looked up and she held his gaze. 'Thank you,' he said softly, and he hoped that she was right.

The eating chamber slowly emptied out. Micah and Cara were the last to leave.

'There's somewhere I want to show you,' she told him when she finally got up from the table and took him by the hand. Then, looking round to make sure no one was there to see what she was doing, Cara hurried him across the eating chamber, out through the archway and down a side tunnel on the other side.

'Where are you taking me?' Micah asked, surprised by her feverish grip and the urgency in her tugging, yet happy for her to lead him. 'Cara, where are we going?'

'Sssshh,' she said, turning and putting a finger to her lips, and his interest grew.

The tunnel narrowed, then split in two and, almost running now, Cara dragged him down the left-hand fork. It started rising steeply and curved round to the right, and all at once they emerged into a small low-ceilinged cave. The pair of them stopped.

'I ain't seen this place before,' said Micah, short of breath.

'It's a special place,' said Cara. She smiled. 'Where we, the youngest of Deephome, come to get away from everyone else.'

Micah looked round him. The cave was dim lit. There were wyrmepelts lying on the glowing floor, while above his head, Micah saw that someone must have lodged pieces of the glowing straw and barkchip into the cracks and crevices of the rock, for the whole lot twinkled like a constellation of stars.

'It used to be an old laundry cave,' Cara was saying. 'But I asked my father if it could be a place for us young ones, and he agreed.' She smiled. 'It's important to have a place of one's own.'

'It's pretty,' said Micah, still looking up at the ceiling.

Cara trailed her fingertips down his cheek. 'And no one will disturb us.' She paused. 'I've told the others to stay away tonight.'

Micah turned and looked at her. Her lips were parted and he could smell that roseblush breath of hers, warm and sweet in his face. In the pink-blue light, her eyes had turned to violet, and they stared at him intently as her hand dropped to his chest. She eased the hacketon jacket from his shoulders and let it fall to the floor. She un-buttoned his shirt.

'Cara,' Micah whispered urgently. 'Are you sure?'

As if in answer, she reached up and pulled the white bonnet from her head and dropped it on top of Micah's clothes. She unfastened her plaits and tossed her head and the ends of her hair flicked against his face, his chest. He untoggled the cloak at her neck, and she flung her arms around him. They dropped together to the wyrme-pelts on the floor.

Cara's bare skin felt soft and warm as she pressed herself against him.

'I'm sure,' she said.

'I love you, Micah.'

Cara rolled over onto her side. Micah did the same, and they were curled up and facing one another, their lips almost touching, sharing the same breath. Micah wrapped an arm around her shoulder.

'But you hardly know me,' he said.

'I've loved you, Micah, from the first moment I saw you walking down that snowy trail towards me. I knew. Don't ask me how. I just did, is all . . .'

'Really?' he said, grinning lopsidedly. 'You like to expand on that, Cara?'

'I don't know,' said Cara, her eyes flicking down, then up, then down again. 'That handsome face of yours.' She smiled. 'The way you held yourself. And them rugged kith clothes that spoke of danger and experience and . . . and such things that I could not even begin to imagine.' She reached across and traced the line of his jaw with a fingertip. 'Things that we're protected from down here in Deephome.'

Micah scritched up closer. 'Tell me more about Deephome,' he whispered, 'for in truth, Cara, I ain't never encountered nothing like this place.'

'You haven't?' said Cara.

Micah shook his head. 'I don't believe you know just how unusual Deephome is, do you?' he said. 'I'm telling you, Cara, it's harsh and brutal out there in the weald. I have witnessed stuff that would turn your hair white. Yet, here's this place – this Deephome of yours – with its well-stocked stores and busy kitchens and hot springs open to all who come here . . . By rights, such a place should not exist at all. Kith should have come and taken it for theirselves . . .'

'But I told you, Micah,' said Cara evenly, 'when such kith have come, my father has asked them to leave. And they have.'

'Your father,' Micah murmured softly.

Cara pulled back a little, rested her head on her crooked elbow and observed his face closely. She cleared her throat.

'It was my father who founded Deephome,' she said. 'I'm sure you realize that.'

Micah nodded.

'He's a stone prophet,' said Cara. 'He left the plains because he was sickened by the wickedness and cruelty he found there. He came to the high country in search of a fresh start in a place that was unsullied and uncorrupted.' She nodded, as if to herself. 'Like all stone prophets, he looks to the stones themselves – their purity and majesty – to inform him in his calling. You see, Micah, all in Deephome are equal, and we look after one another like we look after ourselves.'

Micah frowned. He knew only too well that the weald attracted all sorts; adventurers, grifters, hermits, the wicked and the good . . . Stone prophets were just one among them.

Cara was silent for a moment, and Micah took the opportunity to study her profile. The high forehead and freckled cheek. The soft lips, with their hint of an incipient smile. She was beautiful, this Deephome girl, Micah realized with a jolt – and she loved him.

'Sixteen years ago, when my father was but twenty-one years of age, he went searching,' she said at last. 'Searching for the truth. He left the plains and set off into the wilderness of the weald with nothing but the clothes he wore, trusting in the Maker to provide him with the sustenance and shelter he required . . .'

Micah listened, aware that her words were following a well-trodden path, and he guessed that it was Kilian's own story he was hearing – a story that he had told his daughter so many times it had sunk in deep.

'And the Maker did provide,' she announced, her eyes sparkling with fervour. 'For one entire year, my father roamed the barren landscape, scraping an existence from the meagre pickings of the weald. When he was parched, the Maker led him to water. When his belly growled, the Maker provided him with food. And, having furnished him with shelter through drought and rains and dust-storms, when fullwinter began to bite, the Maker brought him here.' She paused. 'By which time he was not alone.'

Micah pulled himself up onto his own elbow, mirroring Cara's posture.

'He had gathered nine followers along the way,' Cara went on. 'Four men and five women. Lost souls out wandering in the weald for their own reasons.' She paused. 'One of them was my mother. Not that I ever knew her,' she added softly, and Micah saw her gaze slide off into the distance as the past stirred. 'I only have memories of my father,' she said. 'No recollection of her. But my father told me that she was bright and brave and determined, and that he would have done anything for her. But . . .'

Tears filled her eyes. One welled over and trickled down her cheek and Micah reached out and caught it on the tip of his finger. Cara looked at him and smiled bravely.

'She died?' said Micah.

Cara sniffed. 'Like I said before,' she said, 'sometimes the Maker's ways are hard to fathom.'

She eased her arm out from under her head and clasped it to the other, before her, like she was lying on her side praying. Micah took both her hands in his own and squeezed them reassuringly. Cara sniffed again, and resumed her telling.

'So there was my father and me, a baby, and the eight that had joined him,' she said. 'But soon more came, wayfarers and trailsetters who had stumbled across Deephome, and others who had heard rumours of our settlement and come a-searching – the helpless and the dispossessed souls who were lost, but who found their true calling in Deephome. My father offered them shelter and food and, most important of all, protection. And all he asked in return was that, just as he was obedient to the will of the Maker, they should pledge their obedience to him.'

Micah nodded. 'I guess he was lucky to stumble across such a place,' he said.

Cara frowned. 'Micah, have you not been listening to me?' she said, and he heard a sharpness in her tone. 'I told you, luck played no part in this. The Maker guided him, and my father followed. Besides,' she added, 'when he first discovered Deephome, there wasn't nothing here but what's now the store chamber. The rest has been excavated, piece by piece, tunnels joining up the underground caverns. Some big, and some small,' she added, and she sat up and swept her arm round. 'Like this one.'

Micah grinned. 'This one's my favourite,' he told her.

'And mine,' said Cara, twisting round and wrapping her arms about Micah's body. She held him tightly, her chin resting on his shoulder. Then she pulled back and pressed her face close to his. 'I don't want to talk no more, Micah,' she said. 'Kiss me.'

And Micah was happy to obey.

The sound of the horn echoed through Deephome with its deep mournful wail. Cara sat up.

'The sentinel,' she said. 'Someone's been found.'

Micah rolled over onto his back, put his hands

behind his head. He watched Cara as she climbed to her feet, staring intently as she clothed her slim body in the thick skirt and high-buttoned shirt, and imprisoned her long lustrous hair inside the white bonnet.

'You just going to lie there?' she asked.

Micah sat up. His head was fuzzy, still full of the intimacies they'd shared in this shimmering cave, and the warm, comforting presence of Cara's body close to his. He hadn't felt this safe and protected ever. Not back on the plains, not in the high country. Not with Eli.

Not with Thrace . . .

He pushed the wyrmepelt covers back and got himself dressed. He was pulling on his second boot when the horn sounded again, louder now.

'Come *on*. Everyone will be gathering at the stockade, and my father will notice if we're not there,' said Cara urgently, as she headed out of the small cave and back down the narrow tunnel.

Micah grabbed his hacketon and chased after her.

When they arrived at the store chamber, Micah found it thronging with the brothers and sisters of Deephome. In among them was Kilian, his face flushed with anticipation, and Micah found himself wondering whether his and Eli's arrival had provoked such keen excitement.

'Quieten down, all of you,' Kilian was saying. 'You shall discover in good time whoever it is the Maker has brought to us. Now, let us create the right impression by quietly getting on with whatever chores are to hand.'

There was a soft muttering of approval as Deephomers did as they were told. Cara approached her father, and Micah held back, suddenly shy and guilty-feeling, and fearing the prophet might notice that something had changed between himself and his daughter. Kilian turned and appraised Cara then, as if satisfying some unspoken question of his own, he smiled. Micah felt himself flush hot and red, and stared down at his boots.

'Be prepared to lead everyone to the great chamber should I give the signal,' said Kilian.

Cara nodded solemnly.

Her father turned and, adjusting his hat and pulling his grey cloak around him, he stepped outside, where the wind was wailing and the snow falling so thick that the stockade just beyond was fuzzed up and barely visible.

'We need help here,' came a faint call, and Micah recognized the voice of Abel, the dawnwatch sentinel.

He hurried up the snow-covered steps after Kilian and looked down over the sharpened wooden poles of the stockade. Abel was standing at the foot of the rope ladder, one arm supporting a limp, gaunt-looking man at his side.

He was white from head to toe, snow covering every inch. His boots, his wyrmeskin breeches and jacket; his gloveless hands and bare head. And when he looked up, Micah saw that there was even snow on his face, obscuring the sunken grey cheeks and redrim eyes, stuck to the skin that had not warmth enough to melt the flakes as they had settled.

Micah's heart leaped as, from behind the snowy veil, pale blue eyes fixed their gaze on his.

It was Eli. And he was still alive!

Micah wanted to shout for joy, to praise the Maker for sparing his friend's life. But he did not. Instead, he helped Abel and Kilian lift the shivering, half-frozen cragclimber up the ladder and over the stockade. In the store chamber, they half carried and half dragged Eli over to a brazier, and Cara appeared with a bowl of steaming broth in her hands.

'Drink this, brother Eli,' she said, and Micah saw Kilian nod approvingly.

'Cara will look after you now,' he said, but his eyes were fixed on Micah as he spoke, and Micah found it hard to take his gaze.

Kilian turned and strode off across the store chamber as, all around, Deephomers absorbed themselves in various tasks, while clearly listening closely. With a twinge, Micah began to understand Cara's need for the old laundry chamber.

He knelt down beside Eli, who was accepting spoonfuls of the hot broth from Cara and trying to stop his teeth from chattering. Micah smiled and clasped one of the cragclimber's hands.

'It's good to see you,' he said softly.

'I must look quite a sight,' said Eli. He shook his head. 'Don't know what I was thinking, lad. Like some greenhorn, wet behind the ears, I underestimated the savagery of fullwinter. And when it attacked me, I was as defenceless as a newborn grey before a redwing.'

Micah nodded sympathetically. 'How far did you get?' he said.

'Far enough to make the return all but impossible,' Eli said wearily. 'If that sentinel hadn't spotted me . . .'

'Brother Abel has good eyes,' Cara murmured.

Eli nodded, then looked up into Micah's face. 'Much as it pains me to confess it, lad, you were right and I was wrong. We can't move on, not till fullwinter's over.'

'So you're happy to stay in Deephome?'

Eli shivered. 'Happy don't play no role in it,' he said,

'but I accept it's the only option open.' He frowned. 'I guess I shall have to get used to it. And I shall endeavour to make myself useful while I'm here,' he added, smiling at Cara and accepting another spoonful of the soup. Then he paused. 'And how about you, Micah. Are *you* happy?'

Micah looked round at Cara, who smiled back at him. And Micah thrilled inside.

This kithgirl clearly loved him – loved him with all her heart and with an intensity that he recognized. It was how he'd felt about Thrace, yet the kingirl had been incapable of returning his feelings. It was good to be the one who was loved for a change. He would endeavour to earn that love.

He looked back at Cara, then at Eli, and nodded.

'More than happy,' he said.

THIRTY-FIVE

Alsasse and the great blueblackwyrme stood on the broad slab of rock facing one another.

The leader of the whitewyrmes had pulled himself up to his full height, his neck extended and chin raised – yet he was dwarfed by the blueblackwyrme, who fixed him with a sapphire stare. The moon had risen, and it shone down bright and cold and picked out the three ridged tusks at the snout and lower jaw of the immense wyrme as he dipped his muscular neck and thrust his face towards Alsasse.

The whitewyrme recoiled a fraction, both at the meat-rot stench of the larger wyrme's breath, and the power of his voice.

'*You are not welcome here*,' he repeated in the strange guttural tones which Alsasse had to concentrate on to understand.

'*Forgive us*,' Alsasse breathed, inclining his head and lowering his eyes respectfully. '*We do not mean to trespass on your lands, only . . .*'

'*Only what?*' the blueblackwyrme snarled, acrid smoke curling up from his flaring nostrils. In contrast to

Alsasse's hissing whisper of a voice, this wyrme's guttural roar sounded like thick swirling lava as it bubbled up from the depths of his throat.

'*Only we have nowhere else to go, and we need to rest and forage,*' Alsasse answered softly.

The blueblackwyrme's eyes narrowed, and he nodded over Alsasse's head at the colony of whitewyrmes, the spiked barbels at the sides of his mouth quivering. '*How many are you?*'

'*There were nearly twelve hundred when we set off. Now there are barely a thousand,*' Alsasse said sadly. '*And those who have survived are weak from hunger.*'

The blueblackwyrme stared at Alsasse, as though sizing him up. '*Follow me,*' he barked at last, and edged back toward the lip of the crevice he'd emerged from.

Alsasse tried to obey, but his legs gave way and he stumbled and almost fell. The flight had weakened him even more than he'd realized.

Alucius stepped forward. '*I shall go with you,*' he told the blueblackwyrme, and Alsasse noted how the second of the host had cleverly added a harsh and guttural tone to his voice that echoed that of the blueblack's.

The blueblackwyrme dipped his head and, spreading his immense wings, stepped backwards into the crevice and disappeared from view. With a reassuring glance at

Alsasse, Alucius spread his own wings. Then he sprang out from the lip of the crevice and swooped down into the glowing void after the wyrme.

Below the crevice, the walls of rock widened, opening up to reveal a cavern that was vast and bathed in lavagloam. The air was hot and the fumes from the river of molten rock far below were acrid and sulphurous and stung Alucius's eyes. As the blueblackwyrme wheeled around on the thermals, Alucius followed, craning his sinuous neck upwards to observe the strange bluish-grey clusters of nests that dimpled the roof of the cavern high above.

They were large and domed and appeared to be made of baked mud. As the two wyrmes glided up towards them, Alucius could see that the nests were decorated with clawcut patterns; squares and circles and spirals, sun-rays and cross-hatching, and intricate interwoven designs that looked like plaited grass. Each mud nest had twenty or more openings, with hundreds of blueblack-wyrmes flying in and out of them.

This colony, Alucius realized, like the blueblack-wyrmes themselves, dwarfed his own, and must number into the thousands.

Flying close to his escort, Alucius swooped and swerved past countless wyrmes who were feeding on the clouds of iridescent sulphur flies that swarmed in the hot air. They stared at him with their bright sapphire eyes, but seemed content to let the strange whitewyrme in their midst pass unmolested.

With a tilt of his wings, the blueblackwyrme soared up towards the cavern ceiling, where he selected an entrance to one of the great mud domes and disappeared inside. Summoning what remained of his strength and courage, Alucius followed him.

Warm humid air enveloped him and, from the gloom inside the dome, Alucius was aware that there were many pairs of eyes upon him. Looking up, he could see that the interior was terraced, and on the curved ledges, wyrmes of all ages were jostling for position and talking loudly in their harsh jarring voices that were so difficult to listen to. At the centre of the sloping floor, on a bed of yellow lichen and red mossbloom, sat a blueblackwyrme of immense age, judging by his great curved claws, elongated chinspike and the overlapping scales that ridged his back.

A hush fell as Alucius's escort stepped forward. He bowed his head in supplication.

'*Beveesh-gar, the thin-necked snowwyrmes we sighted have arrived at the steam pools. I brought this one for you to see for yourself.*'

The ancient wyrme turned his great head and Alucius

saw that he had lost an eye. The other stared at him unblinkingly.

'*What my scouts have reported is true*,' the ancient wyrme conceded. '*You are indeed odd-looking, and your wyrme calls are strange to our ears.*' Beveesh-gar's eye narrowed. '*But tell me, snowwyrme, what is to stop us breaking those fine wings of yours, and snapping those slender necks.*'

Alucius bowed his head. '*We offer you and your colony no threat*,' he said, forcing a growl into his soft whistling call. '*We ask only to be allowed to rest and recover from our journey. We have travelled far from our lands to escape the taint of the two-hides.*'

'*Two-hides?*' said Beveesh-gar.

Alucius raised his head. '*Man, they call themselves*,' he said, '*but our name for them is two-hides, since they cover their own hide with a second hide.*'

'*Why?*'

'*For protection*,' Alucius said. '*Manhide burns in the sun and offers no warmth against wind or snow. And it tears easily . . .*'

'*They sound weak, these two-hides*,' Beveesh-gar observed, and from the ledges above came growls of agreement. '*So why do you fear them so much that you and your snowwyrmes fled from your roosts in the middle of fullwinter?*'

'*They are many and we are few,*' said Alucius, his yellow eyes trained on Beveesh-gar. '*And what the two-hides lack in individual strength, they make up for in cunning. They have ways to kill wyrmes that we do not understand: holes that open up beneath our feet, invisible entanglements that ensnare us, and thorns that whistle on the wind and tear our flesh . . . And all so that they can rip our hides from our backs and take them as their own. It makes no sense to us, this killing . . .*'

Alucius paused. Beveesh-gar stared at him, saying nothing, waiting for this snowwyrme to continue. And when he did, Alucius's voice was soft and mournful.

'*Some of our number tried to understand the two-hides,*' he said. '*They took their young and gave them their sloughed skin. But those wyrmes have now got the two-hide taint themselves, and are drawn into killing in their own strange ways. And that the colony cannot accept. So, rather than be tainted ourselves—*'

'*You took flight,*' Beveesh-gar sneered. '*And came here.*'

He raised his sapphire eye to the ledges above him. They were crowded now with blueblackwyrmes who chittered and rasped as they made room for the wyrmes still arriving.

'*Hear this, thin-neck snowwyrme. We, the clans of the fire rifts, shall tolerate your presence, but only if you stay out of our way,*' the blueblackwyrme announced, his voice amplified by the curved walls of the mud dome. He leaned closer to Alucius, his head cocked to one side as he fixed the whitewyrme with a penetrating stare. '*But these two-hides,*' he growled. '*They interest me . . .*'

THIRTY-SIX

'She and her farmers need to be taught a lesson,' the eel-mother said, her shrill voice shot with sour recrimination.

The flickering light of the smoking tallow candles played on the wet walls of the kelds' gathering chamber. The air was cold and dank, and the two fat crevicewyrmes coiled round the eel-mother's fleshy shoulders slithered closer for warmth.

'But with the winter caller still gone,' she said, 'we will have to wait till the thaw to make our move.'

Beside her, slumped in a chair of human thighbones and skin, Blue Slake the poisoner gave a slurfing laugh. He raised a claw-like hand and wiped round the hole in his face where his nose had once been.

'Like I always said, you can't trust those who turn to farming,' he muttered.

'It seemed like a good idea at the time,' Cutter Daniel observed levelly. The liquor bottles tied to his coat jangled as he withdrew his left hand and extended his right, so that the dull-eyed slave kneeling before him might complete his nails, filing them to needlepoints.

'But I agree with you. Get too close to the kith and you forget that you are keld.' He reached out and ran a razor-sharp nail across the slave's cheek, drawing blood, then licked his finger. 'But that's no excuse. She agreed to pay us a share if we allowed them to set up on their own—'

'And now those payments have ceased,' Blue Slake interrupted, and shook his head.

'And you know why, don't you?' hissed the eel-mother. 'It's because they've got greedy. They're trading every drop they make with kith on the trail, and leaving none for us.'

'It is an insult,' spat Blue Slake, 'to the keld mistress!'

At the head of the table, the black-cowled figure of the keld mistress raised a velvet-gloved hand. 'The farmers will be punished,' she said quietly.

The three keld turned to her, their eyes glittering with eagerness.

'Punished?' said Cutter Daniel, licking his lips.

The eel-mother's chins wobbled as she caressed the limbless crevicewyrmes round her neck, and beside her Blue Slake the poisoner gave another slurfing laugh.

The keld mistress nodded, and the voice that came from the faceless blackness beneath the hood was soft and honeyed. 'It's high time we paid Deephome a visit,' she purred.

THIRTY-SEVEN

The small greyish-green wyrme scritch-scratched across the stone floor on needlepoint claws. It paused by the tall earthenware jar with the peeling parchment label. Dripping water had left the words *Pickled Linefruit* smudged and barely legible, and corroded the jar's wax seal.

Micah's eyes narrowed. He was seated in the store chamber on an upturned crate, repairing his boots. He had been busy tacking and gluing the sole of his left boot back into place when the tiny creature had poked its pointed snout round the corner of a shelfstack.

As Micah watched, the wyrme sat up and sniffed the air. With its emerald crest raised, it jumped up onto the lowest shelf and scuttled along the row of earthenware jars until it came to the one with the damaged seal. Then, oblivious to the fact that it was being observed, the wyrme reached up and thrust a bony arm through the wax lid. It snatched a glistening yellow fruit, clutched it to its chest and scampered away.

Micah smiled. It wasn't just the grey-cloaked Deephomers who ate well through fullwinter, he thought.

The previous night, he and Cara had eaten glazed sweetmeat pie, thick with gravy, which they'd mopped up with hunks of freshly-baked buckwheat bread. The mood had been happy and relaxed, Cara laughing and looking into Micah's eyes with that twinkling look of hers, almost as if daring him to take her in his arms and kiss her in full view of the other Deephomers. But Micah had held back, as he always did, and suppertime had been charged with delicious anticipation.

As the weeks had passed and their feelings for one another grown stronger, Micah and Cara had taken to leaving the eating chamber separately, then meeting up later in secret. Every night, Cara would steal into Micah's sleeping niche and curl up next to him, smelling of crushed myrtle and roseblush . . . Afterwards, Micah would drift into a deep sleep, and wake up refreshed and contented, only to find that he was alone, for Cara always left him before the earliest risers stirred.

Unlike every other aspect of life in Deephome, where each action was observed and each conversation over-heard, the relationship between the two of them had been kept hidden. And Cara intended to keep it that way: at least until Micah put aside his weald clothes – the boots, the breeches, and the hacketon that Eli had made him - and donned the red hat and grey cloak of a

Deephomer. Her father would never accept him otherwise.

But last night's supper had not been like all the others . . .

Micah tested the boot. The glue had set and the thick sole seemed bonded to the leather uppers. It would need proper stitching with wyrmegut if it was to hold fast on the trail, but it would do for now. He pulled the boot on and, climbing to his feet, turned to go.

'There you are, Micah, lad,' said Eli. The cragclimber was standing by the shelfstack eyeing him levelly. 'Good to see you're keeping your kit in good repair. Come the thaw, you'll have need of it.'

Micah nodded. He didn't have the heart to tell Eli he was now no longer sure he wanted to leave Deephome when the thaw came. He wanted to stay here. Where it was safe. With Cara.

He frowned. 'Have you seen Cara, Eli? I haven't seen her since supper last night when . . .' He paused.

'When what, lad?'

Micah saw that Eli was wearing his thick leather jacket, belted and buckled and buttoned to the throat, and knew that the cragclimber was on his way to the stockade steps to stand and look out into the fullwinter blizzard that had been raging for days now. He would often stand at the stockade, and Micah knew that the cragclimber could not wait to leave the confines of Deephome.

'Oh, it was nothing,' he said. 'It's just that brother Kilian didn't look happy with Cara last night.'

The events of the previous night were playing on Micah's mind. He and Cara had been about to leave the eating chamber as usual, with Micah going one way and Cara going the other, when her father had surprised them. He had loomed over them, his tufted eyebrows knitted together with concern.

'You look flushed, daughter,' he'd told her, and pressed the palm of his hand to her forehead.

'I'm fine, Father,' Cara had said. She'd attempted to pull away, but Kilian had held her head still with his other hand, and maintained the pressure on her brow.

'Don't argue with me,' he'd said, and there was a hard edge to his voice. 'Your temperature is higher than it should be. And your eyes are glittering. You have a fever.' He'd glanced round at Micah, his gaze penetrating, and Micah had felt as if Kilian held him to blame. 'You'd best come with me, Cara.'

'Oh, but Father . . .'

'Cara,' he'd said, his voice cold and clipped, and he had leaned forward and whispered something in her ear that Micah could not hear, and Cara had nodded and climbed obediently to her feet. Then the two of them turned and went, leaving Micah feeling suddenly isolated and unhappy.

What had Kilian whispered? Had he discovered that Cara had been spending her nights with him? And if so, what should Micah do?

He'd wanted to ask Eli for advice. But the cragclimber hadn't been there at table. His friend kept to himself more and more as he waited for fullwinter to pass and, as Micah and Cara had grown closer, Eli had become more distant. And Micah missed him: his company, his terse conversation, his advice . . .

That night, Cara had not come to his sleeping niche, and Micah had slept fitfully. She was not at breakfast either.

'I did see her,' Eli said, turning up his collar and heading off towards the stockade steps. 'Earlier. She was with a couple of others. They were on their way to them thermal baths of theirs.'

'Th . . . thanks,' Micah called after him as Eli stepped outside.

He set off in the opposite direction, walking quickly, but with his head down and avoiding eye contact with the Deephomers he passed. He hurried quickly through the meeting chamber and down the dimly lit tunnel that led to the cave containing the hot spring. Entering the steamy cavern, he heard a low murmur of voices that seemed to be coming from the shadowy recesses on the far side of the empty pool. He ducked down beneath one of the stone benches, his heart thumping.

Through the drifting steam, he could just make out two figures, one seated, the other standing with his back to him. The seated figure spoke.

'Is that enough yet?' It was Cara's voice.

'Just a little more, daughter.' Kilian's voice was low and reassuring. 'It's for your own good. The weakness will pass, and when it does, you'll feel calmer, you know you will.'

Micah wanted to jump up from his hiding place and confront the prophet, demand to know what was going on. But something about the hushed tone of their voices suggested to him that this was something private, something intimate between father and daughter, and that he should not intrude.

'There,' said Kilian at last. 'Now I shall bind it and the wound will soon heal. You have been a dutiful daughter, Cara, and have obeyed without complaint.' He cleared his throat. 'I hope you will not disappoint me in other matters,' he said, and he paused, as if to let the words sink in. 'Now, you rest there a moment while I see to this.'

Kilian turned and walked across the cavern. He was holding a bowl in his hands, taking care not to spill its contents. But as he passed the bench, some of it trickled over the side and dripped to the floor. Micah stifled a gasp.

The bowl was full to the brim with blood. Cara's blood.

As the prophet's footsteps receded down the tunnel, Micah rolled out from beneath the stone bench and leaped to his feet. He ran over to Cara, who sat slumped on a narrow alcove ledge, leaning back against the smooth stone wall behind her, her eyes shut. She was barefoot and wearing a cotton underslip with thin straps over her slender shoulders. It had droplets of blood on it. A bandage was wrapped tightly round the top of her right arm, and several bloodstained linen towels lay at her feet.

'Cara, are you all right?' Micah asked, kneeling before her.

Cara opened her eyes and looked at him blankly for a few moments, then smiled weakly. 'I'm fine,' she said, but her voice was frail and hoarse.

Micah glanced at her pale arms. What he had taken

for accidental nicks and scratches in the lampglow of the sleeping niche, he now saw were fine white scars, the result of deliberate and calibrated cuts. He reached out and gently touched them.

'Cara,' he said softly. 'What are these?'

Cara pulled her arm away, and hugged it to herself with the other. 'It's nothing,' she said, and when Micah frowned, his eyes fixed on hers, she looked down. 'It's for my own good,' she whispered.

'Your own good?' Micah said, his voice louder than he'd intended. His cheeks flushed and his scalp prickled hotly at the thought of the sharp blade slicing into her soft delicate skin. 'How is cutting you meant to be for your own good?' he demanded.

Cara sighed, and a faint smile played at the corners of her eyes, as though the answer was so obvious he was foolish even to ask. Yet she couldn't meet his gaze.

'Cara?' he said more gently, and he took her hands in his.

Finally she looked up, and Micah felt something tugging inside him as he stared into her blue-green eyes. He squeezed her fingers reassuringly.

'Every Deephomer submits to a letting,' she said. 'And they submit willingly, in supplication and with good grace.'

'But why?' said Micah.

'Like I told you, Micah, letting is done for our own good. Father says it restores calm and bestows tranquillity on the restless spirit . . .'

'By taking blood,' said Micah, nonplussed.

'By taking *bad* blood,' said Cara. She smiled again, and pulled one of her hands from his and placed the back of it against his forehead. 'Happen it might benefit a restless spirit like you.'

'Me?' Just the thought of it made Micah shudder. He eased away from her and straightened up. 'I don't know, Cara,' he murmured.

'You've been happy here in Deephome, haven't you, Micah?' Cara asked.

'Well, yes,' Micah admitted.

'You've felt warm and safe and protected here?' Cara's voice was measured and low.

'Yes,' said Micah.

'And what has passed between us, that has made you happy?' Her hand reached out, and her fingers played idly with the cuff of his hacketon jacket.

Micah nodded.

'Then you have to decide.' Cara's gaze met his, and Micah saw those turquoise eyes of hers sparking with emotion. 'Whether you become a Deephomer,' she said.

'Whether you stay here as one of us. Whether you allow yourself to be protected by my father and . . .'

'And?' said Micah.

Cara rose to her feet and put her arms round his neck. 'Loved by me,' she whispered.

THIRTY-EIGHT

Where was Eli?

Micah peered out through the entrance to Deephome, and let out a low groan. The stockade steps were deserted, and snow was falling thick and heavy out of a dark and brooding sky.

Micah pulled up the collar of his hacketon and stepped outside. Snowflakes hissed softly all round him. He climbed the wooden steps of the stockade gingerly and, gripping the tops of the sharpened staves of wood, looked up into the stippled air of the valley gorge. The snow landed on his head, his shoulders, the backs of his hands. Fullwinter's grip seemed tighter than ever, and even the sentinels were only venturing as far as the lowest lookout point at the jutting rock. Micah groaned again.

He'd already checked everywhere he could think of. The great chamber, the meeting chamber, the eating chamber, the kitchens. He'd tried the sleeping galleries, but not only had Eli not been there, but his sleeping niche looked as though it hadn't been occupied for some while. He'd returned to the hot pool, wondering whether the cragclimber had gone there to bathe. But he had not, and the half dozen Deephomers who were there, their heads sticking out of the hot steamy water, had no knowledge of his whereabouts. He'd even ventured into the narrow tunnel that led to the equipment store deep down inside the rock. But the tunnel had proved empty and there was something about the door, thick-cobwebbed by cave spiders, that gave him the creeps.

Now, Micah felt scratchy and bothered. He didn't know what he thought of the letting, or of brother Kilian, or how to take what Cara had told him. He wasn't sure of anything any more. That was why he wanted to talk it over with Eli, for the cragclimber was sure to have an opinion. He would wrinkle his weatherbeaten brow, run his fingers through his hair and fix him with those watery blue eyes of his, and mull over everything, his voice calm and measured.

Yes, Eli would know what to do. He always did.

Micah pulled the stout hacketon more tightly about him and was about to head back into the warmth of the store chamber when there was a commotion of screeches and squawks, and half a dozen pitchwyrmes – in their pearlwhite coats of winter – flapped noisily up into the air. The next moment a hunched snowy figure lurched into view.

'Eli,' Micah breathed, but as the man came closer,

and Micah picked out the grey cloak and the red hat and the thick black beard, he saw that it was not the crag-climber at all, but rather Abel, the sentinel, back from his watch.

Abel tipped back the brim of his hat, sending snow falling to the ground, raised a hand to shield his eyes, then waved. Micah waved back, and when Abel reached the stockade and climbed the rope ladder, he helped him onto the stockade steps.

'Thank you kindly . . . brother Micah, isn't it?' he said, snow falling from his beard as he spoke.

'It's Micah,' he said. 'Though strictly speaking, I ain't no brother. Not yet.'

Abel cocked his head to one side, dislodging more of the snow that had settled on his hat, and looked Micah up and down. 'So I see,' he said. 'You and brother Eli still fixing to leave us come the thaw?'

'Maybe,' said Micah. 'I . . .' He frowned. 'Have you seen Eli?'

'Oh, yes,' Abel nodded. 'He's up by beak rock. Told me he found Deephome a mite too crowded for his liking, and wanted to be alone. I left him staring up at the top of the valley – though on a day like this, there's precious little to see.' He clapped a gloved hand on Micah's shoulder. 'Come, brother,' he said. 'No sense waiting out here in the cold. He'll come back in when he's good and ready. You hungry?'

Micah nodded. He had not eaten since he'd left Cara in the bathing chamber the previous night, and now his belly was grumbling.

Abel patted Micah's back. 'Then let's go get us something to eat.'

They helped each other down the slippery steps. A tall man with salt-and-pepper stubble was standing at the bottom. Abel removed the horn from his shoulder and handed it across to him.

'There y'are, Joel,' he said. 'And you take care now. That snow's treacherous. I wouldn't go no further than the beak rock if I was you.'

Joel thanked him for the warning and climbed the stairs. Abel headed over to the row of hooks along the inner wall of the stockade, and replaced his wet cloak for a dry one. Micah watched him. He imagined himself returning from an early watch, taking off a cold sodden cloak and slipping on a dry comforting one instead, before stepping back into the warmth and security of Deephome.

'I just don't understand it,' Abel was saying, adjusting the ties at the collar of the cloak. 'Why anybody would choose to go back out there into the weald when we've got all this right here.'

They paused in the entrance to the store chamber and stamped the snow from their boots. Ahead of them, other Deephomers were also on their way to the eating chamber, and Abel and Micah joined them, with Abel amiably returning the nods and smiles he was given.

'I been here twelve years now, and there ain't a day gone past when I haven't thanked the Maker for delivering me to the Deephome.' He gave Micah a playful nudge. 'But then I was just a simple farmhand from the plains, not a tough young cragclimber like yourself.'

Micah shrugged nonchalantly, unbuttoning his hacketon jacket as he did so. 'Thing is, Abel, there's a whole weald out there to explore and I'm not sure I'm ready to settle down in one tiny corner of it just yet,' he said, enjoying the measured drawl of his voice, and the the way it sounded like Eli's.

Abel breathed in and Micah heard the sucked air whistling over his teeth. He shook his head slowly from side to side.

'I had me three years at a gutting tarn, knee-deep in wyrme guts, before striking out on my own. I got me this in a scrimshaw den,' he said, pulling up his sleeve to reveal an angry-looking scar that extended down his inner arm from elbow to wrist. 'And I lost these in a liquor hole.' His lips drew back in a clenched snarl that revealed three missing teeth. He snorted. 'Guess I seen all the weald I want to see.'

They entered the eating chamber, that was filling up for the midday meal, and sat down at one of the long tables. Servers appeared beside them and set down dishes. Micah appraised the plate of crisped wyrmeribs and steaming rootbeets that had been placed before him.

'When I stumbled into the deep gorge here, I was all but dead on my feet,' Abel was saying. 'Fullsummer it was. My water bottle had been empty three days and I was racked with a harsh thirst.' He shook his head earnestly. 'But the prophet took me in. Watered me, and fed me. Offered me shelter and protection. I felt like I'd finally found me a home.'

'And the letting?' Micah said quietly. 'Doesn't that bother you?'

Abel paused and picked up one of the wyrmeribs and turned it over thoughtfully in his calloused fingers. His brow creased with thought.

'The letting's just something brother Kilian does,' he said and shrugged dismissively. 'It don't mean much. You feel a bit weak at first, but with fine food like this . . .' He smacked his lips noisily. 'You soon build your strength back up.'

He put the wyrmerib to his mouth and took a bite,

then another, and wiped his mouth on the back of his hand as he chewed hungrily. Micah picked up a wyrmerib of his own. Across the chamber, he noticed that Cara had just entered, supported on either side by sister Abigail and old brother Absolom. She looked fatigued, though there was some colour to her cheeks now.

She glanced up, and Micah's face burned as their eyes met. Then she smiled at him.

And Micah smiled back.

Beside him, Abel's eyes had narrowed, and he was observing Micah with wry amusement. He prodded Micah's shoulder with the end of the stripped wyrmerib.

'Seems like good food's only one of the reasons to stay at Deephome,' he observed.

Thirty-Nine

Micah sat back and leaned against the shelfstack. The great jars with their neat labels and precious contents felt cool against the back of his neck. He ran a hand through his hair. It had grown some since Cara had cut it and was beginning to curl up at the ends and tangle.

Cara. He had hardly seen her since her bloodletting. Once in the eating chamber the day after, since then hardly at all. Despite the sweet promise of her smile, she had not come to Micah's sleeping niche later that night. Nor the next. Nor the one after that. Now a week had passed and, apart from the occasional task they'd shared here in the store chamber, they'd barely spent any time together, and none of it alone.

Sister Abigail seemed to shadow Cara wherever she went, and Cara showed no signs of minding. She appeared sad and disappointed in him, as if Micah had let her down in some way. And when he caught her eyeing his hacketon critically, he knew that she was vexed that he had not agreed to stay on in Deephome.

Trouble was, he could not. He *would* not – not until he and Eli had sat down and talked things over. And for his part, the cragclimber was being frustratingly elusive. There was a distant haunted look to his pale eyes, and Micah knew that the constant presence of eaves- dropping Deephomers riled him. In the chambers, in the adjacent sleeping niches, on the stockade steps; there was nowhere for him to escape. And when Micah did speak to him, Eli always put him off.

'We'll talk later,' he would say, fidgeting with his back- pack. Or, 'Not now, Micah,' as he turned in for the night. 'In the morning.'

And Micah had begun to suspect that the real reason for Eli's reticence was that the cragclimber knew he was going to tell him that he was staying in Deephome for good, and did not want to hear it. And perhaps, Micah thought, that was what he would have told him. After all, it was warm. It was safe. There was food aplenty.

And there was Cara . . .

A small grey-green wyrme poked its head round the corner of an end shelf, its emerald crest raised and quivering.

'It's you again,' Micah said, and smiled. At least there was one thing in Deephome that wanted to be alone with him.

Since Micah had spotted it stealing linefruit from a jar, he had taken to leaving scraps out for the timid little wyrme, and it had responded. It had grown used to him and now sought him out most days in this quiet part of the store chamber.

Micah reached into his hacketon and drew out a hunk of barleybread. The little wyrme approached where he sat, its blackbead eyes bright and darting. Then, quick as a flash, it snatched the bread from his outstretched fingers and scurried off towards its nest, tucked away in some crevice nearby.

'You're welcome,' Micah called after it.

He sat back once more and paused. He could hear voices. Children's voices. They were coming from the other side of the shelfstack.

Micah turned and peered through the chink between a massive jar marked *Cornhoney* and an equally large one marked *Pickled Redbeet*.

There were a dozen or more youngsters – girls in homespun skirts and white blouses and boys in grey cloaks, their red hats lying on the floor behind them. They were seated in a semi-circle on the stone floor, their backs to Micah. Before them, perched on a low stool, was Kilian the prophet. He was telling them a story. His voice was soft yet animated, and his words were punctuated by the movements of his hands.

'A whole hundred of them, there were,' Kilian was

saying, his eyes wide, and the young children gasped at the thought of such an unimaginable number. 'A hundred wyrmes that he kept, raising them up from little'uns. But then, do you know what happened?'

The children shook their heads.

'One of them went missing.'

'Uh-oh,' muttered a small boy.

'So there were only . . . How many of them were left.'

'Ninety-nine,' the children chorused.

'Ninety-nine,' said Kilian. 'Ninety-nine wyrmes. Yet that wyrmeherder, you know what? He could not stop thinking about the hundredth wyrme. The one who had left the herd and got lost. So he went searching for it. He pounded the weald, trekking high and low, far and wide, night and day, till at last he found it, looking lost and alone on a high ledge.'

The children clapped happily.

'He picked up that wyrme and carried it all the way back to his cave and reunited it with the other wyrmes, and he rejoiced that they were all together once more.' Kilian's eyes narrowed and he looked at the children, one after the other. 'Now who do you think that wyrmeherder was?' he asked.

The boys and girls looked at one another, puzzled. Then one of the girls spoke up, her voice uncertain.

'You?' she said.

Kilian laughed. 'That's a good answer, Esther, but no. Not me. Someone far more important than me.'

Again, the children looked at one another. More important than brother Kilian? Who in the weald could be more important than brother Kilian? Then one of the boys looked up excitedly.

'The *Maker*!' he blurted out.

'That's right, Tobias,' said Kilian, nodding sagely, and Tobias glanced round at the others, his eyes gleaming with pride. 'That wyrmeherder was the Maker himself. And despite all the wyrmes He still had, it was the one that He found and brought home when it had gone astray that filled Him with such joy. We are like those wyrmes, and we are all precious to the Maker . . . You, and you, and you, and you, and you, and you . . .' he said, pointing to each of the children in turn, as they giggled back at him. Then he sat back and clapped his hands together. 'Now run along and attend to your chores,' he announced. 'Off you go.' He winked. 'And make sure none of you go astray.'

Laughing and chattering, the children scrambled to their feet and left the store chamber. Their eager voices echoed back along the tunnel. Kilian got to his feet and walked round to Micah's side of the shelfstack.

'So it's you, brother Micah,' he said, looking down at Micah. 'Thought I glimpsed an eye peering through the shelves. Eavesdropping like a true Deephomer . . .'

'I didn't mean to.' Micah reddened, suddenly aware of how nervous he felt in front of Cara's father.

But Kilian smiled and patted him on the shoulder. 'I know that you have been troubled,' he said kindly. 'It's not easy surviving in the weald. Even here in Deephome, there are sacrifices to be made for the good of all. Privacy, certainly. And some freedoms – to do as we please, to go where we want . . . But these are small things indeed compared to the protection that Deephome offers.' He gripped Micah's hand with both of his own and squeezed it warmly. 'To be safe from all the dangers and hardships of the weald, Micah. And to be loved.'

Micah looked into Kilian the prophet's deep brown eyes. There was no accusation in them, no displeasure. Only acceptance. And Micah felt foolish. Of course he should stay here; safe and happy with the other Deephomers, with Cara.

A broad smile spread across his face. 'Happen I'm like that wyrme,' he said.

And Kilian nodded, his intense gaze never wavering. 'Happen you are,' he said, 'brother Micah.'

* * *

That night, Micah slept better than he had for weeks. When he awoke, it was to the sound of the sentinel's horn being blown, loud and fitful. It echoed down the tunnels of the Deephome, filling the caverns with its urgency.

Someone new had stumbled across the valley, Micah thought. Someone new was coming to Deephome.

He reached out for his clothes and paused. There were two piles. One pile was untidy, thrown off in a heap the night before; the worn shirt and breeches, and the fine hacketon that Eli had made. The other pile was neatly folded and untouched; the grey cloak, the homespun breeches and shirt, with the red straw hat perched upon the top. Micah reached out, his hand shaking as it hovered over first one set of clothes, then the next. From outside, the horn sounded again.

Micah seized the homespun breeches and pulled them on, then the crisp shirt, the heavy grey cloak, the straw hat of deep red . . . They felt comfortable, warm, fresh – they made him feel like he belonged. Micah looked down. His hackdagger and catapult lay next to the hacketon jacket. He hesitated, then reached out and picked them up. He put the catapult in the back pocket of his breeches and tucked the knife into his belt. He pulled the grey cloak over them.

He wasn't ready to give up his weapons just yet.

Micah crawled to the edge of the sleeping niche and climbed down the ladder to the floor far below. From outside the sleeping galleries, he heard the sound of movement, lots of movement. Running footsteps. Raised voices. Urgent cries. The Deephomers were gathering in the store chamber.

From behind him, he heard a familiar voice. 'Fixing to stay, I see.'

It was Eli.

Micah turned. The cragclimber was climbing down from his own sleeping niche, his jaw set firmly. He was staring at the clothes Micah was wearing. There was disappointment in his eyes.

'It's . . . I mean . . . they were the first things that came to hand . . .' Micah stopped.

The cragclimber had stepped from the ladder and was eyeing him levelly.

'And Cara?' he said. 'I reckon she must have played some part in your decision to stay.'

Micah nodded. 'I wanted to talk to you, Eli. Discuss things. Things that had been troubling me. About Deephome. About Cara, and her father . . .' He fell still. All that time he'd wanted to tell Eli what he had seen, yet now the cragclimber was in front of him and actually listening, he suddenly felt reticent and shy.

'What things, Micah?'

'I saw her – Cara . . .' He took a deep breath, then suddenly he found himself babbling. 'Kilian had cut her arm. He was collecting her blood in a bowl . . . Letting, Cara called it. But, but it was all right. I mean, she wasn't being punished or nothing. All the Deephomers submit to such letting. In supplication and good grace,' he added, echoing Cara's words, 'so that their restless spirits might be calmed. That's what Cara told me. But then she asked me to decide – to decide whether I wanted to stay or not. And I wanted to talk to you, Eli . . .'

'Calmed, eh?' said Eli, his voice low and expressionless. 'And the blood? What did Kilian do with it?'

'I . . . I . . .' Micah swallowed. He realized he did not know. Hadn't thought to ask.

Eli stared at him, his pale blue eyes boring into his.

'But Eli!' Micah exclaimed. 'Why does it matter anyhow? Besides, it's all right now. Cara's fine. And . . . and I heard Kilian talking to the children . . . He's a good man, Eli. All he wants to do is to look after them folks that have had enough of the trials and tribulations of the weald . . .' He looked down, embarrassed by his outburst. 'He's . . . he's like a farmer, Eli. Leastways, like a wyrmeherder looking after his herd . . .'

'And taking their blood.' Eli's voice was harsh and scathing. There was anger in it. 'Come on, Micah, lad,' he said, brushing past him and striding off towards the store chamber. 'Let's see who the prophet is welcoming into his fold.'

FORTY

Micah and Eli arrived in the store chamber to find Kilian the prophet standing in the middle of the stone floor, his arms folded, and eyes scanning those around him. Cara was standing beside her father. She was dressed in a crisp white bonnet and a freshly-pressed grey cloak, buttoned at the neck.

'Deephomers,' Kilian was saying in a calm but authoritative voice. 'Busy yourselves around the chamber. Do not stare at whoever the sentinel is bringing. No loud cries or clatter . . .' His tufted eyebrows rose. 'For we don't want to startle or overwhelm them. And Cara, make sure the route to the great chamber is kept clear, should we need to use it. Watch for my signal.'

Cara nodded and turned toward the entrance to the tunnel, only to find Micah watching her.

'Cara,' he said simply.

She smiled. 'Micah,' she said, and as her gaze fell upon the clothes he was wearing, her smile broadened. She reached out and took him by the hand. 'So you have decided to become one of us,' she said quietly, but her

eyes were bright and there was an excited tremor in her voice. 'Oh, Maker be praised!'

Beside him, Micah sensed Eli stiffen. He didn't want to look into the cragclimber's face.

'I thought a change of clothes would be good,' he said, and felt Cara's grip on his hand tighten.

She leaned forward and her head brushed the brim of his hat as she whispered in his ear. 'They suit you, Micah. I'll tell you how much . . . tonight.'

Micah blushed and glanced at Eli, but the crag-climber's attention was focused on Kilian. The prophet had crossed the chamber to the entrance and was looking out at the stockade steps.

It had stopped snowing, but the snow that had already fallen lay deep and even on the ground beneath the stockade. He adjusted his hat and was about to step out into the fullwinter cold, when all at once something round and ragged came hurtling through the air, high over the jagged spikes of the stockade wall.

With a muffled thump, it landed at the top of the stockade steps and tumbled down the stairs, leaving a bloody trail in the white snow. At the bottom, it rolled to one side and came to rest at the prophet's feet.

It was a head. A human head, with a thick black beard and panic-filled eyes. A hank of hair had been ripped from the scalp. Blood dripped from the tattered skin at the severed neck.

Micah gasped and wrapped his arm protectively around Cara. Neither of them could look away.

'Brother Abel,' Cara murmured, her voice trembling. Then she turned and buried her face in Micah's chest, and Micah hugged her tightly, feeling her shoulders rise and fall as she sobbed.

All round them the Deephomers were shrinking back. Mothers shielded their children's eyes as best they could, but some had already seen and had started whimpering. One woman was wailing. Someone vomited.

'Cara!' Kilian turned, ashen-faced, and Micah felt Cara pull away from him. The prophet pointed, and his daughter nodded. When Kilian next spoke, his voice was soft but charged with urgency. 'To the great chamber,' he announced. 'Everyone to the great chamber. Gather yourselves inside, seal the doors, then sing, brothers and sisters. Raise your voices to the glory of the Maker, for He shall protect us.'

The air hummed as the Deephomers obeyed, turning and hurrying off to the great chamber, their voices already rising in song. And from every corner of Deephome came low murmuring chants as others did the same – abandoning pots on the kitchen stoves, leaping from the hot springs and grabbing linen towels, hurrying from the meeting chamber and the sleeping galleries.

'That's right, brother Leo,' Cara was saying encouragingly, ushering a grizzled old-timer with a walking stick across the floor of the store chamber. 'Hurry now, sister Bethany . . .'

As the Deephomers left the store chamber, Cara hung back at the entrance to the tunnel. She gave Micah a beseeching look.

'Micah, come. And you, brother Eli. Let my father deal with this . . .'

Trembling with shock, Micah turned to Eli. It was like he was trapped inside a nightmare, powerless to wake. Eli's blue eyes met his.

'Run if you want to, lad,' he said, his hand reaching for the knife at his belt. 'But I'd just as soon take my chances here.'

Cara gave Micah a despairing look, then turned and hurried after the rest of the Deephomers. The store chamber filled with the sound of singing. It was coming from the great chamber. Then there came the scraping of wood on rock as heavy wooden doors were pulled shut, and the voices were muffled.

Micah turned away to see Kilian striding towards him.

'If you'd obeyed me and gone with the others, I could have protected you,' he said regretfully as he strode past. 'Now, Maker have mercy on your souls.'

The prophet disappeared down the tunnel, leaving Micah and Eli alone in the store chamber.

Just then, from the top of the stockade steps, there came a dull thud. Eli spun round to see a small round metal object, smoke hissing from one side as it rolled down the wooden stairs, gathering snow.

'Get down!' he bellowed. He threw himself to the stone floor and covered his head with his arms.

Micah fell down beside him and curled up into a tight ball. This couldn't be happening, he told himself desperately. Not here. Not in Deephome . . .

The explosion was colossal. It ripped through the air, earsplit loud and destructive. It drove a hole through the stockade and reduced the wooden steps to splinters. Snow flew up in clods, hissing and steaming as flames erupted and melted it mid air.

Dense clouds of grey smoke billowed up from the broken stockade and shattered steps. Then, in the midst of the smoke, something seemed to coalesce. Something dark. Something massive.

His ears ringing, his mouth full of dust, and the grey cloak covered in chips of wood and pottery shards, Micah looked up. The shelfstacks around him had collapsed. Vats of oil had been crushed, spewing their contents. Grain barrels had been smashed. Earthenware pots lay broken, their ochre shards engulfed in liquid as rockpears in syrup mingled with wyrmehearts in brine. Charred pieces of wood and lance-like splinters from the stockade were strewn across the stone floor.

One of them had skewered the little grey-green wyrme that Micah had befriended. It lay a little way off, outstretched, motionless. Its beady eyes stared blindly up at him.

It looked smaller in death, Micah thought.

He turned.

The dark shape loomed out of the haze, becoming more distinct as the smoke thinned and cleared; the dark-rimmed eyes, the heavy lakewyrmeskin cape, the monstrous face quilted in crisscross scars.

No, it couldn't be. But it was.

Micah opened his fear-parched mouth. 'The winter caller.'

FORTY-ONE

Micah stared, trying to make sense of what he was seeing. Broken pieces of pottery dug into his chest, his belly. Beside him, Eli was breathing hard.

The winter caller turned his head and his small dead eyes surveyed the chamber.

Light played across the quiltwork of crisscross scars that etched his face. One of his ears hung by a thin twist of skin and flesh. He smiled, and a strand of drool dripped from the corner of his twisted mouth.

Around his shoulders was the lakewyrmeskin cloak, battered and ripped, and as white as the avalanche that had buried him. Beneath its folds, something silver glinted. The eye-gouge. It dangled from his belt alongside other tools. The bone-shears and liver-clamps. Hooks and spikes. Knives with curved serrated blades. He had picked them up from the snow in his massive clawed hands – the same massive clawed hands that had dug him out of the avalanche.

The winter caller had freed himself from his frozen tomb and returned to the winter den, to gather up his precious belongings; to pick up the scent. And he had followed them here, these kith who had killed Redmyrtle, who had escaped punishment – and who had refused to die. Here, to this place that smelled of rich provisions and sulphurous springs.

His gaze fell upon the kith he'd been hunting. Micah and Eli stared back at him. The winter caller took a step forward . . .

Eli leaped to his feet, seized a stone jar and hurled it at the winter caller, who let out a muffled grunt as it slammed into the side of his head. Micah scrambled up, his feet slipping and sliding on spilt fruit, liquor, oil; tripping over shattered pottery and splintered wood. The winter caller bore down upon Eli. With one arm raised, he swept a row of large green jars from a shelf, then seized one end of the shelfstack and sent the whole lot crashing to the floor.

Micah and Eli jumped back, the toppled stack just missing them, but sending sacks and boxes and jars tumbling about their ears. Eli threw another heavy jar at the winter caller, then retreated, his knife now glinting in his hand. Stumbling over the debris, Micah headed in the opposite direction. Then, dropping to his knees, he gathered a handful of broken shards with one hand and drew his catapult from his back pocket with the other.

The winter caller batted away a third stone jar and, shooting out an arm, seized Eli by the neck and threw him bodily across the store chamber. The cragclimber hit the wall and crumpled to the floor.

His fingers trembling, Micah loaded the catapult with a shard, pulled back the drawstring and fired. The shard spun through the air and embedded itself in the back of the winter caller's neck. He didn't flinch. Instead, he pulled a serrated knife from his belt and advanced on the stricken cragclimber.

Micah fired again. And again. Blood spurted from cuts to the winter caller's head as, with his back to Micah, he knelt down over Eli and ripped open his jacket. He raised the curve-blade butcher's knife with its fine-toothed jags, so good for rib-splitting and evisceration, and took aim.

Then stopped . . .

A shard of pottery whistled past his head. It slammed into the wall and shattered.

The winter caller stared at the medallion hanging from the silver chain around the cragclimber's neck. It was oval and, engraved on its worn silver surface, were three names. Hiram. Anya. Darius.

'Darius. Darius . . .' His mother's voice came to him, soft and loving and calling across a summer meadow.

The feel of his father's hand, so warm and strong, leading him home through the rippling grass . . .

Winter. Bitter winds. Endless tramping through the snow . . .

Screams and cries and pleas for mercy.

'Go, son. Save yourself.' His father's voice urgent, full of fear.

Brutal hands grabbing him and dragging him away, down, down into the darkness . . .

'Come, little one.' A voice close to his ear, honeyed, soothing. Promises full of menace. 'I shall teach you the ways of the keld. You will be my special slave.'

Whiplash. Knifecut. Pain . . .

'Make it stop! Make it stop!'

Obedience . . . Reward . . .

Bloodhoney.

The winter caller reached out and tore the medallion, *his* medallion, from the cragclimber's neck. He hesitated. A rich bloodtaint odour was flooding into the store chamber from the tunnel to his right.

It was sweet and rank and pungent. It was the odour of keld.

FORTY-TWO

Micah shrank back behind a fallen shelfstack as six savage-looking figures burst out of the tunnel and into the store chamber. With a guttural roar, the winter caller pulled away from the prone body of the cragclimber and turned to face them.

The figures spread out and circled the massive bulk of the winter caller warily. They were keld like him, raised in the gloom of deep caverns, trained and goaded in the keld way to fight and kill with chilling brutality.

Four of them wore bone masks, their eyes glinting out of black sockets. The other two were bare-faced, openly displaying their hideous disfigurements; a lipless mouth stitched into a permanent snarl, and a face pocked with black-ringed burns from a whitehot poker.

All six of them wore heavy wyrmeskin boots, wyrme-skin breeks and sleeveless wyrmeskin jerkins. On their arms and legs they wore plated armour of wyrmebone ivory, crudely scored with arcane designs. In their hands they clutched their weapons of choice: a heavy harpoon crossbow, a rock-weighted catchnet, a spiked cudgel, a gutting-sabre and a bone-wrench, and long-handled headclamps with zigzag teeth . . .

The winter caller sprang up from the stone floor, his powerful legs propelling him through the air in a head-long leap. Crashing into the keld with the gutting-sabre, the winter caller knocked him from his feet, embedding his serrated curve-blade knife in the eyesocket of the keld's mask as he did so.

The winter caller jerked his knife free and leaped to his feet, swinging his arm in a wide arc as he rose. The curved blade of the knife sliced through the thick wyrmeskin jerkin of the keld with the long-handled clamps. The keld's pockmarked face registered puzzle-ment for a brief moment, before he fell to his knees and slumped to the floor at the winter caller's feet.

The four remaining keld fell back with snarls and high-pitched stuttering shrieks, widening the circle. In the centre of the chamber, the winter caller dropped on one knee and, wrenching the clamps from the dead keld's hands, sent them spiralling across the floor at knee height.

The keld with the lipless snarl screamed as the razor-sharp teeth of the headclamps sliced through his shins. Dropping his spiked cudgel, he collapsed in a heap, flailing wildly about amid the broken jars and spilt provisions, the stumps of his legs spraying blood in a wide arc across the floor.

The winter caller lunged at the three remaining keld, who darted back beyond reach of his massive arm and flashing knife. Grunting with frustration, the winter caller flung his curve-blade knife at the keld with the bone-wrench.

It was the opportunity the other two had been waiting for. As the knife found its target, thudding into the third keld's neck, the keld with the rock-weighted catchnet flung it into the air and his companion raised his heavy harpoon crossbow and took aim.

Too late, the winter caller reached to his belt to draw a hatchet, only for the coils of the net to snag his throwing arm. At the same moment, the crossbow leaped in the keld's hands, sending the harpoon spinning through the air, trailing a length of rope behind it. It struck the winter caller hard, low in the back, penetrating the lakewyrmeskin cloak and emerging out through his chest on the other side.

The winter caller staggered, staring down at the barbed point of the harpoon and at the blood spreading out across his wyrmeskin jerkin. He rocked on his heels, his dark-ringed eyes glazing over. His nostrils flared.

He could smell the rich dark odour of blood. His own

blood. Fresh and pungent. It was the odour of death.

The keld pulled sharply on the rope and the winter caller gave a low groan and toppled backwards, then crashed to the floor. His massive body convulsed for a few moments more before the life left it, and one huge fist uncurled to reveal the silver medallion it had been clasping.

The medallion clattered to the floor.

The two remaining keld closed in on the lifeless body already framed in a growing pool of blood. Their eyes glittered behind the bone masks as they stooped over the corpse and sniffed.

From the shadows behind the fallen shelfstack, Micah rose and crept over to where Eli lay. He knelt down over the cragclimber, who had a deep gash to the side of his head. Micah held a finger to his neck, checking for a pulse.

Eli opened his eyes.

'Brother Eli, brother Micah.' It was Kilian the prophet's voice.

Micah looked up.

Kilian was standing by the entrance to the store chamber. As Micah watched, he picked his way through the splintered wood, broken pots and dead bodies. He clapped his hands and, from behind him, more keld trooped into the store chamber. The prophet was clearly in command. The two surviving keld were dragging the winter caller's body across the floor and into the tunnel.

In the distance, the muffled voices of the Deephomers could be heard, raised in song.

'I'm sorry you had to witness this,' said Kilian, shaking his head sadly. 'But since you have, you leave me no choice.' He clicked his fingers and keld in bone masks stepped forward and seized Micah and Eli. 'Take them to your mistress,' he said.

—⚜—

FORTY-THREE

The choke collar the keld had fastened round Micah's neck tightened as the leash was tugged viciously. Micah stumbled forwards and almost lost his balance as he gasped for breath. He reached up and clawed at the chain at his throat, only for a heavy cudgel to knock his hands away.

'Keep moving,' a wheezing voice hissed close by his ear.

Micah gagged at the foul odour of the keld's breath. It stank of rust and rotten meat and masked, for a moment, the pervasive stench of unwashed skin. The cudgel slammed into his back as the keld urged him on down the dim-lit tunnel.

Beside Micah, Eli struggled to catch his breath as the choke collar round his neck bit deep into the skin. Blood trickled from the wound at the side of his head.

Behind them the sound of the singing in the great chamber grew fainter as Micah and Eli were driven down deeper into the tunnel. In front and behind them, the keld pressed in closer as the tunnel narrowed. Beneath their feet, the rough stone floor steepened. It was slippery with blood from the bodies of the winter caller and the four dead keld that had been dragged down the tunnel ahead of them. Micah skidded and fell, and the choke collar pulled tight as his keld handler yanked him back to his feet.

They came to a door.

Micah recognized it all too well. It was the door that he'd been told led to the old equipment store; the cobwebbed door that had so unnerved him when he'd ventured down this tunnel before.

It was open.

With snarling curses, the keld dragged and prodded Micah and Eli through the doorway. Behind them, the door slammed shut. The air was hot and humid and fetid with unfamiliar fumes. Micah looked up, and struggled to make sense of the scene before him.

They were in a large cavern, about the same size as the great chamber of Deephome above. But the great chamber, with its glowing carpet of straw and magnificent rock formations, had exuded an atmosphere of calm and tranquillity. This cavern was different. The walls were stained a deep red and glistened with condensation. A dozen or so stooped dead-eyed figures, their sweat-covered torsos gleaming, shambled about like sleepwalkers. The wyrmeskin breeches they wore were little more than soiled rags and most were barefoot, though some wore tattered boots.

Kith boots, Micah recognized. Like his own.

In among them, several hulking bone-masked keld screeched commands and lashed out with whips and cudgels as the shambling figures tended to a large apparatus at the centre of the cavern. A pot-bellied vessel of blackened copper was being heated over a roaring fire set in a pit beneath it. At the top of the vessel was an elbow-shaped pipe that was attached to a long snake-like coil of piping, which was immersed in a vat of ice-cold snowmelt, dripping from a thin crack in the cave ceiling. Emerging from the bottom of the vat, the tapered end of the pipe dripped a deep, dark red liquid into a flagon placed under it.

Micah had seen apparatus like this before. It was a still. Back in the winter den, Eli had used one exactly like this to brew his green liquor from a mash of barleygrain, water and yeast. But this was no green liquor that the keld were distilling, not judging by the mash they were using.

As the keld dragged Micah and Eli across the chamber by their choke collars, Micah saw a gaunt kith slave pick up a brimming bowl and carefully pour its contents into a red-stained barrel. It was blood. Deephomers' blood.

Maybe even Cara's blood.

And that was not all. In a recess gouged out of the cavern wall to his left were three large redwing wyrmes, their savage muzzles bound shut; they were shackled by their necks, their tails and all four of their legs. Two kith slaves were crouched over one of the wyrmes. They had made a small incision and were draining the precious flameoil from the glands at the base of its neck into a small pot. Just like the Deephomers, these wyrmes were being used, Micah realized. Farmed by the keld. As he and Eli were dragged past, Micah saw the kith take the pot of flameoil, add it to the blood in the barrel and mix the two together in readiness for distillation in the copper still.

No, this was not green liquor. It was that stuff that Eli had taken from the winter caller's backpack and that they had both drunk when their strength had given out. Micah could still recollect the taste, the smell, the red stain it had left on their lips – and the way it had made him feel . . .

Bloodhoney, Eli had called it.

At the far side of the cavern, they stopped in front of a wyrmeskin curtain hanging from a rod. One of the keld pulled it aside to reveal an opening in the wall of rock.

'Two kith, mistress,' he announced.

'Bring them to me,' came a voice that was soft and honey-sweet, and as he was shoved into this second chamber, Micah was astonished to hear the sound of the Deephomers' singing once more.

He looked up. At the centre of the lamplit cavern, seated on a bone chair slung with tattooed skin, was a woman. She had long auburn hair, flecked with silvery grey, and penetrating turquoise eyes. Cara's eyes. Micah flinched. It was as though he was looking at an older version of Cara herself. But where Cara's face was open and trusting, the face before him was hard and arrogant, yet still beautiful.

'Kneel!' barked the keld.

Micah dropped to his knees. Beside him, the second keld pressed down hard on Eli's shoulders till the cragclimber's legs buckled. He landed heavily, then crumpled and sprawled forward. Micah instinctively reached across to his friend, only to receive a vicious stroke of the lash across his shoulders. He looked up to see that the woman had a whip in her hand.

'Leave him,' she said sweetly. 'A little bloodhoney will soon revive him, and the two of you will be put to work.'

Just then, the wyrmeskin curtain was pulled aside. The woman turned and smiled.

'Ah, husband,' she said. 'Join us.'

Micah looked round. Kilian the prophet was standing in the doorway.

FORTY-FOUR

Kilian looked down at Micah and Eli, who were kneeling on the floor in front of the woman. The two keld guards stood behind them, gripping the ends of the leashes.

'Oh, Carafine,' he said. 'Not the whip. Please . . .' Kilian reached out a hand to Eli and helped him to his feet. Then did the same for Micah. 'I'm so sorry it had to come to this,' he began, his eyes full of sorrow and compassion, 'but you left me no choice . . .'

'Keld,' said Eli quietly. 'You are in league with the keld.' His voice was bitter and tinged with contempt. 'I should have expected no less from a stone prophet.'

Micah looked down at his feet. He had been so wrong about the prophet, about Deephome, about everything. He couldn't look at Eli. He felt foolish and ashamed.

The woman who looked so like Cara stepped forward and struck the cragclimber a vicious blow across the face with her whip. She raised the whip again, but the prophet stayed her hand.

'Please, Carafine!' he insisted. 'You must let me explain . . .'

Carafine's face softened. 'You're too tenderhearted for your own good, husband,' she said gently, but her turquoise eyes were bright with suppressed anger. She returned to the bone chair and sat down. 'Well?' she said, and crossed her arms.

'These kith,' said Kilian. 'They're not like the others, Carafine. They have done nothing wrong. In fact, I had hoped that they would become Deephomers themselves. But unfortunately they witnessed the way we defend ourselves, of course, we can't let them go now . . .'

'Kith are kith, husband,' she said dismissively. 'Thieving scum, the lot of them.' She glared at Eli and Micah. 'So if *they* didn't attack us, who did?'

'Well, it's the strangest thing, my dear,' the prophet said, his tufted eyebrows knitting together. He crossed to the wyrmeskin curtain and drew it aside. 'It seems our attacker was a keld.'

Two more keld stood just outside, waiting to be called. The massive corpse of the winter caller was propped up between them, his scarred head lolling to one side. Carafine leaped up from her chair and strode across the chamber. She paused in the doorway and stared at the body. Her nostrils flared as she sniffed the air.

She turned to Kilian. 'I know this keld. He is an assassin.' Her blue-green eyes darkened. 'He belongs to my sister.'

Micah saw the whip twitch in her hand and the sinews in her elegant neck tighten as her jaw clenched. And when he glanced at Eli, he saw that the cragclimber had noticed too.

'How dare she!' Carafine stormed. 'We've paid our dues to her and her cronies, haven't we, husband? And now she sends her . . . her *creature* here to attack us! I won't stand for it. Come.' She waved her whip at the two keld. 'Bring that *thing*, and follow me. I shall feed it to the wyrmes myself.'

She stepped out of the chamber and the wyrmeskin curtain fell back into place behind her. Kilian turned to Eli and Micah. In the background, the singing in the great chamber of Deephome continued somewhere above them. Micah looked up and saw a small hole in the ceiling. Kilian followed his gaze and smiled.

'It is how I alert Carafine if we're attacked,' he explained, 'by getting the brothers and sisters to raise their voices in song to the Maker. It can be heard perfectly down here in this chamber.' He smiled. 'It is the meek, the defenceless, the downtrodden calling upon the powerful to come to their aid. And the beauty of it is, they don't even know it.' His voice grew suddenly stern. 'And that is the way it must stay.'

He looked at the two keld guards standing behind Eli and Micah.

'Take off the collars,' he commanded, 'then wait outside.'

The guards did as they were told. As they left the chamber, Kilian crossed to his wife's chair and sat down. In front of him, Micah and Eli crouched down and sat back on their haunches.

'So, prophet,' said Eli, rubbing his neck, 'what are you fixing to do with us?'

'If you knew the position I was in, you would understand what must happen now,' said Kilian with a sigh.

'Well?' said Eli. 'How about you go ahead and tell us, preacherman?'

FORTY-FIVE

Kilian sat back and cleared his throat. 'It all began when, as a young man, I discovered these caverns. I knew at once that they would make a perfect dwelling place, concealed as they were at the bottom of a deep gulley – with an abundance of timber, a good water supply and, of course, the hot springs. I already had a following as a stone prophet, eight good souls and true. They had travelled with me faithfully through the harshness of the weald, and joined me in praising the Maker for the purity of the wilderness He had created. They were my flock and I loved each and every one of them.'

Micah saw a look of tenderness in Kilian's eyes. The prophet smiled and sat forward in the chair.

'Imagine our delight when the Maker provided us with such a fitting haven. We worked hard, turning the cracks and crevices into tunnels that linked the various caverns one to the other, and gathering together the simple provisions we needed to survive. We called it Deephome, and we prospered – prospered, that is, until that terrible day when a gang of kith stumbled across our haven.'

Kilian shook his head, and when he spoke, his voice was hoarse with anger.

'They were weald-hardened and heavily armed,' he said. 'They took everything we had: our tools, our provisions, even the clothes from our backs. Then they cut us down and left us for dead. I alone, out of the nine, survived. I'd been shot with a crossbow bolt and would have had my throat slit like the others, had not brother Timon made a run for it and distracted them. I passed out, and when I came round, my wounds had been dressed and I was being nursed by a beautiful young woman.

'That woman was Carafine. Cara's mother . . .'

'Cara's mother,' Micah breathed.

'She told me she'd left her own people and was exploring the valley country for herself when, spotting the carrionwyrmes circling above Deephome, she found me. She tended my wounds – and we fell in love. But when I was well again, she left me . . .

'Of course, I was broken-hearted, but I threw myself into my work. And, with the help of new followers, poor lost souls who had found their way down into the valley, I restored Deephome. But I was terrified that at any moment another gang of hardened kith might find Deephome and murder us all.'

Eli stared at the stone prophet, his face impassive.

'Then Carafine returned,' Kilian went on. 'But she was not alone. For not only was she holding a child, *our* child, little Cara, she had a gang of her own in tow. They were the most brutal, terrifying group of fighters I had ever seen. She handed my daughter to me with the following proposal. I could look after her, raise her in the peace and tranquillity of Deephome, but only if I allowed her mother to set up a keld colony in the deepest caverns below.

'I resisted at first, of course I did. But then I looked into my baby daughter's eyes, and Carafine explained that these keld of hers would protect her, and me, and all the other weak and defenceless souls who had come seeking refuge in Deephome. And I could resist no longer.'

Kilian shrugged.

'All she asked was that, once in a while, her keld receive a little blood from each of us – as well as the right to enslave any kith who attacked us. It seemed a price worth paying to protect my growing flock.' He smiled. 'And it's worked wonderfully well, I don't mind telling you.'

Micah saw a strange glint in Kilian's eyes that made the prophet look almost deranged.

'Of course, I've played no small part in the success of our operation,' he went on. 'Carafine set up the still, but it was my idea to milk the redwings. It makes all the difference,' he added proudly, 'the flameoil in the distilling process. We produce the most sought-after bloodhoney in all the weald. The kith can't get enough of the stuff. We can hardly keep up with the demand, and as you've seen, our stores are overflowing as a consequence.'

Eli nodded grimly. 'Never seen anything like them,' he admitted.

'Precisely,' said Kilian excitedly. 'I go up to the valley country each season, loaded down with bottles hidden beneath my cloak, and my dear sweet Deephomers don't suspect a thing. And if the kith I trade with ever cut up rough, I just retreat back here and let Carafine deal with them . . . Of course, she still thinks we need to pay her sister a share. But I don't agree. So I've stopped paying it. And so what? If the winter caller's the worst they can throw at us, then we're fine. You saw how we dealt with him.'

Micah and Eli exchanged glances, but said nothing.

'And now her blood's up,' Kilian continued, wild-eyed and breathless, 'Carafine will finally deal with that greedy sister of hers! So, you see, in the end, here in Deephome, we're all winners.' He paused and his face fell. 'Or nearly all of us.'

He shook his head. 'The thing is, I can't let any of my precious flock know that they're living on top of a keld colony. Or giving them their blood. It has to remain my secret. Do you understand? If they were ever to find out, they would be both revolted and terrified and would try to flee from Deephome. Then the keld would enslave them and it would ruin everything I've worked so hard for. And I can't let that happen to my dear sweet Deephomers . . .' He paused and looked at Micah. 'Just as I can never let Cara discover who her mother is.'

Kilian sat back in the chair and folded his arms across his chest. His face took on a look of intense sorrow.

'Which is why, my dear brother Eli and my dear brother Micah,' he said, looking from one to the other, 'though it grieves my heart sorely to have to tell you so, neither of you can ever leave this place.'

FORTY-SIX

'I'm sorry, Eli.'

'You ain't got nothing to be sorry for, Micah, lad.' Eli laid a hand on Micah's shoulder. 'Reckon I'm not entirely blameless myself. I should have trusted my instincts and got the two of us out of Deephome, fullwinter or no fullwinter.'

'I was a fool, Eli,' Micah insisted. 'That bloodletting. I should never have believed what Cara told me.'

'You wouldn't be the first to be distracted by a pretty face, and I guess you won't be the last.' The cragclimber sighed, and in the dim red light of the cavern Micah could see the sweat running down his face. 'But picking over past foolishness won't get us out of here . . .'

'Bloodhoney.' The keld's voice sounded from behind them.

Micah turned. Around the cavern – at the copper still, in the wyrme alcove, beside the firepit – the kith slaves downed their tools and lumbered towards the overseer. He was a tall hunch-shouldered man with a lacerated face and ears clipped to points. He held a pewter tray on which a dozen small beakers, the size of thimbles, had been placed. The kith slaves formed a jostling line, their dead eyes fixed on the tray and drool dripping from their lolling mouths.

'Stop shoving,' the overseer barked as he handed out the beakers of bloodhoney, one at a time. 'That's it. Drink it down . . .' He noticed Micah and Eli standing by the pile of firewood they'd been stacking. 'You two. Get in line.'

Two keld in bone masks turned from the still, where they had been supervising the corking of flagons, and stepped towards Eli and Micah. One of them cracked his whip.

'You heard!' he grunted.

Eli and Micah exchanged looks, then joined the back of the line. Eli leaned forward and whispered in Micah's ear, 'Whatever you do, don't swallow the stuff.'

Micah shuddered. He didn't need to be told.

The kith in front of Micah was handed a beaker. Throwing back his head, he downed the bloodhoney in one gulp and returned the beaker to the tray. He turned and shuffled past Micah, a vacant smile spreading slowly across his face as the intoxicating liquor took hold.

Micah stepped forward and stared at the beaker being proffered.

'Take it,' the overseer snarled through serrated lips.

Reaching out, Micah took the beaker. He put it to his lips.

'Drink!'

Micah tipped the beaker back and his mouth filled with fiery rust-taint sweetness. Avoiding the overseer's eye, he placed the beaker back on the tray and walked away, trying hard not to gag. He stooped down at the log pile and glanced back. The overseer and the other keld were walking across to the copper still, and Eli was coming towards him. Micah spat out the bloodhoney which spattered onto the floor at his feet, then covered the telltale stain with a hunk of firewood.

Eli did the same. He wiped a hand across his mouth and scowled. 'That stuff'll kill you, you take it long enough,' he muttered. 'It destroys the mind, but keeps the body going. That's why the keld prize it. And they're not the only ones neither. There's kith out there in the weald that take doses of it for the strength and endurance it gives them.' He pushed a log into place with the toe of his boot. 'But they're playing a dangerous game, lad. Too high a dose and the heart gives out. I've seen it happen.'

He looked across at where the kith slaves were slumped. Work was over for the day, and the ten of them sat with their backs against the glistening cavern wall, breathing heavily and staring into space.

'But as for those poor wretches,' Eli said, 'it's already too late for them. Their minds have gone and their bodies ain't far behind. Not that the keld care, not when it comes to slaves. They'll replace them when the next band of kith show up to attack Deephome.'

From the opposite side of the cavern came the sound of low voices and hicking laughter. Eli looked across at the eight hulking figures, all now unmasked, as they broke into and ate greedily from stone jars.

'In the meantime,' he went on, turning back to Micah, 'they've got that stone prophet up there taking in waifs and strays and getting away with this blood-letting of his. Slaves or fresh blood, the keld win either way. And what makes this keld colony so dangerous is that nobody but Kilian knows it's here.' He shook his head. 'We've got to get out of this cavern, Micah, while we still have the wits and strength to do so.'

'But . . . how?' said Micah. He could still taste the metallic taint of the bloodhoney in his mouth. 'There's only one door to this place. And it's locked.'

Eli glanced round at the wyrmeskin curtain that led to Carafine's cavern. 'The singing, Micah. Did you notice where it was coming from?'

'That hole in the ceiling?'

'Yes, Micah. A hole.' He nodded. 'Leading up to the great chamber . . .'

'The great chamber,' said Micah excitedly. 'You reckon we might be able to climb up there?'

'Not we, Micah. I'm too big. But *you* might make it.'

'You think so?'

'Can't do no harm trying – unless you have a better idea.'

'But what about you?' said Micah, his mouth suddenly dry. 'I can't just leave you here.'

Eli sat back and surveyed the boy coolly. 'Reckon you're going to have to,' he told him. 'Leastways, for a while . . .'

FORTY-SEVEN

'Elders, if I might bring this meeting to order,' Kilian the prophet announced, rapping on the round blackstone table that had been lowered on ropes from the ceiling of the meeting chamber.

The elders of Deephome turned to him, their faces flushed with a mixture of excitement and relief. How good it was to have their leader back among them, safe from harm and as confident and reassuring as ever.

'I know the events of this morning have been traumatic for us all,' Kilian began, his brow creased with concern, 'but once more, the Maker has protected we Deephomers from harm. I only wish I could say the same for our precious stores.'

The five elders exchanged looks with one another, then turned back to the prophet.

'Did we lose much, brother Kilian?' asked brother Anselm. 'The stone jars we traded with the black valley kith were stored at the very back of the chamber . . .'

'And the meats and smoked goods were wrapped and crated,' said sister Rebekah defensively. 'I made sure of that myself before the first snows.'

'The labels!' exclaimed brother Bede, tugging at his grey beard with ink-stained fingers. 'We don't have to do them all again, do we? My scribes have only just finished seeing to the last consignment – those sacks of grain from the western valleys.'

Brother Absolom and sister Grace nodded fervently.

'I'm afraid, brothers and sisters, you must brace yourselves for bad news,' said Kilian. 'The damage has been severe.'

'How severe?'

'What are our losses?'

'Can anything be saved?'

The shocked voices of the elders echoed round the meeting chamber.

'I'm not going to lie to you,' Kilian told them. 'We've lost almost everything.' He shook his head sorrowfully. 'It was a monstrous redwing . . . the largest I've ever seen. It tore our sentinel brother Abel limb from limb.'

'I . . . I saw his head,' murmured sister Rebekah tearfully. 'Rolling down the stockade steps. It . . . it was horrific.' She pulled a handkerchief from the pocket of her skirt and pressed it to her mouth.

'The half-starved creature must have been driven mad by the harshness of fullwinter and invaded our store chamber in search of nourishment,' Kilian said. 'Maker be praised that you and the flock took refuge inside the great chamber in time. As for myself, I followed you down the tunnel, and when I saw the great doors slam shut, I got down on my knees and prayed to the Maker that Deephome be protected.'

He smiled and glanced round the table, gauging the elders' reaction to his words.

'It seems my prayers were answered,' he continued. 'The redwing did indeed inflict terrible damage on us, that is true – and yet, brothers and sisters, the Maker moves in mysterious ways. Those two kith who were wintering with us – the Maker chose them as instruments of His will. They did battle with the wyrme. I heard terrible screams and cries. I smelled burning . . .'

'It must have been awful, brother Kilian,' said sister Rebekah, dabbing her eyes.

'It was,' the prophet agreed, 'but I was sustained by the sound of your voices raised in song.'

The elders smiled across the table at one another and nodded.

'Praise be to the Maker,' whispered brother Bede reverently.

'Finally,' Kilian continued, 'when the store chamber fell still, I ventured inside to find our stores in a terrible state, which is why I put them off limits until I had a chance to talk to you all. The stockade is in splinters and the shelfstacks upturned. And there's blood . . .' He paused and looked round at the elders, each in turn. 'The wyrme has gone. But so too, I'm afraid, have our brave kith friends.' He shook his head. 'The Deephome will never forget the sacrifice they have made.'

The elders bowed their heads and, for a moment, the chamber fell silent. Kilian cleared his throat.

'Now that it's safe for our brothers and sisters to return to the chamber, we must salvage what we can.'

'But we have so many mouths to feed,' Brother Bede ventured. 'How are we going to cope?'

'Have faith, brother,' said Kilian. 'The thaw is almost upon us, and when the snows have receded we shall clear more terraces in the lower valley for barley and set extra wyrmenets across the mouth of the falls. And I shall go forth daily, rather than once a season, into the valley country to preach to the kith and receive alms. The Maker will provide, as He always does, and I shall return each day with riches aplenty until our store chamber has been replenished. Last year was one of our best years. I don't see why this year should not be even better.'

The elders smiled. They were already beginning to

feel reassured by the prophet's optimistic words.

'Now,' said Kilian, getting to his feet, 'after this terrible tragedy, which has left everyone feeling so upset and unsettled, I suggest that we should submit to a letting, that our troubled spirits might be calmed.'

The elders rose from their chairs, their hands clasped to their chests.

'Maker be praised,' they intoned softly.

The elders filed out of the meeting chamber. In the tunnels and chambers beyond, word spread among the Deephomers. They had been saved. Once again, thanks to the prayers of Kilian the prophet, the Maker had protected them. They gathered tools and timber and buckets of steaming water from the hot springs, and were waiting to be allowed inside the store chamber, gossiping about what they might find there.

Kilian walked among them, humbly accepting their gratitude and offering reassurance to those who needed it, while the elders organized the Deephomers into work parties. The prophet was just turning away from old brother Ezekiel, who had particularly close to brother Abel, when Cara seized him by the arm.

'Father, is it true what everyone's saying?' There were tears streaming down her face. 'Micah ... Is he ... ?'

Kilian opened his arms and wrapped them round his daughter, drawing her close. 'I'm so sorry, child,' he said as she sobbed convulsively in his arms. 'So, so sorry . . .'

FORTY-EIGHT

The kith slaves sat in a small group, some with their backs to the cavern wall, others crosslegged and slumped forward. They were dead-eyed and slack-jawed, yet Micah noticed how, having drunk the bloodhoney, their nostrils twitched and flared at the faint shifting odours that wafted across the cavern from where the keld were feasting. Not having drunk the bloodhoney himself, Micah couldn't smell the food, but unlike the slaves, he was clear-headed and focused on what he and Eli had to do.

The cragclimber tapped him on the shoulder. 'Look,' he whispered.

Micah glanced up to see the wyrmeskin curtain in the corner of the cavern billow and shimmer in the flickering red light, and Carafine step out. She was holding the winter caller's bone mask and, as Micah watched, she strode over to the keld and began talking in a low voice. The keld gathered around her in a huddle, nodding and tutting and gesturing as she spoke.

'The keld of the valley country sent their assassin to attack us and now four of our number are dead.'

Carafine's voice rose. 'We kept our side of the bargain and sent my husband to supply them with a share of our bloodhoney each halfwinter, and this is how they repay us! If my sister wants a war, then that is what she shall have!' She brandished the winter caller's mask. 'Let us plan our revenge with an attack of our own.'

The keld closed in around her, their heads bowed as she began to scratch out a crude map of a cave system in the dust at her feet.

Eli turned to Micah. 'Come on,' he whispered urgently.

He got to his feet and crept towards the wyrmeskin curtain, keeping close to the wall, his eyes fixed on the keld. Micah followed, fear fluttering in the pit of his stomach in case one of the keld looked round. Reaching the curtain, Eli pulled it aside, and the pair of them slipped silently into the chamber beyond. The curtain fell back into place and Micah stared in horror at the objects which lay in front of the bone chair.

They were the winter caller's tools, laid out on the stone floor just as they had been laid out on the snow outside the winter den. The bone-shears, the liver-clamps, the tongue-splitter; the eye-gouge that the winter caller had taunted him with . . .

Micah paused. There, at the end of the line, was Eli's

knife and his own hackdagger. And the bone catapult.

Eli bent down and retrieved the weapons, handing the hackdagger and catapult to Micah and concealing his knife beneath the folds of his jacket. He looked up at the hole in the cavern ceiling above their heads.

'Quick, Micah,' he said. 'Reckon we haven't got much time. I'll give you a hoik up.'

He stooped down and laced his fingers together. Micah placed one foot in Eli's stirrupped hands and an arm round his shoulder. With a grunt of exertion, the cragclimber straightened up, raising his arms and lifting Micah towards the ceiling. Micah reached up into the narrow chimney-like opening, his fingers searching for and finding a grip on the rough surface of the rock inside. His arms shaking and muscles straining, he pulled himself up, jamming his knees against the sides of the chimney to brace himself. Micah looked down.

Eli was staring up at him. 'Good luck, son,' he said, and stepped back out of sight.

Micah heard the soft dry swish of the wyrmeskin curtain as the cragclimber left the cavern. He stared up. A narrow tunnel twisted away into darkness, its sides studded with jutting slabs, creating a puzzle of tight fissures and dog-leg crevices through which Micah would have to climb. He took a deep breath and started to worm his way up.

He pushed himself through the first of a series of vertical cracks, each one narrower than the last. The tunnel walls closed around him like a tightening vice, pressing against his chest and back, making it difficult to breathe.

When he feared he could go no further, Micah found a handhold and managed to squirm his way through to a wider crevice above. From here the tunnel snaked up through the rock, its surface shot through with shards of quartz that cut his hands and snagged his homespun shirt. Sweat soaked the soft cloth making it cling to his back, cold and clammy in the chill air. Micah held up a bloodied hand and felt a draught coming from the blackness above. Pulling himself up with aching arms, he squeezed round one final dog-leg and saw that the length of tunnel above was bathed in a soft glow. He climbed towards the light and, emerging from the tunnel, found himself on a narrow ledge high above the great chamber. On either side of him, great jagged stalactites hung down towards the glowing floor, while sparcrystals glittered like stars in the vaulted ceiling above.

A solitary figure in a grey cloak and white bonnet was

kneeling on the floor, head in hands, and rocking slowly back and forth, sobbing.

Micah picked up a shard of sparcrystal that lay before him on the ledge, and slipped it into his pocket. Then, turning as he lowered himself over the lip of rock, he climbed down the wall of the cavern. He jumped down the last few feet and, as he landed on the straw-strewn floor, the figure looked up.

It was Cara, her face tear-stained and blotchy. She stared at Micah in disbelief.

'You're alive,' she gasped.

'Cara,' he said, taking her by the hands and helping her to her feet. 'You've got to help me . . .'

But before he could say any more, she had pulled him to her and was smothering his mouth with her kisses. Micah held her close, and she buried her face in the folds of his shirt and wept.

When finally she was still, Micah cupped her chin in his hand and gently raised her head. He looked deep into Cara's turquoise eyes. There was uncertainty and fear in them, but also a trusting innocence that Micah knew he was about to destroy. Cara looked back at him, her mouth trembling.

'It's about your father . . .' he began.

FORTY-NINE

Cara paused by the lowest sentinel point, the jutting slab of granite known as beak rock. The air had lost its bitter chill and all around her snow was slipping from the branches of the valley trees and landing on the ground with soft thuds. She raised the bone horn to her lips and gave three long blasts before lowering the horn and walking back down the trail to Deephome.

Her eyes were red and raw from the tears she had wept. But they were dry now. She had hoped against hope that what Micah had told her earlier in the great chamber was not true. She didn't want to believe it – believe that her father had been so treacherous. Yet he had lied to her about Micah's death, and everything Micah told her about the true nature of Deephome had made a kind of terrible sense.

She'd had to admit that as she had grown older, she had begun to have misgivings, doubts. There were the frequent bloodlettings, the brutal kith gangs who just seemed to leave when asked to, and her father's mysterious trips to the head of the valley . . . But she had pushed them all to the back of her mind, trusting in her father and the Maker, just like the other Deephomers had.

Hearing Micah's words in the great chamber had been like waking from a dream.

Her heart had been in her mouth as the two of them had crept furtively through Deephome's tunnels to her father's study. There, while Micah kept watch at the door, she had found it, concealed beneath his bed like the evil secret it was. Her father's grey homespun cloak. As she picked it up, she had heard the clinking of glass and, unfolding it, had discovered the secret pockets, dozens and dozens of them, nearly half already loaded with the tiny vials of deep red liquid.

Bloodhoney.

She approached the remains of the wooden stockade, and heard the excited babble of voices calling to one another as the Deephomers took their places. Above them, her father's voice sounded deep and resonating as he called for calm. She stepped between the piles of splintered wood stacked on either side of the mouth of the cavern and entered the store chamber. Her father strode forward to meet her, his eyebrows raised quizzically.

'You sounded the alarm, daughter?'

'I did, Father,' Cara began breathlessly. 'I saw figures on the trail ... men with bone masks, and strange weapons, coming towards me out of the mist . . .' Her voice broke. 'They were horrible, Father. Frightening!'

The colour drained from Kilian the prophet's face. He reached out and placed his hands on his daughter's shoulders.

'Calm yourself, Cara,' he said. 'You know what to do.'

She nodded, her eyes fixed on the prophet's face. 'And *you*, Father?'

'I shall stay here and talk to . . . these visitors,' Kilian replied. 'As I always do.'

Cara's face registered no emotion as she broke away from him. She turned to the Deephomers.

'Let us go to the great chamber,' she said, 'and raise our voices in song.'

Kilian the prophet waited until the last of the Deephomers had left the store chamber. He looked around. The few remaining shelfstacks were all but empty and the broken glass and pottery had been swept up into a large pile in the corner. Despite the thaw in the air, the chamber looked cold and forlorn. The prophet shivered.

Hearing the doors of the great chamber slam shut and singing fill the air, he turned away and hurried from the store chamber. He ran down the tunnel, past the sealed entrance to the great chamber, and on, past the meeting chamber, towards the tunnel that led down to the keld cavern. From the depths came the sound of the door slamming back against the wall, and the pounding of heavy footsteps. A moment later, half a dozen heavily-armed keld emerged, bone masks covering their faces.

'More assassins are approaching,' Kilian told them. 'They must have followed the other one.'

The keld at the front grunted, and all six of them set off for the store chamber, with Kilian following behind. As the sound of their footsteps receded, Micah emerged from his hiding place in the tunnel to the hot spring and headed for the cavern beneath Deephome. It was dark and clammy in the narrow tunnel, and reaching the open door he paused as the hot fetid air of the keld cavern washed over him.

He loaded his catapult with the shard of sparcrystal and stepped inside.

At the far side of the cavern, from behind the wyrmeskin curtain, the sound of the Deephomers' singing mingled with the clash and clatter of tools being thrown about. Carafine's disembodied voice rose up above it all.

'Two attacks in one day!' she shrieked from her cavern. 'This must be my sister's work. Ahab! *Ahab!* I want those assassins brought to me, alive. You hear me? Alive!'

By the copper still, surrounded by sweating kith slaves, the overseer grimaced, his lacerated face glistening in the flickering red light.

'Yeah, yeah, I heard you the first time,' he muttered to himself, then looked up. 'I told 'em, mistress,' he called back. 'Break their backs, but keep 'em breathing.'

On the other side of the still, the only other keld remaining in the cavern snorted unpleasantly behind his bone mask. Eli gazed up from the woodpile from where he had been pretending to work, while watching the cavern door. His face broke into a smile of relief when he saw Micah, then hardened as he reached behind him and drew his knife. He nodded.

Micah swallowed hard and took aim with his catapult.

Swiftly, silently, Eli sprinted across the cavern floor and leaped onto the back of the keld in the bone mask. He yanked back the keld's head and, with one deft movement, slit his throat.

At the same moment, Micah released the drawstring of the catapult. The lump of sparcrystal flashed in the red cavern light. It struck the back of the overseer's head and embedded itself in his skull, sending a jet of blood spurting high into the air. With a low grunt, the overseer crumpled to the ground.

Eli released his grip and let the dead keld fall. Then, wiping his blade on his jacket, he strode across to the wyrmestalls and quickly and efficiently put the three emaciated redwing wyrmes out of their misery. He bent down and seized a stone jar of flameoil, and removed the cork. Meanwhile, Micah, his arms outstretched, herded the dead-eyed slaves towards the door. Eli joined him, trailing a thin line of glistening flameoil behind him. It ran from the stacked barrels of bloodhoney on the far side of the cavern, across the floor and out through the entrance.

Micah and Eli retreated back up the tunnel, driving the kith slaves before them. At the top, Micah steered the kith towards the bathing chamber, while Eli followed, continuing the trail of flameoil as he went.

Moments later, they heard the keld returning, cursing and swearing and rattling their weapons in frustration. Micah and Eli froze. Kilian's voice sounded from the top of the tunnel.

'Tell your mistress that it was a false alarm,' he called. 'I shall have a stern word with the latewatch sentinel.'

'You do that,' an angry voice shouted back. The door

banged shut and there was a sound of grinding metal as it was bolted shut.

Crouching down, Eli pulled his flintbox from his jacket pocket and struck a match.

Micah and Eli exchanged looks.

'Are you sure about this, Eli?' said Micah.

'Reckon we don't have no other choice, son,' Eli told him.

He held the flickering blue flame to the puddle of flameoil on the ground before him. With a soft spluttering sound, it ignited and fire rippled along the line of flameoil like the crest upon a wyrme's neck. Down the tunnel it went, under the thin gap beneath the door, scorching the wood as it flickered past . . .

Kilian hammered on the doors of the great chamber with his fists.

'Cara!' he roared. 'Cara! What is the meaning of this?'

Inside, the singing abruptly stopped and the doors opened. Kilian pushed his way inside, to see his daughter, arms folded, staring back at him defiantly.

'I might well ask you the same question, Father,' she replied, her turquoise eyes flashing with anger.

'Wh . . . what . . . what do you mean?' he said, taken

aback by the sudden change in his daughter. 'You sounded the alarm. Yet there was no one there. I went up to the sentinel point and found nothing. No footprints in the snow. Not a trace of these visitors you said you spotted.'

'There were no visitors,' Cara told him evenly.

Behind her, the Deephomers murmured among themselves.

'I sounded the alarm because we are in danger,' she said, turning to them. 'Not from outside. But inside. Here, in Deephome itself.'

The Deephomers stared back at her, their open trusting faces clouding over with confusion and concern. Cara turned back to confront her father.

'Beneath our feet is a cavern, a secret cavern. It is infested with keld.'

'Keld!' The word echoed round the chamber as the Deephomers turned to one another in horror and disbelief. Above the rising hubbub, Cara's voice was strident and accusing.

'And *you*, Father. You are in league with them. When kith come to Deephome, you don't talk to them, do you, Father? You summon the keld to drag them down to their den and enslave them, don't you? And when you take our blood, Father, it isn't for our health, is it? It's to pay the keld for their *protection*.' She spat the word out. 'Isn't it? Father?'

'Oh, Cara, Cara, how can you say such things?' Kilian protested. 'What's wrong with you?'

'There's nothing wrong with me,' she said, her eyes blazing. 'Leastways, nothing that my conversation with brother Micah hasn't put right.'

'Micah? But—'

Cara turned back to the Deephomers, who were staring at the prophet, waiting, hoping, praying for some kind of an explanation.

'My father lied to you,' she told them. 'Brother Eli and brother Micah aren't dead. He told the keld to take them because they had discovered his secret. The secret he is so desperate to keep from us. But it's over, Father. The lies. The deceit. The wickedness . . .'

The prophet pulled himself up to his full height and stared past his daughter at the Deephomers, his eyes fixing on the faces of each of the elders in turn. 'Rebekah, Grace, Anselm, Absolom, Bede,' he said. 'I know you don't believe a word of this.' He smiled sadly. 'My poor dear daughter is distraught. She was in love with the kith boy and can't accept his loss. We must try to be understanding.'

He took a step toward Cara, but she backed away, tears in her eyes.

'These horrible nightmarish fantasies of hers will fade, so long as we don't indulge her further. There are no keld. There are no slaves. There is no secret cavern, just an old equipment chamber and the ravings of a grief-stricken mind . . .'

'If that is true, Father,' said Cara quietly, wiping the tears from her eyes, 'then who are they?'

She pointed at the entrance to the great chamber where Micah and Eli were now standing. Behind them stood the kith slaves, their mouths lolling open and their dead eyes fixed on the floor.

Kilian turned, and as his eyes met Eli's, the blood drained from his face and he seemed almost to shrink into himself. His shoulders slumped, his mouth fell open and, for a few moments, he seemed incapable of speech. Around the great chamber, the Deephomers stood in stunned silence as they stared at the two kith that the prophet had told them were dead, and at the ghoulish faces of the other kith the prophet had told them he'd persuaded to leave.

White-faced and trembling, Kilian fell to his knees. Hands clasped before him, he looked up beseechingly at his daughter.

'Cara, I can explain . . . Everything I did, I did for you. For you, my daughter.' He looked round, but no

Deephomer met his gaze. 'I only wanted to protect her
. . . To protect you all – the meek, the defenceless, the
downtrodden . . .'

At that moment, there came an earsplitting
explosion from beneath the great chamber. The blast
shook the floor, shattered stalactites and sent
sparcrystals raining down on to the stunned
Deephomers. Another explosion sounded. Then
another . . .

Wild-eyed and shaking, Kilian looked across at
Micah and Eli in the doorway. 'What have you done?'
he wailed.

FIFTY

A ball of fire from the exploding keld cavern rose up through the twisting tunnel and erupted from the opening high up in the wall of the great chamber. It spread out across its vaulted ceiling in a rippling tide. Sparks and flaming globules of red liquid rained down onto the glowing straw that covered the floor of the chamber, setting it ablaze. A carpet of flame came towards the Deephomers.

Screaming, weeping, clutching at one another, the Deephomers were forced back towards the cavern doors and spilled out into the tunnel beyond. The fire followed them.

Micah and Eli fell back on either side of the doors as the Deephomers jostled and elbowed their way through.

'Cara!' Micah shouted, forcing his way into the chamber against the surge of fleeing bodies. 'Cara!'

She was standing close to the wall, head in hands, as flames lapped at the hem of her grey cloak. Kilian stood a little way off, his arms spread wide in supplication and a look of utter despair on his face. His clothes had caught alight. Flames rose up his cloak, flickering in his face, setting his hair on fire. He stared at his daughter, oblivious to the inferno consuming him.

'Forgive me, Cara,' the prophet pleaded. 'I . . . I did it for your mother. I loved her. Even though she was wicked, I loved her . . .'

Micah leaped forward and swept Cara up in his arms. 'Don't look,' he whispered as he ran with her from the burning chamber.

'FORGIVE ME!'

The prophet's anguished screams echoed round the empty chamber as Micah hurried after Eli and the shambling kith slaves up the tunnel to the store chamber, while, clinging to Micah's neck, Cara sobbed uncontrollably.

Thick black smoke and crackling flames filled the passages and chambers behind them as the fire spread over the glowing straw that carpeted every part of Deephome. In the sleeping galleries the flames spread from the floor, up the ladders and into the niches, setting the straw-stuffed mattresses ablaze. In the eating chamber, the benches and dining tables burst into flames as vats of cooking oil exploded in the kitchen chamber beyond. As the ropes from which it was suspended burned through, the stone table in the meeting chamber fell from the ceiling to the floor with a colossal crash, while in the bathing chamber, the pools were surrounded by rings of fire as the straw-strewn floor burned.

Coughing and spluttering, Micah stumbled blindly through the smoke that filled the store chamber and staggered outside. In his arms, Cara gasped for breath. Eli was just ahead of them, crouched down beside the remains of the stockade, his soot-blackened face staring after the kith slaves.

They were lurching up the trail that led to the head of the valley, tripping and stumbling, sometimes falling to the ground and getting up again, as they scrambled mindlessly towards the pale sun. The sound of their low groaning voices echoed against the steep valley sides as blind instinct and the bloodhoney coursing through their veins fuelled their escape from Deephome.

'Couldn't stop 'em once they caught a whiff of that halfsummer breeze,' Eli said, glancing round at Micah. He shook his head. 'Not that I had the heart to anyway – not given what those poor devils have been through.'

Clustered in small groups in front of the cavern entrance and perched on rocks at the sides of the trail, the Deephomers looked unhappy and bewildered. The sun was low in the sky, the pines and cedars casting long slanted shadows across the melting snow. Above beak rock the waterfall shimmered in the evening light, the torrent of water swollen with freshmelt. Fisherwyrmes were diving in and out of the pool below, while two crested manderwyrmes drank at its edge.

'It's what we've been waiting for, Micah, lad,' the cragclimber smiled. 'The thaw.'

Micah set Cara gently down. She looked across at the Deephomers. They were gathered around the elders, who were wringing their hands and shaking their heads and calling on the Maker for guidance. Several were kneeling, their heads bowed and arms upraised, while others stood in shock, staring at the cavern mouth from which a thick black pall of smoke was rising up into the warm valley air.

'We can't stay here,' Rebekah the elder was saying. 'The prophet is dead. I shall go to the western valleys. Follow me, brothers and sisters.'

'The high plateau,' exclaimed Bede. 'Come with me to the high plateau.'

Anselm and Absolom both nodded, but Grace the elder barged them aside. 'I shall go to the east,' she said. 'The kith traders will welcome us there.'

The Deephomers started falling into groups behind their chosen elders, casting regretful looks back at their burning settlement. Cara watched them, then turned back to Micah, her turquoise eyes were hard and clear.

'Take me with you,' she said.

FIFTY-ONE

Two whitewyrmes appeared in the halfsummer sky. One was young and skittish, soaring high and swooping low; the other was older and more measured, flying levelly with slow rhythmic beats of its powerful wings.

Once it had begun, the thaw was swift. Warm winds had blown in from the west, gently forcing fullwinter's frozen grip on the high country to yield.

The blanket of snow covering the weald had thinned, turned lacy and fragile, and melted away. Water dripped from every branch, every boulder, every overhanging rock; pools and lakes lost their impenetrable covering of ice. Rivers and falls flowed once more, roaring noisily through the valleys, turbulent and milky blue. And, in every crack in the mountain rock – from the narrowest crevice to the broadest valley – life stirred.

Manderwyrmes and bluewings emerged from their rock nests in the cliffsides, and circled in great flocks. Squabwyrmes scuttled over the scree, while herds of lumbering greywyrmes came up from their winter hides and roamed across the high plateau, their broad backs warmed by the watery halfsummer sun.

High above, at the summit of the loftiest of the jagged peaks, the distinctive silhouette of a Methuselah pine stood out against the clear blue sky. The ancient tree, that had seen more than five thousand fullwinters come and go, had a broad folded trunk and stout branches. Some of them were twisted like wood shavings, some beanpole straight; some were decked in dark green needles and clusters of cones, others stripped and dead and scoured pale by snow and sun. Below them, the trunk of the tree was anchored at its base by immense serpentine roots that gripped the pitted sides of the steep rock and delved down deep into its fissures and cracks.

The two whitewyrmes circled low over the Methuselah pine, their wings grazing its uppermost branches as they inspected it with keen yellow eyes, before soaring back up into the sky. The older wyrme opened his mouth and let out a long sighing call, like wind in long grass. He swept his wings back and arrowed back down towards the tree, his eyes fixed on the upper branches that were bleached and vertical and grew straight as candles.

Spotting the approaching wyrme, a small colony of carrionwyrmes, perched in a row along a knotted branch like dirty washing on a line, screeched with rage for a moment, before taking to the air and flapping noisily away, their tatterwings black and ragged against the flawless blue of the sky.

The older wyrme landed on the branch they had vacated. He folded his wings. The younger wyrme landed beside him, and the pair of them looked up at the cluster of thin straight branches above them, which pointed up at the sky. The older wyrme spoke again and the younger wyrme nodded, before leaving the branch and climbing up the trunk, his claws sinking into the rough bark as he did so. Pausing, the wyrme ran a curved talon up and down the length of first one branch, then the next, then the next – before hesitating at the one after that.

He glanced back at the older wyrme, who nodded in agreement. The young wyrme turned back to the branch and drew back his head. He opened his jaws and released a jet of yellow flame that he directed up and down the length of the branch.

It steamed and darkened, but with instruction from his companion, the young wyrme was careful not to hold the stream of fire on one spot for long enough to char the wood. Droplets of resin bubbled at the surface and spread out to form a thin film that sealed the wood and made it sheen. Up to the very tip of branch the wyrme aimed his jet of flame, then down again, back and front. The air filled with a sweet clean fragrance that made the older whitewyrme's nostrils quiver.

Suddenly, with a loud rasping crack, the branch split along its length.

The young whitewyrme closed his mouth and drew back, surveying the damage ruefully. Then, at the older wyrme's instruction, he moved on.

The second branch he selected did not crack when he scorched it. Nor did it buckle or warp, and when the older wyrme below was satisfied that the branch had been tempered to perfection, he instructed his young companion to use his claws to slice through the branch at its base, cutting it from the tree. And this he did.

With the length of wood clutched in his foreclaws, the young wyrme launched himself off the Methuselah pine and flew after the older wyrme, who turned to check he was being followed. The older wyrme's nostrils flared and streams of white smoke plumed back in the air. His jaws parted and he growled his congratulations.

The young wyrme chittered back – grateful, eager, proud.

FIFTY-TWO

Thrace and Hepzibar were standing face to face at the centre of the cavern floor of one of the upper wyrme galleries. Thrace gripped her kinlance in her hands and took a step forward. Arching her back and bracing her legs, she thrust the lance out to the side in one swift decisive movement. In front of her, the younger kingirl mirrored her movements, her hands gripping the shaft of an imaginary lance.

A gentle breeze whispered round the twisted pillars and ruffled their ashgold hair, bleached and sheened by wyrmesmoke. Thrace twisted round and jabbed back behind her with the other end of her kinlance, and once again Hepzibar mirrored her.

'*Good,*' said Thrace, the sound soft in the back of her throat. '*But twist the lance, little one. Like this.*'

Hepzibar's dark eyes narrowed as they fixed on the flexing of Thrace's slender fingers, and the kinlance spinning in her grip.

'*Then the wound will be deep . . .*' Thrace paused as she saw the young kingirl's eyes widen. She straightened up and placed her kinlance in the crook of her arm.

'*I think that's enough for now, Zar,*' she said with a smile.

Hepzibar frowned as she looked back at the older kingirl. '*But there isn't much time,*' she said. '*You said so yourself. The thaw is here and I need to learn quickly.*'

Thrace met her gaze. '*You're doing well, little one,*' she said encouragingly. '*And once Asa has finished your kinlance, you will learn even quicker.*'

Hepzibar nodded thoughtfully. '*Well, if we are finished,*' she said, turning to go, '*I'll go and see how he's getting on.*'

Thrace watched her leave. Hepzibar wasn't just a quick learner, she thought; she had a natural talent. They were fine traits. But the young girl was gentle-hearted, and Thrace wondered whether she would prove to be a good fighter.

Leaving Thrace in the small gallery behind her, Hepzibar stepped out into the larger chamber beyond, its far side open to the elements, jutting slabs sticking out high above the ground below and the wind whistling through the fluted columns between them. She made her way across the floor of the chamber.

'*Oi,*' came a sneering voice, and Hepzibar's stomach churned. It was Kesh. She tried ignoring him, but he only called out the louder. '*Oi. Hep-zi-bar,*' he said, breaking up her name like it was something ridiculous. '*Where you off to?*' Kesh snorted unpleasantly. '*Not that it matters,*' he said, '*since you and that little wyrmeling of yours don't even have a lance.*'

Hepzibar could feel herself blushing from the tip of her chin to the roots of her hair. She wished she could think of something clever to say, but her head was full of shame and anger and embarrassment, and she could not.

'*Zar.*'

The voice was soft and reassuring, like barley rustling in a warm breeze. Hepzibar turned to see Asa sitting at the foot of one of the great twisted pillars. Aseel was by his side.

'*Asa,*' said Hepzibar. '*I was hoping I'd find you here.*' She was aware that Kesh was listening. '*How's it coming along?*'

'*Your kinlance?*' Asa said, then glanced round at Aseel. '*Nearly ready, I think.*'

The young wyrme returned his attention to the length of ancient pinewood that he was holding in his claws, and continued scraping a curved talon over its surface, removing the last of the bark and smoothing the annealed wood beneath. The older whitewyrme watched critically, then turned to Hepzibar. His eyes grew wider.

'*Asa is about to sharpen the ends,*' he told her. '*Then the lance must be primed.*'

'*Can I help?*' Hepzibar asked gravely, trying hard not to hear Kesh's snort of derision.

Aseel nodded, and she sat on the floor and watched as Asa put the finishing touches to the length of wood with his claws. Then, when Aseel was satisfied it was ready, Asa opened his jaws and, twisting the lance in his claws and biting down, began to chamfer the first of the ends to needle-sharp points against his teeth.

The timber – seasoned for thousands of years and tempered with fire – cut well. There were no splinters, no knots, no fibrous twists. Instead, as he continued to turn the wood against the razor-sharp edge of his teeth, thin shavings coiled away from the wood and fluttered to the floor. Slowly, patiently, under Aseel's watchful eye, Asa honed both ends of the lance to lethal points, then handed it to Hepzibar. She tested its sharpness with the ball of her thumb, her heart racing.

'*Call that a point?*' came a sneering voice, and despite herself, Hepzibar looked round. Kesh was standing behind her, looking over her shoulder, a look of contempt tugging at his face. '*That ain't sharp enough to skewer a squabwyrme.*'

Hepzibar looked away. She stared down at the lance. Her hands were shaking so badly that it slipped from her grip and clattered to the stone floor.

Kesh snorted again. '*Useless,*' he snarled, ignoring the way Asa and Aseel were eyeing him. '*You won't be no good in a fight, a little girl like you. No good at all. Fact of the matter is, you just ain't cut out for it—*'

Asa growled menacingly, but Hepzibar's cry of anger drowned him out as she grabbed the lance and leaped to her feet in one movement. Her dark eyes fiery and intense, she shoved Kesh back hard against a twisted pillar. He banged his head on the rock and, dazed, looked down at the small furious kingirl before him, surprise turning suddenly to blind rage.

His hand went for his knife – but Hepzibar was too quick for him. Gripping the lance tightly, she jabbed the sharpened end at Kesh, forcing him back against the pillar till his shoulders were pressed against the rock. The point of the lance prodded the soft skin at the base of his neck.

Hepzibar stared into Kesh's frightened eyes. Her lips were small and hard; her knuckles were white.

The three wyrmes looked on. Asa trembled. Azura braced herself, ready to attack, but paused when she saw Aseel's eyes darken menacingly.

Hepzibar felt the anger inside her crystallize into a single thought. One little thrust. That was all it would take. One shove of the lance in her hands and her tormentor would be dead . . .

'*Seems she might be good in a fight after all*,' came a soft voice.

Everyone turned to see Thrace standing beside Aseel, her own kinlance in her hand – everyone, that is, except for Hepzibar, for she had not heard her. It was only when the older kingirl reached out and took hold of the lance, and pulled it from her grip, that Hepzibar realized she was there. As Kesh put his hands to his grazed neck, she suddenly felt self-conscious, foolish. Ashamed.

Hepzibar turned to Thrace. She saw the kinlance she and Asa had just finished held in the kingirl's hand along with her own, and frowned uncertainly.

'*I . . . I'm sorry* . . .' She fell silent, fearful suddenly that Thrace might keep the lance as punishment for her outburst.

But Thrace smiled and held out the lance to her. Then she turned to Kesh.

'*You were lucky that time*,' she told him. '*I would advise you not to push that luck.*'

Kesh stared at the kinlance back in Hepzibar's hands, his fists clenching and unclenching in his shame and humiliation. He'd been bested by a girl. A little girl. He looked up at Thrace's face. It was hard and severe; her eyes bored into his. His own eyes narrowed to thin slits. Then, with a low grunt at the back of his throat, he turned on his heels and stomped off across the chamber and outside.

Thrace turned to Hepzibar, her appraising gaze upon the younger girl's half-finished lance. '*Looks like it's ready to be primed,*' she observed.

Hepzibar turned to Asa and Aseel.

'*You know what to do,*' Aseel said, his voice rustling like fallen leaves.

Hepzibar nodded. She'd known that this moment would come. Thrace had told her about it.

To be truly effective, the tips of the kinlance had to be steeped in the venom of the kinrider's wyrme. Afterwards, any kith so much as scratched by such a kinlance would endure slowdeath. Hepzibar knew that once her lance had been treated there would be no turning back. She, like Thrace, would be ready to defend the weald from the kith.

Under Aseel's instruction, and with Thrace looking on approvingly, Asa sat back on his haunches and Hepzibar knelt before him. Asa opened his mouth. Hepzibar gripped the middle of the lance and placed one end between his gaping jaws.

'*Position the lance between the upper and lower fangs,*'

Aseel told Hepzibar, then turned to Asa. '*Bite down gently,*' he instructed.

Both Asa and Hepzibar did as they were told. The points of the upper and lower fangs pressed into the wood, then punctured the surface.

'*Now, bite harder,*' Aseel told Asa.

As the younger wyrme clamped his jaws shut, venom started to pump from his fangs. It soaked into the porous wood through the pinprick holes and trickled over the surface. And when the first end had been saturated, Hepzibar turned the lance around and they primed the second.

Hepzibar took the lance from between Asa's jaws and climbed to her feet. Thrace stepped forward and placed a hand on the younger girl's shoulder. She was smiling, though her eyes glittered with emotion.

'*Now you are true wyrmekin,*' she told her.

FIFTY-THREE

'*One of us must act as their guide,*' said Alsasse.

Aylsa and Alucius exchanged glances.

The leader of the whitewyrme colony turned from one to the other, his eyes narrowing. '*Aylsa has consented to accompany the blueblackwyrmes,*' he said. The ancient creature's barbels trembled. '*As second of the host, Alucius, I cannot afford to let you go.*'

It was just before dawn, and the three whitewyrmes were standing on the edge of the gorge of the blueblackwyrmes. The air smoked and the fiery glow of the molten lava, which ran deep down below the fissure of the rock, stained their whitescale bodies red.

'*I still think that, since Beveesh-gar is sending one of his own sons, I should go with them,*' said Alucius. His voice was soft, but the admonishment was clear.

'*You think that I am not up to the task, Alucius?*' Aylsa commented.

'*Of course I don't think that,*' Alucius said softly. He turned his yellow eyes to Alsasse. '*It is just . . . I miss the valley country so much, and I had hoped to see it again.*'

Alsasse nodded, wisps of white smoke coiling from

his nostrils. '*I understand,*' he said. '*I, too, pine for our home. But we must all make sacrifices . . .*' He paused. '*And I will not be able to lead the host for much longer.*' His intense gaze remained on the second of the host until the younger wyrme looked away.

Alucius bowed his long graceful neck. '*I understand,*' he said, his voice soft as trickling sand. He stared back across the dark broken slabs of rock to the east, his eyes glowing a deepening shade of amber. The sun was just breaking over the distant mountains. Back there, beyond this harsh landscape of fire and rock, was their abandoned home – the ancient wyrme galleries.

Would they ever be able to return to them? he wondered.

Certainly, Alucius had to concede, the blueblack-wyrmes had been generous. They had accepted the whitewyrmes into their territory without rancour. The colony had been allowed to scrape roost-holes out of the hard black rock beside the algal lakes, and to hunt and graze in the rock crevices to the north. So long as the whitewyrmes kept themselves to themselves, the blueblackwyrmes had tolerated their presence.

But when fullwinter had slipped into halfsummer, Beveesh-gar had summoned Alucius to the hive nest in the gorge. Surrounded by his clan, the old blueblackwyrme had turned his one good eye on the whitewyrme before him.

He had made a decision, he'd growled in the harsh glottal voice that Alucius still had to strain to understand. He wanted to examine one of these so-called two-hides for himself. So, now the thaw had come, he intended to send out a hunting party to get one – dead or alive, he didn't care - and they needed a guide.

This wasn't a request, Alucius knew. It was a command. So he had returned to the leader of the host and volunteered . . .

Alucius looked up. The sun had broken free of the mountains that seemed to be anchoring it, and had risen into the pink and grey streaked sky. Alucius heard gruff voices behind him. He glanced at Alsasse and Aylsa, then turned to see four of the hulking blueblackwyrmes emerging from the gorge. They pulled themselves up on their powerful foreclaws in that way they had, before standing up straight, their thick necks braced and wings spread out behind them, towering above the smaller whitewyrmes.

'*You are ready?*' said Hasheev-gul, sixth son of Beveesh-gar.

Alsasse nodded. '*Aylsa will be your guide,*' he said.

Beveesh-gar turned and looked the female

whitewyrme up and down, and for a moment, Alucius thought that he might object. But the leader of the blueblackwyrmes merely nodded.

'*The flight is long?*' he growled to her.

'*Many dawns,*' Aylsa replied.

'*Then let us begin.*'

The blueblackwyrme flexed his mighty wings and stepped back over the lip of the gorge with his three companions. They disappeared from view down into the fiery abyss for a few moments, before soaring back up on the furnace-hot updraughts.

Aylsa turned to Alucius and Alsasse, a tremor passing through her long sinuous body. Then she spread her wings wide and, with rapid wingbeats, took to the early morning air.

'*Good fortune,*' Alucius called after her, his voice like a windwhisper through a wyrme gallery.

'*There,*' said Aylsa, raising her head and pointing ahead.

The four blueblackwyrmes flying on either side of her followed her gaze. They had flown for days, through night after starlit night, the sun rising before them each morning as they'd continued east. Aylsa was nearing the end of her strength, though the blueblackwyrmes seemed untroubled by the long flight. Now they were high up in the sky among thin wispy clouds. Far below them was a deep rift valley, the sides steep and orange-red and pocked with shrubs – and at the far end of the valley were the tell-tale twists of smoke from a fire. A kith fire.

As they came closer, Hasheev-gul turned to Aylsa, his sapphire-blue eyes narrowing to slits. *'That smell,'* he growled. *'Pungent. Sour. Rank . . .'*

'That's the taint of the two-hides,' Aylsa replied, her nostrils flaring. *'The entire valley country reeks of it.'* A shudder passed through her long slender body. *'The smell of death.'*

The blueblackwyrmes beat their powerful wings with long slow movements, their massive heads steady on their short necks, and their great forearms flexed and raised, the curved talons ready to strike. Aylsa spread her own wings wide and rose above them as they started down the valley.

There were five of them – two women and three men. They were sitting round the fire, cooking; cooking wyrmeflesh. As the four blueblackwyrmes barrelled towards them, one of the men turned and shouted an alarm; others raised their heads and looked up. One of the women climbed to her feet and stood staring, her face white with shock.

Hasheev-gul swept back his burnished blueblack wings, slashed at the air with his talons and went into a dive. The others went with him.

Aylsa hovered above, her heart pounding. They were dangerous – all two-hides were dangerous – yet the blueblackwyrmes had chosen to ignore her warnings. She watched the four huge creatures home in on the two-hides seated round the fire, their jaws wide and dazzling white flame roaring before them.

The two-hides scrambled to their feet and scattered. But not fast enough.

The first of the blueblackwyrmes lashed out with a taloned hand, slicing through the neck of the oldest of the men. The second pursued a fleeing young woman, his fiery jet of flame setting her outer hide and hair alight. Hasheev-gul seized the second woman in his claws, soared back high into the air – then let go of her, and she tumbled back down to the ground, screaming . . .

Aylsa dropped down lower in the sky, willing the attack to be over. The stench of blood and burning flesh rose up to meet her.

Soaring back up into the air, flanked by his companions, Hasheev-gul threw back his head and roared at Aylsa, '*Are these the puny creatures from which you fled?*'

Just then, from below, came the strange metallic crack of the two-hides' weapons. The thorns of the two-hides flew past the startled faces of the blueblackwyrmes before, with a soft meaty thud, one of them found its target.

Aylsa's cry of pain rang out, loud and anguished, but the blueblackwyrmes did not hear it as they rose and scattered across the sky. Nor did they see her left wing collapse, or the metal bolt from the powerful crossbow that had severed the flight-tendon lodged in the scales at its base.

The whitewyrme flapped her right wing as hard as she could in a desperate attempt to remain aloft. But it was hopeless. She went into a spin, and tumbled over and over, buffeted by the wind, down, down.

The last thing Aylsa remembered was a blur of green and brown, and vicious scratching at her skin as she crashed through the upper boughs of a stunted tree . . .

Aylsa opened her eyes.

It was late. The sun had travelled across the sky and was down by the horizon, a red ball quivering above the jagged mountain ranges in the distance.

Aylsa turned her head and looked awkwardly round. She was lying on her front at the bottom of a tree: the tree that had broken her fall – and saved her life. Broken branches lay about her, jabbing into her side. She pulled herself up on all fours, untangled herself from the mess of twigs and foliage, then limped out from the shadows of the tree. Her wing was throbbing, and she remembered the two-hides' thorn that had struck her.

She glanced round, wincing as she did so. And there it was, grey and hard, still lodged in the bone at the base of her wing. Twisting her neck round, Aylsa opened her mouth and clamped the end of the thorn with her fangs. She pulled. The pain made her yellow eyes deepen to a glowing red. She pulled again, harder. The thorn moved a fraction. With her eyes shut, she clenched her jaws and tugged at the thorn which, with a soft grinding sound, abruptly came free, and she tossed it aside.

With her head raised, she tried to flap her wings. The right wing lifted and braced and swept back and forth; the left wing remained limp at her side.

Aylsa sighed miserably. It would take time to heal.

She looked round for the blueblackwyrmes, but they were nowhere to be seen, and for a moment she was furious that they had abandoned her. But then her gaze fell upon the tree.

Perhaps they *had* looked for her, she wondered. Looked, but not found . . .

With her left wing dragging on the ground, she started walking. Every step was an effort. Her body felt as though it had been pummelled with rocks. She looked about her as she went, but there was no sign of the blueblacks, nor of the two-hides. She cocked her head and sniffed at the wind.

But she could *smell* them.

Cautiously now, she kept walking. Then she saw it. A body, broken and bleeding, wrapped over the top of a boulder. A second body lay beside it, the skull caved in where it had struck the rocky ground. A soft sad clicking sound trilled in the back of her throat. She came to the fire, set in a circle of rocks and all but spent. A third body lay burnt and smouldering beside it.

Aylsa turned away, and was about to leave this place of death, when she heard something. She paused. The sound stopped, then started again. It was a soft whimpering noise, weak and plaintive, and it was coming from a pile of backpacks and belongings stacked up together on the far side of the fire.

The great whitewyrme stepped cautiously towards it. The whimpering grew louder. She dipped her head and nuzzled at the heap. She sniffed. Whatever was there smelled sweet, like milk, like dry hay. She sniffed some more, and her nose drew her to a blanket, which she took in her mouth and plucked it away, and chittered with surprise.

It was a two-hides, small and shivering. A male. He looked up into her face with large green eyes and let out a little cry. And his body shook again, uncontrollably. Aylsa trembled. She opened her mouth and exhaled, her breath warm and sweet. The two-hides closed his mouth and, wide-eyed, stopped shivering.

Aylsa sniffed at him again, then looked up at the sky. Stars were twinkling in the deep indigo darkness.

She looked back down at the small two-hides, her barbels trembling. Then she lay herself gently down, her body wrapped around the small defenceless creature, who had started to cry.

'*Hush, little one,*' she purred.

Fifty-Four

The keld mistress slowly eased apart the folds of scorched wyrmeskin curtain to reveal the figure concealed inside.

The head was hideously burned. The hair had turned to soot and the scalp below was blistered; the skin of the forehead and temples had melted like tallow-wax. With delicate fingers, the keld mistress opened the swaddling wyrmeskin a little more. The nose had gone, and the lips were red and black like strips of raw meat.

'Oh, sister,' she whispered, her honeyed voice soft and soothing, as if talking to a young child, 'what happened to you?'

She bent down, bringing her hood-shadowed face closer to the blackened figure.

'Carafine,' she whispered. 'Can you hear me?'

The small chamber was completely burned out, scorched by the explosion and flash fire that had ripped through it. Her sister had managed to wrap herself in the wyrmeskin curtain as the inferno struck, but even this had not been enough to save her.

The keld mistress stared at the burned wreck of the

face. It looked like some kind of effigy; like a grotesque molten image fashioned from wood and leather and wax. Then the lips moved.

The keld mistress leaned closer.

Her sister's breath was warm, but faint. A soft gurgling rattle came from the back of her throat, then a single rasped word.

'Kith . . .'

The keld mistress drew sharply back. 'Slake!' she called, her voice strident with imperative. 'Slake, where are you? Bring the bloodhoney . . .'

Blue Slake was in the larger chamber, hunched up in a woven basket that was harnessed to the back of a hefty broad-shouldered kith, who was wearing a heavy lakewyrmeskin cloak and bleached bone mask. The air was hot and still thick with smoke, and the poisoner was finding it hard to breathe through the ragged hole where his nose had once been.

In the shadowy alcove beside him was the eel-mother, her two leashed crevicewyrmes squealing and growling as they tore into the charred remains of what looked like three dead redwings. Her own bone-masked kith stood beside her, passive, breath rasping.

Cutter Daniel, four dead-eyed slaves in attendance, stood on the other side of the smoke-blackened chamber. He was poking thoughtfully at a large heap of ashes with a length of iron, occasionally pausing over the hoops of metal he found among them. Then he reached up and ran a finger over the sweaty rock above it. Something red and sticky gathered under the nail, which he sniffed, then tasted.

'Their entire stock must have gone up in flames,' he mused.

'Bloodhoney!' The keld mistress's voice was insistent. '*Now*, Slake!'

Cutter Daniel looked round. 'Slake,' he hissed. 'The mistress wants bloodhoney.'

Stirred from his reveries, Blue Slake tore his eyes away from the remains of what, to his expert eye, looked like an extremely impressive liquor still. He had to hand it to young Carafine; by the look of it, she must have been producing an excellent yield of bloodhoney. Before the fire . . .

The black-cowled figure of the keld mistress appeared in the mouth of the small cavern and beckoned to him.

'Coming, mistress,' he called, his voice slurfing through the hole in his face.

He kicked his heels viciously into the sides of the kith carrying him. The kith dropped obediently to his knees. With fumbling fingers, Blue Slake unshouldered the leather straps, then clambered out of the basket. He limped across the sooty, debris-strewn floor, past charred bodies, pulling a bottle of bloodhoney from the inside of his tasselled jacket as he went. Entering the cavern he paused as he saw the keld mistress bent down over the charred body.

'Carafine . . .' he murmured.

'Just give me it,' the keld mistress hissed, reaching up.

And when Blue Slake made no move, she snatched the bottle from his hand and tugged out the cork stopper with her teeth. Then, spitting it aside, she turned back to her sister. With her hand beneath the wyrmeskin, she gently raised her sister's head; she put the bottle to the burnt swollen lips, and tipped it.

'Drink,' she said, her voice tender, encouraging. 'Just a little sip . . .'

The viscous red liquid trickled into Carafine's mouth, and she swallowed, then swallowed again. The keld mistress withdrew the bottle, but Carafine's blistered mouth pursed and puckered expectantly, and the keld mistress gave her a little more to drink.

Carafine's eyes opened, turquoise set in red. 'Sister,' she rasped, her gaze hardening as she stared into the shadows beneath the black hood.

The keld mistress looked back into her sister's eyes, so like her own, and she smiled.

Carafine did not smile back. 'Why did you send him?' she said, her voice frail and cracked, accusatory.

'Who?' the keld mistress asked gently.

'Who? Who?' The eyes grew wider. 'The winter caller. I recognized him. Why did you send him here?'

The keld mistress frowned. 'The winter caller was here?'

'Don't pretend you didn't know,' Carafine told her, the words desiccated and raw. 'You said I could set up for myself, as long as I paid you. And I kept my part of our bargain. Every halfwinter I gave you your share. But then you sent your assassin . . .' Animated by the bloodhoney, Carafine's husked voice was indignant.

The keld mistress shook her head. 'That husband of yours has not been paying us, sister, whatever he might have told you. That is why we came . . . and found you like this.'

'Kilian didn't pay you?' rasped Carafine with a shudder. 'But why?'

'Oh, sister, sister,' said the keld mistress softly. 'How many times have I told you, you can't trust kith . . .' She paused. 'I did send the winter caller, though,' she admitted softly. 'But not after you. I sent him after the kith who had killed Redmyrtle. He was following their scent.'

Carafine snatched a wheezing breath. 'Redmyrtle is dead?' she whispered, then her eyes widened as a thought took hold. 'The winter caller was following their scent?' she muttered, struggling to say the words. 'When my keld killed the winter caller, they captured two kith – a cragclimber and a boy. Kilian told me their names . . .'

She fell still, and swallowed. She looked imploringly at her sister, who put the bottle of bloodhoney to her lips once more.

'Eli Halfwinter,' she rasped, her turquoise eyes flickering. 'And Micah . . .' The words were getting softer, more indistinct. 'They set the fire . . .' she whispered. Her eyes dulled and flickered. 'They did . . . this.'

The keld mistress reached up and removed the black hood that cowled her head. The face beneath was as white and opalescent as moonstone. Snowwhite eye-lashes, mistwhite hair and smooth polished skin, shot through with tiny bluish veins like marbling through alabaster. It was a bloodless, ice-frosted face out of which two pale turquoise eyes stared down malevolently at the black flame-wizened body wrapped in the wyrmeskin curtain.

'I warned you, sister.' The honeyed voice emerged

from between white lips. 'I warned you not to throw your lot in with a stone prophet.' She reached out and her hands closed round her sister's throat. 'But you thought you knew better,' she purred. 'You thought you could farm kith. And look where it's got you.'

The keld mistress's turquoise eyes hardened as her fingers tightened.

'You killed the winter caller,' she suddenly hissed, as a wheezing gurgling sound escaped from Carafine's mouth. 'And let the kith he was hunting escape.'

Carafine shuddered, the blackened stubs of her fingers clawing weakly at her sister's arms as the keld mistress strangled the life out of her. Finally she fell still. The keld mistress released her grip, pulled the hood back over her white face and rose to her feet.

The other keld were watching from the doorway. Blue Slake and Cutter Daniel exchanged looks. The eel-mother cleared her throat and her two crevicewyrmes hissed at the end of their leashes.

'What now?' she asked.

From beneath the black hood, the keld mistress's voice sounded, rich and sweet and deadly as bloodhoney.

'We find Eli Halfwinter and the boy, Micah,' she whispered silkily. 'And we kill them.'

FIFTY-FIVE

Cara shivered. She pulled the homespun cloak tightly round her and held it shut at the neck. Her clenched fingers looked pale and bluish against the bunched grey material.

'You cold?' Micah asked.

'A little,' said Cara. She shivered again and smiled. 'But I'll soon warm up when we light the fire.'

Micah slipped his arms from the sleeves of his hacketon and, skitching up closer to Cara, draped the jacket around both their shoulders. Cara nestled against him.

'Better?' he said, turning and kissing her lightly on her cheek.

'Much better,' she said, and she kissed him back, on the lips.

'Soon as Eli gets back and gives the all clear, I'll light the fire and get it blazing,' Micah said. 'Thing is, Cara, out here in the weald, you got to be careful. Fires can attract attention . . .'

He felt Cara shiver again, and press more closely against him.

They were sitting on a broad ledge of rock, halfway up the side of a tall crag of yellowish sandstone. It had been an arduous day's journey up out of the valley of Deephome, over the rocky plateau and into the mountains to the west. But Cara hadn't complained once. When at last they'd stopped for the night, and Eli had gone out to check the lie of the land, she had helped Micah collect brushwood for the fire efficiently and with a good eye for what would burn well, even though Micah could see how tired she was.

He reached into the folds of her homespun cloak and found Cara's hands, and squeezed them tightly.

'You did good today,' he said.

'I did?' she said, her voice a mixture of surprise and pride.

'Real good.'

Cara looked up at the sky. 'It's all so big and strange and new out here in the weald,' she said. 'After Deephome . . .'

'It takes time to get used to life on the trail,' said Micah, nodding.

He looked into Cara's blue-green eyes. They were full of innocence and trust . . . Trust in *him*. And Micah felt a sudden overwhelming tenderness for this kithgirl who had lost everything, yet was so resolute and brave. She needed him, and he would not let her down. He leaned forward and kissed her again.

'Things will work out, you'll see,' he said gently, and slipped an arm round her shoulders. 'Eli knows what he's doing. Halfsummer is the time for harvesting the bodies of those wyrmes that didn't make it through fullwinter, and honouring them by putting to full use what they have to give.' Micah smiled. 'That's Eli's way. He doesn't hold with hunting and trapping, but he'll take what the weald freely offers up. We'll use every part of the wyrmes we find – the teeth, the wingbones, the pelts, the flamesac – and trade them for what we need in scrimshaw dens.'

'Scrimshaw dens?' Cara repeated, a quizzical look on her face.

'Scrimshaw dens are like stores,' Micah explained. 'Weald stores. Where kith gather to barter and trade. And once we've gathered enough of value, then we'll be able to visit a scrimshaw den ourselves, and trade. For pots and mugs and blankets and such. And we'll get you some new clothes, Cara. Proper weald gear rather than these things,' he said.

Micah's ran hand over Cara's grey cloak, and he looked down at her moccasins, already scuffed and battered from a single day's journey. He squeezed her shoulder.

'In the meantime,' he told her, 'I'll stitch some

wyrmehide onto those shoes of yours and strengthen the heels and toes. I've still got needle and thread in my pocket from repairing my own boots.'

'You'd do that for me?' said Cara, her eyes glistening.

'Of course,' said Micah, returning her gaze. 'You've got to look out for one another out here,' he said. 'Eli taught me that.'

'He's taught you a lot of things . . .'

'He has.'

'Will you teach me?'

Micah reached out and drew Cara back close to him, then pulled the hacketon jacket around them. 'I shall,' he said.

Just then, there was a raucous high-pitched noise that echoed far above them, bouncing off the rock cliffs and out across the plateau below. It was answered by low booming roars from somewhere out in the dark.

'What was *that*?' Cara said, her voice breathless.

Micah looked up. 'Screechwyrmes,' he said. 'See?' He pointed to half a dozen creatures, pale silver in the moon-light. They had wide angular wings, broad mouths and bony protuberances at the tops of their skulls, and were circling the mountain crag above. 'They shriek like that when they hunt, Eli says.' He turned back to Cara. 'Sounds scary – but they're harmless enough.'

Cara reached up to the back of her neck and raised the collar of the wyrmeskin hacketon. 'I've lived my entire life in Deephome,' she said softly. 'In fact, until today, I had never been beyond the top sentinel post. I used to stand there and watch my father go out into the valley country to preach to the kith.' She paused, frowned. 'At least, that's what I'd thought he was doing . . .'

She stopped, and Micah looked up to see that tears had gathered in the corners of her eyes and were running down her cheeks.

'I still can't quite believe it.' Her voice was low and expressionless. 'Draining our blood and giving it to the keld to make that foul bloodhoney of theirs . . . And all the while he had us praising the Maker and singing to Him in the great chamber . . .'

Suddenly giving way to tiredness and despair, she slumped against Micah. She buried her face and wept quietly, and Micah felt the juddering rise and fall of her shoulders.

'He made a mistake,' he told her.

A bad mistake.

He recalled how, suddenly finding themselves without their prophet, the Deephomers had traipsed off in their different directions, their bodies stooped and faces pale and drawn with shock. Most of them had decided to throw in their lot with one or other of the elders; a few of them went it alone. It seemed so long ago now, yet it had only been that morning.

Eli had hung back, waiting to see where the others were heading, before turning to Micah and pointing off in a different direction entirely.

'We'll go that way,' he'd said, 'out of the valley country. To the west, where the whitewyrmes are said to dwell.'

In Micah's arms, Cara's sobs began to lessen and she fell still. For a while, neither of them spoke. Cara kept her face buried in Micah's chest, while Micah looked over her head at the white impassive moon.

When Cara spoke at last, her voice was thick and husky from crying. 'What do you think my father meant?' she said.

'What do you mean?' asked Micah, though he knew well enough what she was asking.

Cara pulled away and looked at him. 'When he asked me to forgive him, he said he did it all for *her* . . .' she said. 'My mother. Even though she was wicked.' She swallowed and wiped the back of her hand across her eyes. 'He said he loved her, even though she was *wicked* . . .' She frowned. Her turquoise eyes grew wider. 'What did he *mean*?'

Micah couldn't meet her gaze. Cara had her mother's face, her mother's eyes . . .

'My mother died when I was a child,' she went on. 'So he can't have meant her. Can he? And anyway, she wasn't wicked. Not my mother. She can't have been . . .' She grasped at Micah's hands. 'So what *did* my father mean?'

Micah shook his head.

He had told her everything in the great chamber – everything except the truth about her mother. When she had found the grey cloak her belief in her father had finally been shattered. And that was enough for her to bear. He hadn't told her about Carafine then, and he wouldn't tell her now. He wouldn't tell her ever.

'I don't know,' he whispered gently.

Cara nodded, the movement barely visible, and Micah was unsure whether she believed him. But it didn't seem to matter. She reached out and tugged at the lapels of his hacketon, pulling Micah down on top of her as she lay back, and she kissed him and kissed him . . .

Eli had returned a little while later, with the carcasses of two squabwyrmes he'd come across swinging at his side. He'd reported that the country around them seemed quiet, and they'd lit the fire and roasted the wyrmes and then, exhausted, had bedded down for the night.

The moon rose higher, and when Micah rolled over onto

his back it shone in his face like a bright beacon. He opened his eyes.

Beside him, Cara stirred. She nestled into him, her head on his chest and her hands clasped together. Micah tugged at the wyrmeskin hacketon that was draped over the pair of them, shielding her eyes from the glare of the moon, and Cara sighed contentedly.

Looking back at the moon, he caught sight of movement in the darkness. Something was out there, flying, and as it flapped across the white surface of the moon, Micah recognized the familiar dip of a sinuous neck and the way the arched wings rose and fell.

It was a whitewyrme. A whitewyrme with a rider. In the far distance, the long spike of the kinlance dissected the orb of the moon for a moment, then the silhouette was gone.

Micah thought of Thrace.

Cara glanced up at him from the shadows. 'Why, Micah,' she said, 'your heart's racing.'

She smiled, her eyes sleepy and tangles of auburn hair framing her face.

Cara. His sweet trusting Cara.

'Is it?' he said.

The story concludes . . .

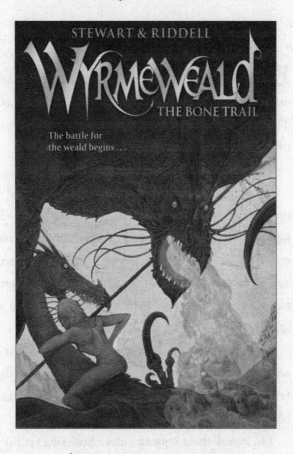

AVAILABLE NOW

Read on for an extract . . .

ONE

Eli Halfwinter surveyed the mountains that rose up out of the mist ahead. Fullwinter's grip had relaxed. The snow and ice had mostly gone. The green shoots of halfsummer were sprouting.

Eli's eyes narrowed.

The summit was a good day's climb by his reckoning, and the way looked perilous steep. The high sun cast long shadows down the ochre-brown rockface that were like stains. Eli glanced north along the range, then south. The mountains seemed to stretch off into the distance for ever, and he was loath to set out on such a detour.

Looking up, the cragclimber saw dozens of wyrmes flitting round the cragtops and upper ledges. Striped orange manderwyrmes. Spikebacks. Metallic bluewings.

He heard their squeaks and chitterings echo off the wall of rock as they pitched and dived in search of insects.

He looked down again, scouring the lower reaches of the mountains. His gaze fell upon a jagged black crevice away to the south. It was a cleft through the rock, large enough for wyrmes to pass through. The scree at the entrance looked trampled, and it was spattered with wyrmedung.

This was what he'd been looking for. A wyrme trail.

One of the migration routes that linked winter hideout to halfsummer pastures.

As Eli approached, he found that the crack in the rock was narrower than he'd thought – just wide enough for the great lumbering greywyrmes to pass through in single file. He stepped into it.

The sun was snuffed out like a candle flame and the air felt chill. High above his head was a thin slit of blue sky. The rock was sheer and dark at his sides, and at the most constricted points of the trail had been chafed and grazed by the flanks of the migrating herds. The shadowed track doglegged sharply to the left, then right again, then opened up.

Eli found himself on a small stretch of flat sand. It was enclosed by vertical rockfaces that rose up around him, curved and ridged like giant hands. Behind him was the narrow opening he'd entered. In front of him, blocking the way ahead, was a great pitted boulder. Except it wasn't a boulder. It was a greywyrme.

Massive. Recumbent. And dead.

The corpse was lying on its side, the back bowed and turned away, the long neck and thick tail curved round towards him, and between them the four limbs, outstretched, clawstiff. The head of the creature was draped over a slab of rock, its great maw gaping open to reveal rows of yellowpearl teeth. Deep empty black eyesockets stared back blindly at him.

It was a bull male, seventy summers old by the looks of it, perhaps even older than that. Eli rested a hand on the hard cracked skin of the greywyrme's flanks. It hung loose over the framework of jutting bones beneath.

The creature must have died just before the start of fullwinter, and its body been covered with thick snow that had protected it from carrionwyrmes and other scavengers, and frozen it solid. With the thaw, the wind whistling through the ravine had dried the body out, mummifying the remains and rendering its skin and flesh too brittle and desiccated to be of use.

But the teeth and claws, now they were a different matter . . .

Eli straightened up. He pulled his rucksack from his back and set it on the ground. He loosened the ties. He pulled out a small hammer, a pair of pliers, then unsheathed the knife at his belt.

The claws of the greywyrme's hindfeet were brown and nubbed, but beneath the pitted surface Eli knew they would be fine-grained and make for excellent carving. They would bring high rewards at a scrimshaw den. He set to work.

The knack was to slide the point of the knife in at the back of the toe, where the curve of the claw left a small gap between the knuckle and the scaly skin, and twist.

Eli jerked the handle round and the blade sliced through the tendons like they were yarns of wool. Then, keeping the knife in place, he gripped the claw with the pliers and wrenched it back hard, twisting as he did so.

There was a dull cracking sound and the claw came away from the foot. He turned it over in his hand appraisingly, then set it down on the sand.

Eli removed all twelve of the claws from the hindfeet.

Then he moved on to those at the front.

These were longer, sharper. Paler. They would make a fine set of pickspikes. Eli took a swig of water from the watergourd at his side, mopped his brow, then set to work again.

He started humming. It was a plodding tuneless rendition of something he'd once heard. He wasn't even aware of doing it.

When the last of the front claws had been extracted, Eli pushed back his hat and turned his attention to the teeth. He peered into the dark yawning hole of the creature's maw, then reached inside. He ran his finger tips over the spike of an eyetooth, the chisel-edge of an incisor.

Using his knife, Eli drove the blade down between the teeth, one after the other, and sawed into the gums.

He worked swiftly and efficiently. When the final cut had been made, Eli straightened up. The teeth were loose now. Setting the knife aside, he seized a front tooth with the pliers, then *tap-tap-tapped* at the gum with the hammer. Slowly. Gently. Taking care not to crack the enamel. Until, with something almost like a sigh, the gum finally gave up its grip on the roots and the tooth came free.

Eli turned it over in his hand, then laid it down next to the claws. It was a fine specimen, and he would have liked to point out its qualities to the boy – the fact that its size alone would furnish a dozen knife handles, and that its grain, even finer than the greywyrme's claws, would make for flawless carving.

But Micah was not there. He was off on the high bluffs to the west with the girl, Cara.

They needed time on their own, the youngsters. Eli accepted that. Especially Micah, after everything he'd been through that fullwinter past – not to mention the couple of seasons before that with the kingirl, Thrace. It had been a tough year, and that was a fact. But they had survived. Him and the boy. And now Micah had Cara to look out for . . .

Eli smiled. Young love. There was no accounting for it.

Eli Halfwinter on the other hand was a loner. He'd learned the hard way that most kith could not be trusted. They would cheat and rob you as soon as look at you. They would kill you over a small nothing. No, so far as Eli was concerned, he was better off steering clear of other folks.

He glanced back down at the tooth. Though he sure did miss Micah to talk to.

Returning to the gaping jaw of the greywyrme, Eli removed the rest of the teeth in rapid succession. He stood back, wiping the sweat from his forehead, and surveyed the haul. Then, swallowing drily, he unhitched the gourd from his belt and took a long slug of water.

It was hard work. Despite the chill, he was sweating.

He took another swig from the gourd and was fixing it back to his belt when he saw it.

The broken shaft of a harpoon. It was sticking out from the base of the greywyrme's neck.

Eli had assumed that, given its age, the wyrme had

died of natural causes. Certainly he hadn't been looking for evidence of injury. Yet there it was. A harpoon. A kith harpoon; the backslant barbs at its base bore testimony to that.

The harpoon was of a type fired from a kind of upright crossbow, favoured by those kith who went hunting for big game. The tip of the blade had penetrated the soft underskin of the greywyrme between the adamantine creases, and punctured its lungs. The ancient creature must have died instantly and, despite himself, Eli was impressed with the cleanness of the kill.

But why bring down so magnificent a creature, then fail to butcher it for meat and strip it of the valuable bone and ivory to barter with in a scrimshaw den? he wondered. It surely made no sense.

Eli shrugged, and was about to stow the claws and teeth in his pack when he noticed the small wound at the base of the creature's throat.

The flameoil sac had been removed. Eli frowned. His mouth grew taut with rising anger.

The kith hunters hadn't been interested in food or ivory, just the tiny gland in the greywyrme's throat.

Returner's wealth.

Small, easy to carry and highly prized. Apothecarists down on the plains would pay handsomely for greywyrme flameoil and its supposedly miracle properties. Anyone returning from the high country with a full pack of the stuff would have their fortune made – never mind that they were responsible for the slaughter of countless wyrmes.

Eli hawked and spat. The thought of it turned his stomach.

He wrapped the teeth up in an old blanket along with the claws, and stuffed the whole lot inside his rucksack before hoisting it onto his back. The pack was heavy, but at least he had honoured the magnificent greywyrme by using what it had to offer.

When it came to moving on, Eli found that the curved back of the greywyrme was pressed against the crevice, stopping up the gap in the rock like a cork.

He had no option but to climb over it if he was to continue his journey. Reaching up, Eli gripped the folds of the wyrme's vestigial wings, then clambered onto the creature's back. He was about to climb down the other side – but then stopped.

His jaw dropped. The trail ahead was blocked.

Before him, like a rockfall of huge grey boulders, were hundreds and hundreds of greywyrmes. They were crammed into the narrow ravine, their throats cut and flameoil sacs removed.

Eli swallowed numbly. These kith hunters had been clever, he could see that now. They must have tracked the herd across the pastures on their long migration to their fullwinter hide in these mountains, and as the old bull wyrme had led them through the ravine the hunters had struck. They had shown no mercy. They had slaughtered the entire herd. Male and female, young and old alike, sparing not a single one.

And for what? For an ointment that supposedly reduced the signs of ageing . . .

Eli's face had turned a dark raw red. His lips trembled and his pale-blue eyes glistened. He was going to have to be late meeting up with Micah and Cara at the stickle falls. He would turn back, find another way through the mountains. He could not face clambering over all these bodies; all that needless death.

'Oh, Micah,' he whispered, 'I'm glad you're not here to see this.'